"Masterfu
stores onl
mystery t
you!"

"[A] darn good murder mystery."   —MyShelf.com

"The mystery is complex and captivating . . . The pace is quick. The plot is tight and fun. And Shelton's writing is a joy to read; her prose has an easy rhythm to it, her narrative style is both witty and engaging, and her dialogue is snappy and rings true."   —The Season

Crops and Robbers

"Shelton has dished up yet another tasty mystery . . . Readers will also get a nice taste of a potential love triangle between Becca's artsy love interest and the principled police officer who's willing to wait in the wings."   —Mojave Desert News

"Very fascinating . . . First-class writing and characterizations along with a lot of homegrown food and jam and jellies that will make your mouth water."   —Once Upon a Romance

"I have loved this entire series . . . No matter the weather outside it is always a perfect time to visit Bailey's Farmers' Market and catch up with all the characters that have sprouted warmly in our hearts."

—Escape with Dollycas into a Good Book

continued . . .

Fruit of All Evil

"A delicious mystery to be savored . . . [A] delightful continuation of the story line featuring feisty and smart amateur sleuth Becca Robins." —*Fresh Fiction*

"Spunky Becca should appeal to fans of Laura Childs and Joanne Fluke." —*Publishers Weekly*

"Fun characters and a great setting are the highlights of this series full of homegrown goodness." —*The Mystery Reader*

"A unique setting and interesting characters . . . You can enjoy Paige Shelton's Farmers' Market Mysteries for the stories, the characters, the humor. *Fruit of All Evil* beautifully blends all of those elements in a delightful mystery." —*Lesa's Book Critiques*

Farm Fresh Murder

"Watching jam-maker Becca Robins handle sticky situations is a tasty delight."
—Sheila Connolly, *New York Times* bestselling author of *Golden Malicious*

"Becca is a genial heroine, and Shelton fashions a puzzling and satisfying whodunit. The first in a projected series, *Farm Fresh Murder* is a tasty treat." —*Richmond Times-Dispatch*

"An appealing heroine . . . As satisfying as visiting the farmers' market on a sunny afternoon."
—Claudia Bishop, author of *A Fete Worse Than Death*

"A breath of summer freshness that is an absolute delight to read and savor . . . A feast of a mystery." —*Fresh Fiction*

Merry Market Murder

PAIGE SHELTON

BERKLEY PRIME CRIME, NEW YORK

THE BERKLEY PUBLISHING GROUP
Published by the Penguin Group
Penguin Group (USA) LLC
375 Hudson Street, New York, New York 10014

USA • Canada • UK • Ireland • Australia • New Zealand • India • South Africa • China

penguin.com

A Penguin Random House Company

MERRY MARKET MURDER

A Berkley Prime Crime Book / published by arrangement with the author

Berkley Prime Crime Books are published by The Berkley Publishing Group.
BERKLEY® PRIME CRIME and the PRIME CRIME logo are trademarks of
Penguin Group (USA) LLC.

For information, address: The Berkley Publishing Group,
a division of Penguin Group (USA) LLC,
375 Hudson Street, New York, New York 10014.

ISBN: 978-0-425-25235-2

PUBLISHING HISTORY
Berkley Prime Crime mass-market edition / December 2013

PRINTED IN THE UNITED STATES OF AMERICA

10 9 8 7 6 5 4 3 2 1

Cover illustration by Dan Craig.
Interior text design by Kristin del Rosario.

For Uncle Tim—you were one of the first ones to welcome me to the family. I'll never forget your kindness and silliness and your genuine enthusiasm over each new Becca story. Thank you. Until we meet again.

Acknowledgments

Many thanks to:

My continually amazing agent, Jessica Faust, and editor, Michelle Vega. I'm sure I frequently test their patience, but they never show it.

My family—whose support and humor are always perfectly timed. Please don't ever change.

And an extra-special thank-you to the Farmers' Market Mysteries' readers. I can't even begin to tell you how much I appreciate your support and friendship.

One

"The rumors are true. He does look a little like Santa Claus,"
I said to Allison as we watched the bearded man working
inside the cargo box on the back of the short freight truck.

"He's a sweetheart. I really like him. I'm glad he'll be
here this year. I can only imagine what this week's going to
be like," Allison said.

"Crazy?"

"But in the best way possible."

Allison—my fraternal twin sister—and I stood next to
each other in the Bailey's Farmers' Market parking lot, right
outside the building that housed Allison's manager's office.
The temperature was cool but not cold, just about right for
our pocket of South Carolina in late December. Even though
Bailey's wasn't currently stocked with harvest-season fresh-
from-the-farm fruits and produce, holiday shopping at the
market had been brisk all month. Christmas was now a week

and a day away, and comfortable temperatures, along with the white-bearded man's freshly grown and recently harvested trees, probably meant we'd all be even busier than we had already been.

"Having a Christmas tree farmer here is a perfect fit," I said.

"I agree. I can't believe we haven't done it before. When I heard that Denny"—she nodded toward the man with the beard—"was donating all the trees for the parade, the idea of asking if he wanted to sell at Bailey's seemed so obvious. I was so glad he wanted to join us that I gave him an exclusive contract with no space rental fees."

The parade was Monson's annual Christmas Tree Parade, held on our short but quaint downtown Main Street. For two evenings every December, the town came together to celebrate the season by consuming holiday goodies and walking up and down the street to admire and bid on decorated trees. Before this year, those who wanted to donate a tree to the parade purchased their own trees and ornaments, placed their creations on display, and then hoped for big, lively bids on their masterpieces. All money made from the auction was donated to a local charity, and the winners got to take home their trees, decorations and all. I'd never once decorated a tree for the parade; I was a bidder, not a tree artist. And though I'd never bid high enough to win, all of the town's residents found a way to donate a little something to the cause. I loved everything about the parade, even the part I'd been volunteered for this year—baking a few hundred jam-filled cookies.

"I guess he looks like Santa would look if Santa were a little thinner and wore jeans." I amended my earlier appraisal.

"Yes, that's true."

Denny Ridgeway hefted a huge, perfect green tree from inside the truck and handed it down to a woman waiting below. She was tall and thin underneath her plaid flannel shirt and khakis, but she handled the tree expertly. She turned and transferred it to a shorter, wider, beardless version of Denny, who carried it into a roped-off area next to the truck. By the time the shorter man came back to the truck, Denny had passed another tree to the woman, and their relay continued. Their movements were seamless, but they'd probably done such a maneuver more than a few times before.

Denny's white, bushy hair, beard, and eyebrows did not disappoint. He was as close to a natural Santa as anyone I'd ever seen. I'd heard about him and his farm for years; they were both legendary. He was the best pine tree farmer in the state; the trees were the best trees in the entire world, at least according to some. He didn't emphasize the fact that he looked a lot like Santa by wearing red suits and a big black belt, but I'd heard that he never shaved the beard. His paunch wasn't as paunchy as it should be, either—about twenty more pounds would be needed to accomplish the look perfectly.

Today, he wore jeans, a long-sleeved black T-shirt, and tennis shoes. He also wore a woven cord choker necklace, which reminded me of my hippie father. Something about the entire three-person troupe reminded me of my parents, actually.

"You have to get Dad and Mom down here to meet him. I bet they'd get along," I said.

"Probably," Allison said. "Come on, I'll introduce you."

I followed Allison around parked cars to the side of the parking lot.

"Ms. Reynolds, always nice to see you," Denny said as he jumped off the back of the truck and wiped his hands on the front of his jeans. The woman and man with him seemed relieved to have a momentary break in the action. They looked at each other and smiled. The woman stepped back a little and the man pulled an arm across his chest as if to stretch his shoulder.

"Allison, please," she said as she shook Denny's hand. "And this is my sister, Becca Robins. She has a jam and preserve stall in the market."

"Any chance you make strawberry?" Denny asked.

"It's my specialty," I said.

"I'll be by to get some today. I love fresh strawberry preserves."

"Great. I look forward to it." I smiled. His face was ruddy—not from the bite of North Pole cold, but from the labor of moving the trees. I really didn't want to notice that his bright green eyes twinkled when he spoke. I was sure it was my imagination anyway.

"This is my sister, Billie, and my brother, Ned." Denny nodded at his coworkers, bringing them back toward us.

"You all look thirsty," Allison said.

"We brought some water bottles," Denny said.

"We have a water hose we're going to connect and run out to you for the trees, but you're more than welcome to fill any of your drinking jugs or cups from water inside the office building. We have vendors inside the market who also sell soft drinks. Make sure you tell them you're working here. The market owners like to help reimburse any drink discounts the vendors give."

"That's great. Thank you," Billie said, her own bright

green eyes twinkling, but not as much as Denny's. Up close, she was still tall and skinny, but also strikingly pretty, with a heart-shaped face and only slightly wrinkled, milky-white skin. She wasn't young, but she still pulled off "fresh-faced" as if she were. She wore a green beret over short, brown hair, which curled up around her ears and away from her face.

"You're welcome," Allison said.

"This is a great place," Ned, the only brown-eyed sibling, added. "I've heard about Bailey's for a long time. I'm sorry I haven't been here before. We're just far enough away that we don't come around very often."

Ridgeway Farm was about a half hour away from Monson. I'd never taken the trip up into the hills to see the farm that I'd heard described as, among other stellar things, stunningly beautiful and a sight to behold.

"We're very proud of Bailey's," Allison said. "And we're thrilled to have you all here."

Billie and Ned excused themselves and set out in search of the soft drinks. As Allison and Denny discussed the logistics involved in having a space at the market, my interest wandered to the trees and the other items still inside the truck. Most of the trees had been unloaded, but there were still a few waiting, their green branches forming a dark mini-forest in a back corner. I also noticed five or six tree stands, an ax, and some wicked-looking spiked implements about ten inches or so long, which had rolled to the edge of the opening.

The air in the immediate area smelled so delicious that I kept taking deep pulls through my nose. I'd had moments with many things pine scented, but I'd never been around such a high concentration of the real stuff. The trees smelled so fresh and . . . piney. This smell could never be mistaken for a cleanser or a car deodorizer. There was something more to it, something that was mixed with natural elements like dirt and oxygen to form its own smell that was easy and comforting to the senses.

"You okay?" Allison asked with a laugh.

Until I opened them, I hadn't realized that I'd closed my eyes.

"Oh. Sorry. The smell. I don't think I can get enough," I said.

"Never smelled a pine tree?" Denny asked with a smile.

"Well, I suppose I have, but I've never had . . ." Suddenly it seemed disloyal to my family to tell Denny Ridgway the reason I'd never had a real pine tree for Christmas. Fortunately, Allison jumped in.

"Our mother's allergic to them. Sneezes like crazy when she's around them. We grew up with artificial."

Denny laughed, but it didn't sound like ho, ho, ho.

"That happens," he said.

"And then . . . well, Becca's life hasn't made a real tree all that convenient. She's getting there, I suppose," Allison said.

"Well, if you'd like a real tree this year, you may find one here, or come up to the farm. I'll give you a personal tour and we'll cut one down together."

I looked at Denny for a long moment. Finally, I said, "I can honestly say that right at this moment I can't think of anything I'd rather do. That sounds just wonderful."

"We'll plan on it then. How about the Sunday after the parade festivities?"

"May I bring a friend?" I asked.

"Of course! Bring anyone." He looked at Allison. "You should come up, too."

In the middle of the invitations, Brenton, Bailey's home-made dog treat vendor, drove a path down the lot next to us. His truck was newer than most of the rest of the vendors', but it was still faded and pocked with plenty of scratches and dings.

Brenton Jones was probably one of the nicest, most easygoing people I knew. He was quiet, friendly, and always wore a New York Yankees baseball cap. I didn't know much about his personal life because he was usually more of a silent observer than a vocal contributor. I had never once heard him say a bad word about anyone. I had also never once seen him shoot a dirty or disgusted look at anyone. He might not have a perpetual smile on his face, but he certainly never looked hateful.

Until that very moment.

As he steered his truck slowly past us, his focus was on the side panel of Denny's much bigger tree truck. No matter that the parking lot was precariously full of cars—Brenton had his eyes glued to the truck, so much so that I had an urge to step forward and see what it was he was looking at, but I stayed put.

Fortunately, Denny's back was to Brenton so he didn't see Brenton's evil eye, but neither Allison nor I could have missed the disgust, followed by dismay, followed by what looked like a flash of anger cross Brenton's face. And even when Brenton noticed we were watching him, his expression didn't soften. In fact, his mouth tightened and he jerked the steering wheel so hard in the other direction that his tires squealed.

Denny turned when he heard the noise and stepped protectively in front of us. Of course, there was no real danger, and no damage was done, because all we saw at that point was the back of Brenton's truck. Denny had no idea who the driver was.

"Thought something might be coming this way," Denny explained as he turned back to face us.

Neither Allison nor I commented, but I had no doubt that she'd be in search of Brenton the second she was finished here. She continued the conversation like she hadn't noticed anything unusual. I tried to follow her lead, but I was sure I wasn't able to hide my distraction as well.

Maybe I'd misinterpreted the entire thing. Maybe Brenton didn't want to spit on Denny's truck. Maybe his dog biscuits hadn't turned out well this morning and he couldn't let go of the frustration. Maybe he was just in a bad mood.

But Brenton was never in a bad mood. Whatever was behind his behavior must have had something to do with the delivery truck, Ridgeway Farm, Denny, or perhaps someone else who worked there. What could have caused one of the most laid-back people I'd ever known to be so visibly perturbed?

My thoughts and Denny and Allison's conversation were interrupted by the arrival of another vehicle. This time it was a Monson police cruiser moving slowly down the same aisle Brenton had taken. The driver moved carefully and purposefully toward the small office building. There was a spot there just for him. Well, there was a spot there just for the police. It was just that this officer visited the market more than any of the others.

Sam Brion, my "most recent love interest"—this is the

way he introduced himself when I told him I thought I was too old to have a "boyfriend"—exited the cruiser. At first, he didn't notice the three of us noticing him.

"Trouble?" Denny asked Allison.

"I doubt it. He and Becca are dating." She sighed. "Though sometimes I suppose it's troublesome for him."

Denny laughed. I didn't.

Once Sam was out of the cruiser, he looked around in that intense, police officer way he did whenever he arrived somewhere. He couldn't help himself; he always had to get the lay of the land, even if there were no imminent threats.

He was in full cop mode, his uniform perfect and his hair slicked back with something I'd yet to be introduced to. He wasn't telling me the product's name. He only slicked back his hair when he wore the uniform. When he wasn't working, his brown hair curled and made him look very non-police-like.

Sam turned and reached back into the cruiser. He pulled out a bright-red box with a large green-and-red bow.

"Ah, someone's getting an early gift," Denny said.

The look on Sam's face made me smile. I didn't know what was in the box, but I knew that whatever his reason for being at Bailey's, it had nothing to do with police work. He was on an errand that included a big box that was far too flashy for his style.

He looked up and finally saw the three of us. His eyebrows rose before he waved and then leaned back onto the cruiser. It was his way of telling me that he didn't want to interrupt the conversation and he'd wait for my signal or for me to join him.

Just as I was about to excuse myself, Billie and Ned came back, their arms loaded with a variety of soda cans.

I was momentarily alarmed by the look on Billie's pretty face. Her eyebrows were together in a tight knit of concern, and she looked at Denny with something akin to panic.

"Everything okay?" Allison asked Billie.

Billie's eyebrows unknit and then rose high. "Oh, everything's fine," she said with way too much breath. Everything wasn't fine, but she clearly didn't want either Allison or me to know what had bothered her. Billie pinched her mouth shut and looked away from everyone.

"Okay, well, let me know if you need anything," Allison said.

"I'm sure everything's just fine," Denny said. He didn't think everything was fine, either, but he was trying to cover for his sister.

The uncomfortable vibe was erased by Allison's ringing phone and Denny's movement up and onto the truck. Time to get back to work.

I sniffed a couple extra times, convinced I could become quickly addicted to the scent of real pine, told Denny I'd talk to him later about the trip up to his farm, waved good-bye to Allison as she hurried away, and then went to greet Sam. The mysteries of the past few minutes dissolved quickly from my mind when he opened the box and told me the contents were especially for me.

Two

"She's out of control," Sam said.

"Mm-hmm," I said, my mouth full of cookie. I hoped my noise sounded like a disagreement. I didn't think she was out of control at all.

"Yes, she is," Sam said. "I didn't even know she cooked."

I swallowed. "Technically, this would be baking, not cooking. She's very sweet to *bake* these for me."

"You know, she asks me every day if we're still together. I've never seen that woman scared of anything, but for some reason I think she's scared we'll break up."

I laughed. "I don't see that hap . . ." I stopped speaking.

Sam smiled and leaned back against the cruiser again. "It's okay to say you don't think that's going to happen, Becca. Even if it does happen—which, by the way, I don't see that outcome, either—it's okay to believe enough in our relationship that you've started thinking that it might, just might, be something . . . lasting. I was going to say 'permanent,' but I thought you might faint or pass out if I did."

I smiled and then put the rest of the cookie in my mouth. Sam and I had talked about my poor success rate in all things romantic. I'd been through two marriages and two divorces and had most recently broken up with someone who was wonderful (even Sam thought he was wonderful). But the timing for Ian and me had been wrong. Considering that Ian was ten years my junior, we'd decided that the timing might never be right. We promised each other that our friendship would continue. For a while I thought our friendship would work, and then I sensed a strain and thought it wouldn't. Neither of us were quite sure how to be just friends, but lately it seemed we'd been able to reconnect without that difficult-to-understand, and even more difficult to explain, romantic tension between us. It was still too early to tell, but I hoped our friendship would ultimately be successful.

So did Sam. In fact, he encouraged it.

But there was no doubt in my mind, no question as to my feelings for the guy leaning against his police car, his hair slicked back, his uniform perfectly pressed, his job steady and real (though Ian was gainfully employed, my two ex-husbands had struggled with this). I was whipped, head over heels, in deep—whatever you wanted to call it. This was the guy for me, and I was pretty certain there'd never be another one to take his place.

I just didn't like to say that out loud. Yet.

"I'm working on it," I said after I finished the cookie.

"I know you are." He stood straight again. "Vivienne wanted me to give these to you." He repeated what he'd said when he handed me the box. "She was extremely relieved to hear we are still together, and I think she wants to bribe you with her cook . . . baking, not to dump me."

Vivienne Norton was one of Sam's fellow Monson police officers. She was burly in a manly way, but wore a thick coat of makeup and her hair bleached in a poufy, Marilyn Monroe blonde color. She was tough and more the silent type than anything. And, apparently, she could bake cookies—at least Christmas cookies—like a pro.

"Well, I'm certainly not dumping you today. These are delicious. Tell her it worked," I said. I reached for a frosted reindeer.

"Good. I'm glad." Sam looked at the truck across the lot. "So, Bailey's is selling Christmas trees this year?"

"Ridgeway Farm is selling. Bailey's is giving them the exclusive space. When Allison heard they were donating the trees for the parade, she wanted to do something for them. Denny Ridgeway, the owner—the guy heaving the tree off the truck—is a South Carolina legend, and the farm is apparently stunning. From all accounts, Denny's a great guy. He invited us—you and me—up to the farm to cut down our own tree. On Sunday."

"That actually sounds great," Sam said, pleasant surprise, and maybe something else, lining his voice.

Though he was much more confident about our relationship than I was willing to express out loud, he wasn't without a few issues of his own. There was a sad story in his past, a story that involved a fiancée who'd met a horrible demise. I still didn't have the full story—he didn't want to talk about it very often—but I knew it was ugly. I'd eventually know exactly what happened.

It was partially because of that tragedy, and the serious nature of his job, that Sam had missed out on a lot of great times. This was unfortunate, because he was a fun person. We were getting there together though, one fun moment at a time. Of course, those moments could only occur when we weren't in the middle of fighting off a vicious murderer or when I wasn't bugging him to share the details of a crime with me. I was fascinated by everything about him, including everything about his job. And, much to my surprise, he was also fascinated by everything about me.

We'd only been together as a couple for a little over a month, but it had been an intense few weeks, filled with emotion and the recognition of feelings we'd both had for a long time, but hadn't either seen clearly or been able to act upon.

We were still in "that" part of the relationship: the over-the-top, breathtaking, and sometimes overwhelming part. My family thought all this fascination with each other would mellow, but I wasn't so sure. I hadn't ever been quite so *fascinated* by anyone.

"We'll have fun," I said.

We were interrupted by Barry of the Barry Good Corn stall inside Bailey's. He walked with effort, his big and not-so-young body becoming more and more difficult to maneuver with each passing season. He seemed to be pushing himself to move quickly today, which was something he rarely did. He had his eyes to the ground and was headed straight for Sam's cruiser.

"Barry?" I said.

He stopped, looked up, and then noticed the car.

"Hey, Becca, Sam." He glanced at me, at the box of

cookies, at Sam, and then toward the back of the stall he'd used to exit the market.

"What's up, Barry?" I said.

Sam set the box of cookies back onto the car. He noticed Barry's jumpy behavior, too.

"Oh, fiddle," he said. "It's not a police matter, but maybe you should head in there, Sam."

"Why's that?" Sam asked as he took a step away from the cruiser. I moved with him.

"Brenton's pretty upset. He was yelling at Allison," Barry said. "I keep my cell phone out in my truck. I was coming out to call Brenton's ex-wife. I didn't know what else to do. He's becoming an unwelcome distraction, I'm afraid."

I always find the moments that my perception is completely altered startling and bizarre. I had no idea Brenton had been married, and I'd known him for years. Brenton yelling at my sister didn't jibe with . . . anything. There were moments when I thought he should maybe be a little upset about something, but he shrugged off those moments, usually with a friendly lift of his baseball cap and a gentle smile.

But his earlier behavior in the parking lot hadn't been what I was used to seeing from him, either. Something must have happened—something horrible—to set him off. But what could possibly change him so much?

Sam looked at me.

"Don't you dare tell me to stay here," I said.

"I was going to ask you to call Brenton's ex-wife with Barry," Sam said.

"I can handle it by myself. I'd use your phone, but I don't know the number. It's on one of those . . . what are they called . . . speed-dial memory thingies, and my phone's in my truck," Barry repeated.

"Of course. Thank you, Barry," Sam said.

As Barry stepped away, Sam and I hurried toward the market. The entrance was about halfway between us and the Ridgway Farm trio, but going through the back of the same stall that Barry had come through seemed like the better idea.

The canvas wall was also the outer wall of Ian's metal yard art stall. I hadn't seen him yet today, but he didn't spend as much time at the market as he had when he was first building his business. He'd purchased some land and was in the process of turning it into a lavender farm and an art studio, so extended time spent anywhere didn't happen often.

Sam lifted the wall of the tent and entered the empty stall through the opening. He held the flap for me but his attention was now focused inside the market and on the ruckus across the aisle.

"Brenton, that's not reasonable," Allison said. "Come on. Please come to the office with me and we can discuss this."

Allison was good at everything, including situations rife with anger, but for the first time in a long time I thought I heard uncertainty in her voice.

Sam and I moved behind her and to the edge of the aisle. No one paid us any attention, but everyone, vendors and customers alike, was standing and watching the showdown, if that's what it truly was.

"I just know the rules, Allison. I know that I'm supposed to get a vote. I would have argued and voted no. I would have convinced everyone else, too. They shouldn't be here," Brenton said.

"You do get a vote, Brenton, but this was an unusual circumstance. This isn't a permanent vendor. Come with me to my office and I'll point that part of the contract out to you."

"I don't want to go to your office. I want them out of here."

"Who does he want out of here?" I asked Abner, the wildflower man, though I thought I knew who he was talking about.

"Those Christmas trees folks," Abner said.

"Why?"

Abner shrugged. "Dunno. Allison's been trying to get that out of him or get him out of here. Brenton's causing quite the scene."

"Sam," I said as I put my hand on his arm.

"Already on it," he said.

He had taken a step forward, and the thought that that was the first time I'd "taken advantage" of his position of authority flitted through my mind. I wanted him to be the police officer and get the situation in front of us handled. Something was wrong with Brenton; his tone was threatening toward my sister. I didn't know how long the show had been going on, but it was time for it to be over, and Sam was here, in uniform and everything. My prompting him forward had been almost an unconscious maneuver.

Sam threaded his way around a couple of curious customers and was standing next to Allison a few seconds later.

"Allison," he said in greeting.

She looked surprised to see him, but her face neutralized quickly.

"Sam," she said.

"Brenton, how're you doing?" Sam turned his attention to the angry man in the Yankees cap.

"I'm not happy, but this isn't a police matter, Sam," Brenton said.

"I don't know. Someone sure seems to be disturbing the peace around here."

Brenton's eyebrows came together as he looked hard at Sam. A moment later, he looked around at the crowd that had gathered. It was as if he finally noticed the audience. He shuffled his feet, lifted his cap, and then put it back on his head.

"I'm not happy, that's all," he muttered.

Allison put her hand on Sam's arm, but kept her glance toward Brenton. "I'm sorry about that, Brenton, and I want to better understand what's going on. Come on, come with me to my office."

Brenton hesitated, but only briefly. He looked at the crowd and then at Sam again. "Sure. Okay, sure."

The disturbance was suddenly over and the crowd began to disperse and return to minding their own business and shopping lists. I joined Sam just as he asked Allison if she wanted him to attend the meeting with Brenton.

"No, Sam, he's harmless. He's just having an extraordinarily bad day, and I'm truly concerned about him. We'll be fine."

Sam didn't like that answer, but he didn't push it.

I didn't know what to think. I agreed with Allison, but something had made one of the mellowest men ever behave as unlike himself as I thought possible. I didn't say anything, but thought that Sam and I would follow behind Allison and keep watch by the entrance of the market, which just happened to be right where Sam's car was parked. We could trail and spy on them casually.

"Hey," a voice said behind me, stopping us from executing my sneaky plan.

"Linda, hey," I said.

"Hi, Linda," Sam said.

As my neighbor vendor and best friend, Linda was like family to me, and she and Sam had grown closer since we'd started dating. She baked fruit pies and played the part of prairie woman perfectly in her pioneer skirt and apron. She sometimes wore a bonnet, too, but as I'd become used to lately, the bonnet had gone missing and her short, blonde curls were free and bouncy.

"That was interesting," she said.

"Do you know how it started?" I asked.

"Yeah, I was close by the whole time. I was talking to Abner when Brenton got to his stall. He was agitated, stomping around, rough with his inventory, hurrying and putting bags of dog biscuits up on his tables, but not neatly. It was strange. I was going to go talk to him when Abner and I finished, but then that woman walked in."

"Which woman?" Sam and I asked at the same time.

"The one who works with the Christmas tree guy."

"Billie?" I said.

"I don't know her name; she wore a green beret. She walked by and when the two of them saw each other, they froze and stared—hatefully—at each other. I thought one of them might leap for the other one and we'd have some sort of brawl to deal with, but then the guy who works with the trees—the one who doesn't look like Santa—joined her.

He acted surprised to see Brenton, but he directed the woman out of there. They must know each other, and they must not like each other. At all."

"How did Allison get involved?" I asked.

"She just happened to be walking by and Brenton yelled her name to get her attention. He got everyone's attention. He yelled at her for letting the Christmas tree people sell at Bailey's. He was adamant that he was supposed to have a vote about which vendors were welcome at Bailey's—that we were all supposed to vote."

"That's true," I said to Sam. "We vote on new vendors, but I'm certain there's an exception for temporary parking lot vendors who aren't paying for their space. I haven't ever looked closely at my contract, but Allison was probably right, there's probably some clause."

He nodded, and we both looked back at Linda.

"Well, he wouldn't let up and he wouldn't tell her why he was so upset they were here. I think you two came in around the third round of back-and-forth," she said as she paused and thought a moment. "It was all so un-Brenton."

"I agree," I said.

"There must be some sort of ugly history between Brenton and the Ridgeways," Sam said.

"Yeah, there's something there," Linda said. She continued a beat later. "Don't mean to be insensitive, but since you're both here together, you two still coming to dinner the day after Christmas? Drew can hardly wait to use his new grill. I didn't know where to hide it or how to wrap it, so he got his gift early." Drew was Linda's almost-two-months-returned and almost-brand-new husband. I'd been her number one back in July—our term for maid of honor—right before he'd left for Navy SEAL duty to someplace secret and dangerous. He was almost as amazing as she was, and they'd both been easygoing about my boyfriend . . . uh, love interest . . . switch-up. They had been as good of friends with Ian as they were with me, but they'd managed to remain friends with us both and with Sam, too.

"We're planning on it," I said as Sam smiled and nodded.

"Good. Well, I need to get back to work, but we'll talk later. I really hope Brenton's okay." Linda hugged me quickly before she turned and wove her way back to her stall.

The Ridgeway trees hadn't been at Bailey's long enough to have contributed to our burgeoning crowd, so I chalked up the number of accidental bumps and excuse me's I was getting to the pleasant weather and the growing holiday spirit. It didn't feel like a big summer crowd, but a good-sized fall crowd at least. I wondered if the addition of the trees would give Bailey's vendors a record December.

It was too late to follow Allison and Brenton. I turned to Sam, who was lost in thought, his face serious as he looked in the direction of the front office and the parking lot. He turned back toward me a second later, but I spoke before he did.

"You need to go check some things out? You need to maybe go ask some questions and see if you can figure out what was up with Brenton? Am I right?"

"Exactly." Sam smiled.

"I know how you feel."

"Yes, but I do such things in an official capacity. You're just nosy."

"Hopefully you'll share whatever you find out."

He raised one eyebrow and then said, "Come get your

cookies. Vivienne might shoot me, or at least lock me in a holding cell, if I don't make sure they're in your hands."

We ventured back toward the parking lot and his cruiser. The door to Allison's office was shut tightly and neither Sam nor I could hear any loud voices. We both veered close enough to listen.

Just as Sam handed me the box of cookies, though, the Bailey's Farmers' Market world was disrupted again.

Bailey's was on the edge of Monson, on a two-lane high-way that led into the small center of the town in one direction and eventually to Columbia in the other direction.

A truck came rolling in from the direction of Columbia. It turned in to the Bailey's lot and lumbered slowly forward toward the side of the parking lot opposite of where the similar Ridgeway truck was parked.

I noticed Denny, Billie, and Ned as they stopped moving the trees. Denny jumped down from his perch and joined Billie and Ned as the three of them stood in their own small group, pointing at and discussing the incoming truck.

On the side of the new truck, written in bigger, bolder letters than were used on the side of the Ridgeways' was "Stuckey Christmas Trees."

Tree illustrations also decorated the panel, which made the Stuckey truck much prettier than the Ridgeway truck.

"Uh-oh," I said.

"What's up?" Sam said.

"I'm pretty sure Allison mentioned that the Ridgeways had an exclusive, that there wouldn't be any other tree sellers at Bailey's."

"You mentioned that to me. Maybe it's a fluke. Maybe the Stuckey truck isn't here to sell—maybe there are some mechanical issues and the driver just had to stop some-where? He could just be here to shop."

"Yeah, that's probably it," I said. I hoped that was the case.

The Stuckey truck came to a loud, squeaky, air-brake halt. The man who got out of the driver's side looked noth-ing like Santa. He was tall, thin, and wiry, with short, dark hair and a beaked nose, which somehow fit his long face. He stood next to his truck on one side of the lot as Denny stood next to his on the other side. They both had their hands on their hips as they stared at each other, reminding me of an Old West showdown. I could almost hear the whistle of the *Ponderosa* theme in the background; if they'd had guns, both would have drawn them by now.

"Or maybe there's a big problem," Sam said.

We were all about to find out just how big.

Three

"I have the paperwork," *Reggie Stuckey said, the tone of* patience gone from his voice. He'd seemed like such a pleasant guy until Allison told him that he wasn't contracted to sell his trees at Bailey's, and that Ridgeway Farm had the exclusive right.

Fortunately, this crisis was happening in the parking lot and not inside the market. The only customers privy to it were the ones who'd either just driven onto the lot or come out of the market and were curious about the small gathering beside the nicer-looking tree truck.

Reggie Stuckey had shaken everyone's hand, including Denny Ridgeway's. There was no doubt that the two of them didn't like each other, though Denny was less obvious about his feelings than Billie and Ned were.

The gathering consisted of the tree farmers, Allison, me, Sam, and Brenton, who'd come with Allison out of her office. I stood toward the back of the crowd, and I was able to watch Brenton's attitude change as the conversation continued. He was pleased that there was some sort of disagreement. Specifically, I suspected he was pleased that the Ridgeway group was somehow bothered or inconvenienced or something. I hoped Allison had been able to get to the bottom of his problem.

"I have paperwork, too, Reggie. I had meetings with the Bailey's owners and later with Allison. They assured me I was going to be the only Christmas tree seller at Bailey's this year," Denny said. His patience was also being tested, though he was still trying to sound unperturbed.

Reggie blinked a couple times, but didn't back down.

"I didn't have meetings, but I certainly have the paperwork. I did everything by phone." He looked at Allison. "I only talked to the owners, though," he said to her.

She nodded.

As I've already noted, Allison's pretty good at everything. She'd been unduly challenged in the last hour, but she was still cool and collected, her long, dark ponytail still in place and smooth. I'd been concerned enough for her that I'd already run my hands through my short, blonde hair about a hundred times. I was trying to stay quiet and keep calm, but I wasn't sure how much longer I would last.

"Do you have the paperwork on you, Reggie?" Allison asked.

"I think so," he said before he turned and climbed back into his truck.

"You want me to send Ned back to the farm to get our contract?" Denny asked Allison.

"No, I've got a copy of that one. Of course, I wasn't in

on the conversations between you and the owners, Denny, but I'm sure that they and I specifically discussed that you were to be our exclusive tree seller. I know that's what your contract says. Exclusivity is definitely something you talked about with them as well as me, right?"

"Yes, of course," Denny said.

"I'm afraid I don't have the contract, but I can call my office manager and have her fax it over to you. I can ask her to bring it over if you'd prefer," Reggie said from the truck's driver's seat.

"Faxing would be fine." Allison looked at Reggie as he scooted off the seat again. She bit her lip as she looked quickly at Denny and then back to Reggie. "Look, there's some sort of confusion or mistake. I'm sorry to both of you, but I will get this figured out. Reggie, I'm not going to ask you to leave, but would you mind not unloading your trees until I get a look at the contract?"

Reggie's face was getting redder by the second, but he'd been able to keep his tone of voice fairly calm. Only he knew for sure whether or not he had a right to be upset, and I thought he realized that Allison was trying to do the right thing.

Before Reggie could answer, Denny said, "Reggie, if you're supposed to be here, I'll help you unload, okay? Let's just give Ms. Reynolds a second or two to sort everything out."

Denny's reputation as a kind and generous businessman had just shown in a big way. At first Reggie's face got a little redder, but then he calmed; his shoulders seemed to relax and his cheeks faded to something a little less red.

"Sure, sure. I'll call my gal," he said.

"Who did you speak with from Bailey's? Which owner?" Allison said to Reggie.

"I'm terrible with names, but I'll see what my notes say. It was some woman, though. What's your fax number?"

As Allison wrote down the fax number for Reggie, it felt like a good time for the group to disband. Denny led Billie and Ned back to the other side of the parking lot. Sam gave me the cookie box and distractedly told me good-bye. I had no idea what sort of police work or investigation might be involved in what had just gone on at Bailey's, but I knew he'd be on the case.

"Where'd Brenton go?" Allison asked as I waved at the back of the police cruiser.

"I didn't know he was gone. I didn't see which way he went. What's up with him, Al?"

"Come to my office."

Allison's desk was unusually clear. December was normally her "spring cleaning" month. It was when she sorted through her files, dusted under her computer, and de-cluttered her desk. Other than the inclusion of the tree vendor, or vendors, as the case may turn out to be, this December probably wasn't much different than any other.

"He wouldn't tell me why," she said. "He just doesn't like the Ridgeway people."

"Brenton likes everyone," I said. We sat across from each other, one on each side of her desk.

"Not everyone, apparently."

"And how in the world could anyone not like the Ridgeways? They're so . . . nice, and Christmas-y. They're a South Carolina tradition and legend."

"I agree, but we might be misjudging them. I was going

to ask Denny if he would tell me what his ties were to Brenton, but then Reggie Stuckey pulled in."

"Would the owners really have offered an exclusive to both Denny and Reggie? That doesn't sound like the way they do business. They're pretty good at that stuff."

As if on cue, the fax on the small, wide, file cabinet behind Allison rang and connected.

"No, never, and I know something weird is up," Allison said. "There are no female owners. They don't even have a female working in their office."

"Doesn't sound very forward thinking," I said.

Allison laughed. "No, they're not sexist. It just happens to be that way. They did give me this job, and I'm pretty sure I'm female. They're good guys."

"So, Reggie said he talked to a female owner." I thought about his words and tone. "Al, he didn't sound at all like he was lying. Why would he, anyway? To pack up one of those big trucks and haul around a bunch of trees? Sounds like a lot of work just to cause some sort of stir or inconvenience."

She gathered the fax and then turned back toward me. "I have no idea."

She spread the contract pages out on the desk. There were three pages of mostly legal jargon, what was deemed necessary in our brave new litigious world.

"Well, it's definitely our contract," she muttered without looking up. She ran her finger down the first page and then moved to the second page, where she stopped halfway down.

"Hang on," she said.

She reached to her side and opened a file drawer. She pulled out another contract and set it on the desk. This one's pages were stapled together.

"Look at this," she continued.

I stood and peered at where she was pointing.

She flipped up the first page of the stapled contract. She put her right index finger halfway down that page while her left index finger was still on the second, loose page of the faxed contract.

"Look at the Ridgeways' contract—I marked the 'exclusivity clause' with a small line, a checkmark of sorts, just for my own sake. That line that I drew is on the Stuckey contract, too. Exactly the same line, in the same spot."

"Reggie Stuckey duplicated the contract? How? That's not a very bright move. It took you less than five minutes to figure it out," I said.

Allison flipped to the last pages of each contract.

"This contract is meant to be used for all temporary vendors. Throughout it, the language is simply 'Bailey's Farmers' Market' and 'Vendor.' Until the last page. There, the vendor's business name and the name of a representing officer are typed in on the computer. The Stuckey contract is identical to the Ridgeway's except for the vendor and representative signature names."

"So, Reggie . . . wait, I'll say someone . . . copied everything, but used Wite-Out on the names and retyped them in?"

Allison laughed. "Yes. Look, you can even see the difference. The contract is, of course, written on a computer. You can see how someone actually rolled the Stuckey contract through a typewriter and added the names. The fonts are slightly different and the *g*s drop a little."

"Where in the world does one find a typewriter nowadays? And how in the world did whoever did this think that they wouldn't get caught?"

"I don't know," Allison said in response to both questions.

I sat back down as Allison continued to inspect the contracts.

"Are you just going to kick him out?" I asked after a moment.

"I probably could, based on this alone, but I think I'd better get the owners involved. I'll tell Reggie not to set up until tomorrow, that the owners want to come out and first talk to him personally. The owners will want to get the police involved, too, I'm sure. It's illegal to forge documents, but I'm not sure how illegal."

"I can help on the police end," I said, pulling out my cell phone to call Sam.

"Hang on," Allison said. She pointed at the contracts. "Let me talk to the owners first. Let me make sure it wasn't us or them who somehow did this."

"What? Something more is bothering you, I can tell," I said. I wasn't using our twin intuition as much as I was just noticing the deep thought–invoked creases on her forehead.

"I just don't understand why anyone would do this. I'm trying to picture the sequence of events. If Reggie wants to sell trees at Bailey's, he calls me or the owners directly, and he's told we've given an exclusive to someone else. Even if he knew who the exclusive was for, why would he bother to go to such extremes, and how did he get the contract?"

"We have a mystery on our hands."

"We always have a mystery, it seems. I'm glad this one doesn't involve a dead body," Allison said.

"True," I said, but I'll never forget the wave of disquiet that ran down the back of my throat, though my chest and then chilled my toes. I'd never been one for premonitions but I was a big believer in jinxes. And as sure as I was that Vivienne Norton, burly Monson police officer, knew how to bake Christmas cookies, the next morning I knew that the wave of wonky I'd felt had been a jinx falling into place and affecting just about everyone involved.

Four

"I have no idea where Reggie went," Allison said. **"After you** and I talked yesterday, I called the owners and then came out to let him know that they'd be by this afternoon to talk to him. They told me not to call the police, either. They had an office temp helping out last month during a big paperwork filing crisis—their words, not mine—and the temp employee was a female. They wanted to talk to her before they talked to Reggie, so they told me to hold off. I came out to talk to him but he wasn't here."

I stepped onto the running board on the driver's side of Reggie's truck and peered through the side window. The cab wasn't like some big-rig cabs I'd seen with a living/sleeping space in the back, but it was plenty roomy. The driver and passenger seats were both covered in black-and-red-checkered fabric that had seen much better days. A sturdy, green Thermos was on its side on the passenger seat, and the smoky cigarette smell I thought I noticed coming through the closed window was confirmed by an open pack under the Thermos. I could even see a few flecks of tobacco next to the pack. I confirmed once again that the door was locked before I hopped down and hurried over to the passenger side.

"I checked it, too," Allison said. "Locked."

It was locked tight, no matter how many times I tried the handle.

"You haven't seen him at all since earlier yesterday?" I asked as I rejoined her on the driver's side.

"No. I haven't really asked around, so I don't know if anyone saw him leave in another vehicle, but if he has trees inside the truck, shouldn't they be aired out or something?"

"I have no idea." I looked toward the Ridgeways' setup. They'd completely unloaded their truck the day before, and I'd already noticed a number of buyers leaving the market with trees. Denny, Billie, and Ned were currently sitting in lawn chairs arranged in a triangle formation. They all wore a similar version of what they'd worn the day before, and instead of soft drinks, each held a steaming mug. "Maybe we should ask Denny."

"Yeah, I hate to bother him but they aren't terribly busy right at the moment." She lifted a foot to step forward.

"Denny!" I said as I cupped my hand around my mouth. "You have a minute?" Then I signaled him toward us.

"I could have walked over there," Allison said.

"This is more efficient," I said. "You were just going to come right back. It's okay for me to be a little uncouth. Anything to help."

To my surprise, Allison nodded before she said, "Good point. Thank you."

"That's my girl," I said quietly so Denny wouldn't hear as he joined us.

"Allison, Becca! How are the two of you today?" he asked cheerfully. If he had problem with the Stuckey truck's continued presence in the lot, he didn't show it.

"Hi, Denny," Allison said. "We're great. You all as comfortable as possible over there?"

"Yes, ma'am, no complaints."

I tried to erase the sudden suspicion in my glance. He didn't sound phony at all, but he had to be at least somewhat upset that the Stuckey truck was still on the lot. Maybe Denny truly was as neighborly as he appeared to be, or maybe he was just being patient in the hope that the matter would be resolved before the day was over. Either way, I thought he was a little too cheery.

Allison smiled. "Denny, I'm sorry to bother you, but since you, Billie, and Ned have been out here pretty consistently for the last couple days, I wondered if you saw where Reggie Stuckey went. I haven't seen him since yesterday."

"I don't think I did." He rubbed the back of a finger over the side of his jaw, making his beard swing like a clock's pendulum. "I'm pretty sure the truck's in the same spot as when he parked it, and I don't remember anyone coming by to pick him up."

Allison squinted up at the cab. "Would he be inside?"

Repeating my investigative maneuver, Denny stepped up on the running board and peered inside the cab. "He's not in there. There's no secret hidden spot or anything." He jumped down.

"What about the back?" Allison led the way down the side of the truck and toward the cargo load.

"He'd be pretty uncomfortable if he was in there with little to no ventilation. I doubt it," Denny said.

"What about the trees? I didn't look inside but if there are trees in there, are they being harmed by the lack of ventilation?"

"They could be, but if he gets them out today they'll probably be fine."

For a long few moments, the three of us stood behind the truck and looked up at the back doors.

"Should we just open it and get the trees out for him, or at least give them air—if that will help them?" I suggested.

Denny shifted his weight from one foot to the other, but didn't say anything. He was hesitant and uncomfortable; he would want to be careful about overstepping his bounds.

"No one answered when I called his office this morning. We haven't seen him since yesterday. It's almost noon." Allison looked at the time display on her phone. "I don't think it's necessarily time to be worried, but I can't help it—I *am* worried. If it's not locked, I'm going to open the back and just take a look."

"Here, let me help," Denny said resolutely. He stepped forward and moved the arm mechanism that kept the doors closed. It clicked with no resistance. "It's not locked."

He stepped backward as he pulled on the door. We were greeted by the scent of pine, but it was different than yesterday's sense-stimulating earthiness. This time, it mixed with other, less wonderful smells, too. The temperature had been warm enough to make the closed-up inside of the truck stagnant and stuffy, which gave the air an automatic dusty thickness.

There was something else, too, something I didn't readily recognize but I probably should have.

I scrunched my nose. "What *is* that?"

"I don't know," Allison and Denny said together.

As if to answer my question, a dark liquid trickled out of the truck and to the asphalt below. It probably didn't make a noise, but I watched the trail of red drops, and in my mind they plopped loudly when they hit the ground.

"That . . . that looks like blood," Allison said.

"Oh no," I said.

Somehow and with no organization, suddenly the three of us were up and inside the truck. We each managed to grab a tree or two and throw them out the back. A mere few seconds later, we finally found Reggie Stuckey. He was on his back in the middle of his own tree truck, a thick stake through his chest.

Reggie Stuckey would not be selling trees from Bailey's this year, or any year in the future, for that matter.

"Reg, oh, Reg," Denny said from his knees. He avoided the puddle of blood as he felt Reggie's neck for a pulse. He looked up at Allison and me. "He's gone."

"Becca," Allison said as she looked at me.

I didn't need any further prompting. I pulled out my phone and called Sam.

"It's an outdoor tree stake," I overheard Denny tell Sam.

I was back a bit from the two of them but I could hear their conversation. I was sure Sam knew I was eavesdropping, but he hadn't signaled me to go away yet, so I hadn't.

Sam and I had been through some scary—and down-right horrifying—moments, but we'd been friends at the time, not a couple. My previous "as-friends" bold behavior included asking him questions about cases that were none of my business. Even then he'd answered more than he should have, but I now wondered just how much I would be able to get out of him. Would our pillow talk turn to things murderous and criminal, or would he become more protective of his information, and more protective of me knowing things?

Time would tell.

"Is it a standard stake? Something all Christmas tree vendors sell?" Sam asked.

"Well, we all sell something like it, though I'm not sure what kind exactly was used on Reggie," Denny said. "Most natural-tree vendors would definitely sell something like it, though."

He was saddened by his competitor's demise; that much was obvious. The two of them hadn't displayed congenial friendship the day before, but Denny had been completely shaken by Reggie's murder. We all had, but there was something tender about his reaction that made me curious about their history. I'd mentioned my observation to Sam when he arrived.

"Becca," a voice said from behind me.

"Officer Norton, hello," I said. "Considering the circumstances, it feels strange to thank you for the cookies, but thank you. They are—well, mostly were—delicious."

"You're welcome. You have a minute? I'd like to ask you some questions."

I glanced toward Sam and Denny and then looked at Officer Norton. "About the . . . about Reggie?" I said.

"Yes."

"I thought Sam would be questioning everyone."

"Well, considering that the two of you are a couple, it wouldn't be prudent to have him talk to you. He sent me over."

"Good point."

I had warily liked Vivienne Norton when I first met her. I found her intimidating in ways that I didn't usually find women intimidating. She wasn't the only female officer on the small Monson police force, but she was the only one I'd ever had dealings with. Her muscular build was something she must have had to work hard to maintain, but I wasn't aware of a gym in Monson or the surrounding areas. She probably had to be diligent about maintaining her bleached hair and thick makeup, too. She was such a boatload of contradictions that for a long time I wasn't exactly sure how to behave around her. I'd realized, though, that she and I were much more alike than we were different. She worked the job of her dreams, she worked hard, she wanted to be the best she could be at her career, and she chose to the look the way she did, just like I chose my wardrobe of overalls and mostly forgotten makeup.

I'd been surprised by her continued enthusiasm about my and Sam's relationship, and I liked her even more for it. Although she was thrilled that Sam and I were a couple, I had no doubt that Officer Vivienne Norton would throw me to the ground and cuff me if she ever thought I was guilty of a crime.

"Come on," she said as she looked toward Sam and then back at me again. "Let's go somewhere away from everyone else."

I followed her to the edge of the Bailey's lot, the side farthest away from the entrance and a good twenty feet back from the Ridgeway setup. Because of their big truck, Officer Norton could conduct her interview in private. We were hidden from everyone except those driving by on our side of the adjacent two-lane highway. Given close inspection, it might have looked like something unusual was going on in the parking lot, but it was typical for it to be full, so passersby didn't even give the market a second glance.

"You found Mr. Stuckey's body?" she asked me.

"Yes. Allison and Denny Ridgeway were there, too." I sounded way too defensive already. I'd found a few dead bodies in my time, and Officer Norton had an accusatory tone to her voice, emphasizing that she remembered my involvement, peripheral though it might have been. I cleared my throat.

"Tell me the events that led up to you opening the back of his truck. Why did you—the three of you—decide it was something that needed to be done?"

"We couldn't find Reggie," I said. "And we were worried about him and about the trees."

I explained that we'd checked the cab, that Allison had said that she hadn't received an answer when she'd called Reggie's office that morning, and that the Ridgeways hadn't seen him.

"So, Mr. Ridgeway said that the *three* members of his group hadn't seen Mr. Stuckey? He was specific about all three of them?" she said.

I thought back. "I think he said 'we,' but I don't know if that was meant to be specific to the three of them. I don't know if he really knew if the others had or hadn't seen Reggie."

"What dealings did you have with Reggie Stuckey?"

"None. I'd never seen him or met him before yesterday. I've probably heard of his farm, but I can't remember when. I've often heard about the Ridgeway Farm."

"Those Ridegway trees are amazing," she said as she jotted in her small, black notebook. There was a rising tone to her voice, as if she wanted me to add something.

I didn't know what exactly to say, so I just went with, "Uh-huh, that's what I've heard for years, and the ones they brought to sell at the market look perfect."

She looked up from the notebook. "You've never had a Ridgeway tree?"

"I've never had a real Christmas tree. Mom was allergic."

"That's a shame." She *tsk*'ed and shook her head.

Now I felt like defending my mom. *But she was good with finger painting, never cared if we made a mess*—or something along those lines. I cleared my throat again.

"So, what do you know about the contract between the deceased victim Reggie Stuckey and Bailey's Farmers' Market?"

"Nothing specific. I know that both Denny and Reggie thought they had the exclusive right to sell trees at Bailey's this year, but I don't know the contract details," I said, quickly and easily. Even I was impressed by my smooth lie. I would tell Sam later about my meeting with Allison and our inspection of the two tree vendor contracts. When I told him, he would tell me that I should have told Officer Norton and he'd pretend he was irritated that I hadn't. But I didn't care. Evidently, she already knew something about the contract was bothersome and I didn't think that she was intimating that Allison was involved with Reggie Stuckey's murder, but she was curious about people who were a part of the market, curious about something my sister had been involved in creating. I'd give the full information to Sam and he'd know the right way to deal with it. I didn't want to risk saying anything that might—even a little bit of might—make Allison look in any way involved.

"Did you hear the argument yesterday in the parking lot?"

"Yes, but it was more a slight confrontation than an argument."

"Can you tell me exactly what you remember?"

"Sure." I told her what had been said between the parties involved. It hadn't been a particularly angry meeting; more tense than angry, but it could have become more heated if Allison hadn't been able to stall everyone for a day or two.

"What do you think would have happened if Reggie Stuckey had been found to be lying about his selling-at-Bailey's status?" Officer Norton asked.

"I guess Allison would have asked him to leave."

"Why would someone go to such lengths to lie about being a vendor? It seems so elaborate and wasteful. His truck was packed with trees, and they might not be sellable at this point," Officer Norton said, but she wasn't really asking me a question. She was pondering aloud.

Nonetheless, I said, "I don't know."

Since I was facing the entrance to the market, I saw when Brenton turned his truck in to the lot. I also noticed the expression on his face. I was almost certain it bore the same crankiness from the day before, but this time it only lasted a brief instant. Then the disdain transformed into something that caused his face to become as pale white as I'd ever seen. He slowed the truck slightly and looked furtively around the lot.

Officer Norton noticed me noticing Brenton, so she turned and watched what I was watching. He was a good fifty feet away and he wore the ever-present Yankees cap, but there was no mistaking his changing expressions.

"What's his name?" Officer Norton asked as she raised her notebook, but didn't take her eyes off Brenton.

"Brenton Jones. He makes homemade dog biscuits."

"Hmm. I've heard of him. I think I need to have a chat with him. You won't be leaving town or anything anytime soon?"

I laughed, but then cleared my throat again when I saw she wasn't joking. "No, ma'am."

"Good."

I watched her advance toward Brenton, and I followed right behind. Brenton's behavior had garnered my full attention, and if he wasn't going to tell Allison what was bugging him, maybe I could just overhear the problem. However, there was no real place to hide. Though we were in the parking lot, it didn't seem wise to dart around the parked vehicles. Besides, attempting to hide while the police were investigating a murder would not only irritate the police, but Allison, too. I moved toward Officer Norton and Brenton, but tried to look casual.

Brenton's truck had been moving slowly, and with a lift

of her hand, Officer Norton stopped him completely. She moved the notebook back into writing position as the two of them spoke through his open driver's-side window.

I stopped beside an old blue Volkswagen Bug. Thinking that my faded overalls would blend in with the equally faded paint job, I crossed my arms and stood very still. If all was going according to plan, I was hiding in plain sight.

And I didn't hear a thing. I couldn't read their lips, either. I would have to move closer, and then I would be caught and dismissed by Officer Norton. Nonetheless, I decided I needed to take the risk.

As I moved one foot forward, though, Brenton put an end to any secrecy. He threw the truck into park and then cannoned himself out of it.

"Denny Ridgeway is the killer," he yelled to Officer Norton as he pointed at the still-living tree vendor.

If it had been any other person, or perhaps at any place other than the Bailey's parking lot in Monson, South Carolina, Officer Vivienne Norton would likely have pulled out her gun and done whatever it took to subdue Brenton and his sudden raging anger.

Instead, she kept her stance firm and her gun in its holster.

"Back off," she said, loudly enough that I heard it from my spot beside the car.

"I'm telling you, Denny Ridgeway's the killer. Reggie Stuckey was killed by Denny Ridgeway!" Brenton said, as he stomped his foot way too far in Officer Norton's space. He hadn't backed off.

"That's enough," Officer Norton said. I hadn't noticed

when the notebook had disappeared, but I saw her hand had finally moved to the still-holstered gun.

"No, no, it's not enough! He's the killer. Arrest him!"

I'd seen Sam shoot people before. In fact, he'd once aimed a gun my direction, though it had been hard to hold that against him since I'd been cradling a bloody ax. But I'd never seen him use the force that he worked hard to build in his body. He was in amazing shape—he worked out almost every morning in his own basement gym. And though I knew it must have had something to do with being the best police officer ever, I'd never seen the need for such effort—until now.

Somehow, Sam came from wherever he'd been and moved behind Brenton. With movements that were so fluid and quick it was difficult to understand exactly what I was seeing, he had Brenton up against his own truck and then the man's wrists cuffed behind his back. If Brenton tried to resist, I didn't see it. Sam had manhandled him as though Brenton had no strength whatsoever. Sam wasn't gentle but he wasn't rough either, just confidently forceful.

He glanced in my direction, his mouth and eyes tight. He wasn't happy about what he'd had to do, but he was trying to let me know that it was necessary. Not that he needed to explain anything to me.

I liked that he wanted to, though.

"You'll get the details to me later?" Allison said. As stealthily as Sam had darted to Brenton, Allison had moved to my side.

I nodded.

"I can't understand what's happening with Brenton. It's

like he's a completely different person than the one who has been working at Bailey's for all these years," she said.

I nodded. I didn't have any idea, either. I could speculate, but if I'd learned anything at all, it was that too much speculation without substance could sometimes drive you down the wrong path, and it would definitely drive you at least a little crazy.

Five

It crossed my mind to follow Sam and Brenton downtown to the small police station located on Main Street, but I stayed at Bailey's. The police didn't shut down the market; they just disrupted it slightly and in waves. Officer Norton stayed, and a couple other officers were called in. They questioned a number of the other vendors, though I got the impression the police didn't learn anything new. Many vendors hadn't paid much attention to the Christmas tree trucks, and no one seemed to have additional information about what had happened to Reggie. His body was removed, but his truck remained; a crime scene unit was called in from Columbia to search it thoroughly for evidence. I was sure I'd have to either give them a new set of fingerprints or let them know that the Monson police had a set on file. Once again, I was in the position of needing to be eliminated from suspicion. I wondered if there was a limit to the amount of times I was allowed to be eliminated, or if I'd automatically be placed under suspicion at some point.

The official police and crime scene unit vehicles were curious sights, but the customers weren't to be deterred. Plenty of people thought it was just another good day to shop at Bailey's, and they ignored whatever was going on in the parking lot and put their energy into filling their shopping bags.

After a trip to an Arizona market last summer, I'd become interested in jalapeño peppers. My farm wasn't set up to grow them, and we had a couple small pepper vendors at the market, but I'd found a small farm not far from my own that grew a large variety of peppers—jalapeños, habaneros, and milder green and red varieties. I hadn't been able to convince Levon Sanchez to open a stall at Bailey's, but he had lately become one of my most important suppliers. I'd created a jalapeño-mint jelly that sold well during the fall and looked to become my big December seller, if the past couple of weeks were any indication. The green color of the jelly along with the word *mint* coincided with what many December shoppers were looking for.

"Oh my! Those are so pretty!" a woman in the most magnificently floppy straw hat I'd ever seen said as she picked up a jar.

"Thank you," I said.

"I want ten. I'm going to put pretty red bows on these little devils and give them to people I like. I haven't yet decided what to give people I don't like. Any suggestions?"

I smiled and then realized that she wasn't joking. Her long, thin face was serious underneath the drooping brim of the hat.

"Gosh, I don't know," I said.

"Well, if you have any ideas, I'll be shopping all day; you track me down and let me know, okeydokey?"

"I will," I said. We completed the transaction, and I placed the ten jars of jelly into her Bailey's shopping bag.

The shopping bags had been Allison's idea. They were made of slick canvas, sewn with handles sturdy enough to carry heavy loads. They were about a foot and a half tall by a foot and a half wide when flat, but could unfold to add a good seven inches of depth. They were emblazoned with "Bailey's Farmers' Market" across the top and had a picture of fruits and vegetables illustrating the bottom half. They'd become one of the more popular items at the market, but Allison refused to mark up the price to anything above break-even. She'd become concerned about the number of plastic and even paper bags leaving the market and wanted a better, more environmentally friendly solution. She had no idea that the bags would become so popular, that people would come to Bailey's just to buy a bag, and that they'd also be used as holiday gifts, but she was pleased by the developments.

"Thank you, darlin'. Now, I need some mushrooms and I can't remember which direction to go for mushrooms. Oh! I could give poisonous mushrooms to the people I don't like." Fortunately, this time she laughed. "The look on your face! I'm kidding. Besides, I know your mushroom people don't sell poisonous mushrooms."

I smiled genuinely this time. "You got me, but no, I don't think we have any poisonous mushrooms. We have two different stands, each of them selling their own specialties. They're both down there." I pointed to my left. "They're at the very end of the aisle."

We told each other thank you, and I watched her quick steps as she hurried away. Never a dull moment at Bailey's. Returning customers were like familiar friends and family. New customers were surprises that never ceased to add excitement to the day.

"I have the best job in the world," I said quietly.

"No, the second best. I have the best," a voice said, pulling my attention to the other side of my stall.

"Ian! Hi," I said.

"Hey. I do have the best job, by the way," he said. His arms were crossed in front of his chest as he leaned on the sturdy pole between my stall and Linda's.

"That's good to hear. How are you?"

"Very well, thanks, but I came by to see how you were doing. I heard about Reggie Stuckey."

"I'm okay. It's never good to find a dead body, though."

Ian's face became serious as he inspected me. "You sure you're all right?"

"Yeah—it's a terrible tragedy and it's tacky to say, but I didn't know him. I'm sad for what happened, but he wasn't a friend."

"I met him. He was a nice guy."

"I should be asking if you're okay then."

"I'm fine. I'd only met him because I'd looked at his place before I purchased the land I ended up purchasing. He'd been trying to sell his tree farm for a long time."

"Really? It wasn't a successful farm?"

"That wasn't it. According to the numbers he showed me, it was doing okay—not great, but good enough to make a living. He told me he was just tired of all the hard work."

"Poor guy."

"Yeah. It's sad."

If we'd still been dating, I would have quietly told him I'd share more with him later. I'd tell him about the contract issue and the scene in the parking lot. I was caught between wanting to share and knowing it was no longer appropriate to do so. Habits were hard to break.

"Anyway, if you need anything, just let me know," he said a beat later, maybe sensing my wave of uncertainty.

"Thanks, Ian. You, too."

"Hey, you need to come out and see both George and Gypsy. Soon, according to George's instructions."

Before Ian had purchased the land he was tilling, planting, and transforming into a lavender farm, he'd lived in the apartment above George's garage. George was older and wonderful but had horrible vision. When Ian built his new home/warehouse, he made a space just for George. And Gypsy was the black cat I'd accidentally adopted when she was a clingy kitten and had just missed my truck's tires as I pulled into a driveway. She and George had fallen immediately and deeply in love. The three of them—Ian, George, and Gypsy—were very happy together.

"Bring Hobbit and Sam," Ian said genuinely, though I sensed there was more he wanted to say but maybe couldn't quite find the words.

Yeah, despite both of us being grown-ups and Ian, at least, being mature enough to handle just about any situation, we were still figuring it out.

"Thanks, I will. Soon."

I'd heard that Ian and a mutual friend we'd made, Betsy, had become a couple. She'd attempted to manipulate her way into Ian's life before he and I had broken up, but at that specific moment I noticed that the raw sense of betrayal I'd felt over her actions suddenly didn't sting as much.

Ian smiled one more time before he turned and left, and then I laughed a little at myself. When I gave it more thought, I'd realize that Ian was, of course, being friendly and supportive, but he'd also come over to my stall to try to communicate something else, something he couldn't quite yet get out. It was probably something about Betsy.

We'd get there.

"What are you smiling at?"

"Mamma, what a great surprise!" I said as I leaned over the front display table and hugged Mamma Maria, a pie vendor from the Smithfield Market I'd met as the result of my snooping into the first murder at Bailey's.

"It's good to see you, Becca," Mamma said as we disengaged. "I heard about the tragedy, though. You doing all right?"

Mamma Maria made and sold piled-high meringue and cream pies. She herself was as stacked as her pies, and she didn't hide her assets. Today she wore tight jeans and a low-cut, short-sleeved shirt that would have given her cleavage the starring role if it weren't for her platinum-blonde ponytail and bright-red lipstick, which somehow got top billing. She'd been dating Bailey's peach vendor, Carl Monroe, for over a year now and we'd all become friends.

"I'll . . . we'll all be okay. It's good to see you, too," I said. "I haven't made it out to Smithfield, and I haven't seen you here for a couple months. What's new?"

"Sounds like we've both been busy. Nothing much. Carl and I are still together . . . living together actually," she said.

"Well, that's new!"

"We're happy, Becca. Our plans aren't *not* to get married,

but we're just taking it one day at a time. We're not in a hurry. I moved to Carl's peach farm. I wanted to tell you myself."

"That's a wonderful place," I said.

"It is. And when we have some sort of soiree to celebrate our 'next step,' you and Sam will, of course, be invited."

"Thank you! I look forward to it. We'll be there."

"Good. I'm off to talk to Allison about getting my own stall."

"What!? You buried the lead! You're moving to Bailey's?"

Mamma laughed. "I think so. Part-time, at least. My Smithfield customer list is too big to abandon completely, but I think I can make it work at both places."

"That's even better news than your good news." I smiled.

In another life and time, I doubted that Mamma Maria and I would have become friends, only because I doubted we would have ever met. The farmers' market way of life attracts a diverse crowd. People can have little in common except for the fact that they work together outside, but that becomes enough to create some tight, lasting farmers' market friendships.

Okay, so Ian and I, and Mamma Maria, all had the best jobs in the world.

"I'm looking forward to being around here more," she said. "Maybe I can help keep you out of trouble."

"I doubt it," I said.

There wasn't time to chat further. Mamma waved and winked as she backed away from the table to make room for a small group of eager customers who'd heard about the jalapeño-mint jelly from "a lady in a big, crazy hat."

The day turned out to be even busier than I thought it would be. I sold out a couple hours too soon. I had to write up orders for both the jalapeño-mint jelly and more strawberry preserves. I had a supply at home, but between the jams, jellies, and the remaining cookies I'd committed to baking, it looked like I had a busy couple evenings ahead. Since there was literally nothing more I could sell and I had plenty to do at home, I decided to leave early. I put a "Sold Out" sign on my front table and left a piece of paper for people to fill out if they wanted to place an order, then threw my empty inventory boxes into the back of my truck.

The aisles of the market weren't packed, but they were busy enough that I had to weave through the crowd a little bit as I sought out my sister. Before I left, I thought I should make sure she was okay. One curve in the flow of traffic led me toward Brenton's stall. I was surprised to see him there, crouched to the ground and looking through a box of his dog biscuits.

I hesitated, but only briefly. "Brenton?"

He looked up and then grimaced slightly. "Hi, Becca." He stood and stepped toward me. "Look, I've apologized to Allison, but I'm truly sorry for my behavior these last couple days. Really sorry."

"Sure," I said. I knew Sam had cuffed him and taken him away, but there had been no reason to arrest him. He'd been disruptive, but no real harm had been done—unless, of course, Brenton was somehow responsible for Reggie's death. But if Sam had thought as much, Brenton wouldn't be back at Bailey's. "You okay?"

"I'm embarrassed, but I'm fine. I reacted to something that I shouldn't have reacted to and I behaved in a way I didn't even know I had in me. I don't have any evidence that Denny Ridgeway killed anyone. I should never have made such an accusation. I should never have lost my cool. Again, I'm sorry."

"'S'okay. You want to talk about it?"

"No. Thank you, though."

I couldn't think of one thing to say that would make him spill the beans. I wanted to, but I bit back my curiosity. "If you need to talk, call me, find me, whatever."

"I appreciate it. Sam said the same thing. He's a good guy, Becca."

"I agree."

Brenton looked away and down at the box on the ground. It was an obvious dismissal, but I wasn't offended. Whatever he'd been going through, it had been rough. I understood how he felt, but I reluctantly stepped away from his stall. Maybe in time he'd be able to talk about it. Maybe Sam would tell me what he'd learned.

As I continued down the aisle, I was distracted by Jeannine, the egg lady. She wore an off-kilter Santa hat as she stood with her back to the aisle. She was looking at the small stack of egg boxes behind her. There wasn't much left to sell. She'd had a busy day, too.

"Everything okay?" I asked her.

She turned and glared at me in the way that she glares at everyone. Jeannine was short and strong, and leaned more toward paranoid than friendly. Though we usually wore about the same amount of makeup—none—her closely cropped hair was dark and unruly and she was older than me, but I didn't know her exact age. We'd all thought the Santa hat was a strange addition to her cranky attitude, but we'd become used to it.

"No, Becca, everything isn't all right. Someone stole some eggs—some brown eggs, to be specific."

"Really?"

"I'm missing a half dozen that I know I didn't sell and I know I had with me when I got here this morning."

Jeannine Baker's farm-fresh eggs were delicious. There's a noticeable difference in the taste of farm-fresh eggs and a store-bought-not-fresh-from-the-farm eggs, and Jeannine had a slew of loyal customers. I knew firsthand that she'd created a financially successful farm, but could never tell her about my accidental snooping. She saw conspiracy theories everywhere and would frequently misinterpret someone's accidental, sideways glance for something suspicious or evil. Telling her I'd seen her bank records once when Sam and I thought she'd gone missing and were searching her house might make her so angry that she'd never be able to forgive me. Of course, I wouldn't want someone seeing my bank records, either, and I wasn't paranoid. It was just best to keep the secret.

"Oh, that's too bad. Are you sure?" I asked.

"Of course I'm sure. I count my inventory twice every morning and I keep a running count throughout the day." She held up a notebook with frayed corners.

"I'm sorry about that, Jeannine. Were you away from your stall at all?"

"Yes, I took a small break earlier." Her mouth pursed tightly. "That must be it. Someone must have seen Barry in here and known that he's not as vigilant as I am. They must have somehow snuck around back and grabbed them." She moved her front table enough that I took it as an invitation to join her in the stall.

I doubted that anyone had stolen six eggs, but Jeannine definitely would pay close attention to her inventory. There must be some mistake, though I wasn't sure I wanted to be

the one to discover what it was and point it out to her. Nonetheless, I stepped into the stall.

"Look there." She pointed to the ground underneath the
back wall. There were distinct skid marks on the dirt floor,
as though someone had scooted into the stall on their knees.

"Don't you go through here to get your eggs in and out?"
I asked.

"I do this." She pulled up the canvas wall and secured
the corner of it with a hanger hook, similar to what most of
us used. "I walk only on this path. Those skids or marks or
whatever weren't there this morning."

The space she walked through was to the side of the marks,
far enough away that her route shouldn't have caused the digs
in the dirt.

"I never go that way over there. Ever," she continued.

An evenly worn path marked her entry and exit. It was
obviously the path that she always used, and though I hated
to admit it, it was clear that something or someone had
disturbed the other space. But it would be impossible to
attribute the marks to an egg thief. Bailey's was an open-air
market; people could access the backs of the stalls easily,
and so could animals. It wasn't rare that someone would
turn around and find a surprise visitor—dogs, cats—in
their stall. Bo, the onion guy, even had a skunk visit once.

"Do you want to call Allison? Let her know there might
have been a problem?" I asked as I took out my cell phone.

I was surprised she didn't immediately say yes, but she
thought about it and then shook her head. "No, it's just six
eggs. It's my fault for taking a break. I'll be better about
watching, and maybe I'll rig something up to catch the thief
next time."

"I am sorry, Jeannine. It's always unsettling to have something stolen."

"It won't happen again, I guarantee it."

I nodded.

I helped her get everything back into its proper place and arrange the small amount of remaining inventory before I exited the stall and took the final path to Allison's office. Disappointingly, but not surprisingly, she wasn't around. I knew that she must be busy and I didn't have anything urgent, so I didn't try to track her down. Instead, I ventured back toward my truck, which I'd parked behind my own stall.

The trip back held fewer distractions. Jeannine didn't see me wave as I passed by her space, and I couldn't see Brenton for all the customers in front of his. Traveling through the market was often a slow, diverging process. It was good to finally make it out my own back canvas wall.

Before I climbed up to the driver's-side bench seat of my truck, I opened the door and rolled down the window a couple inches. The old, handle mechanism worked better when I did it that way.

I hoisted myself up and closed the door. It wasn't until I'd turned the key that I noticed something sitting on the passenger side of the seat.

I actually said "Huh?" aloud as I glanced at the small item. It took a second to understand what it was, but when I did, I followed up with, "Uh-oh."

Of course I couldn't be completely certain because, really, one pretty much looks like all the others. But I thought that perhaps I'd found one of Jeannine's missing brown eggs, and for a minute I wasn't quite sure what to do about it.

Six

The egg was unquestionably brown-shelled, but it also had parts that were green and red. For a long moment, I stared at it and thought about what I should do. Though it was a harmless egg, it was not something I'd ever found on the passenger side of the truck's seat—or anywhere, for that matter—which made its presence foreign and alarming. Anything that I hadn't put there would have been at least surprising. I never locked the truck's doors because I usually didn't carry anything valuable inside it, and the lock mechanisms, like the window, didn't always work smoothly. It was rare, though, that anyone ventured inside it without an invitation or first giving me a heads-up.

It was the decorative nature of the egg, though, that finally caused me let down my guard and pick it up.

And it really wasn't an egg; it was just an eggshell, the insides having been released through one of the holes that had been put in it at either end. It was like something I'd made in elementary school, when we'd put holes in raw eggs and then blown out the insides so we could decorate the shells. If I remembered correctly, I'd broken a few to the point of being unusable before I'd been successful. This shell had green and red bands colored around it with what I thought was marker and a paper clip hook through the shell close to one of the holes. It was a Christmas ornament; something that a kid had probably made. Who, though? My nephew, Mathis? Had Allison snuck it into the truck to surprise me? I doubted it. That wasn't her style. Besides, Mathis would want to give it to me himself, and I didn't think he was quite old enough to create such an item.

I turned the shell slowly. The red and green bands alternated, and in between two of them was a line of writing. I had to hold it just right to make out the black-inked numbers. I was pretty sure it read "1987."

"Huh," I said aloud again as I pondered what I knew about the year 1987. The one and only thing I could think of was that that was the year that Ian was born. "Ian?"

No, this wasn't Ian's style, either. Besides, he was an artist. Any eggshell he decorated wouldn't be so amateurish.

"And Ian wouldn't steal eggs from Jeannine. He'd buy them," I rationalized aloud.

I thought about calling him, but that idea felt uncomfortable. I'd just ask him the next time I saw him. I also thought about going back into the market to ask some questions: Had anyone noticed anyone by my truck? Did anyone know anything about the egg? But I didn't want to have to explain my surprise to Jeannine. I was pretty certain the egg had come from her stall, but there was no way to prove whether it had been purchased or stolen. Jeannine might want a full investigation into the matter, and it just didn't seem that important.

No matter who had left the egg in my truck, I had to assume that it was a gift. I might appreciate it, given a little time to get over the nature of its bold, intrusive, and secretive delivery.

Finally, I sat it back on the seat and drove home to Hobbit. I'd see what she had to say about it.

As I steered the truck down the two-lane highway toward my small farm, thoughts of the egg gave way to thoughts about Christmas, the tree parade, more jelly, and the dozens more cookies I had to bake.

The jelly and the cookies would happen, one jar and one dozen at a time. I just had to take the time in the kitchen. The two parade days were always days that I looked forward to, and this year was no exception. I would bid on some trees, and I would lose because my budget wasn't quite as large as those of the highest bidders. The money always went to a great cause, so it was good to be outbid, and good to know that people in and around Monson were so generous.

Sam and I would attend together this year, which would give us both a chance to think creatively about decorating our own tree. Our own tree? My heart skipped a little at the idea, but not so much that it scared me. It was a new life to get used to, and something I was finding that I wanted more with every passing day.

My parents were in town this year, too. Though Mom would sneeze her way through the parade, she had never missed one unless she and Dad were away on an RV adventure.

My entire family would be together this year, and though we weren't much into gift giving, we were all very into family. I did always try to think of a little something special as gift for them and for close friends. Often, my gifts were something made in my kitchen or something from the market. Jalapeño-mint jelly, along with some bread from Stella, a Bailey's baker, would be perfect. I'd need to put some jelly aside today if that's what I chose to do.

And, there was Sam. Our first Christmas together as a couple. What in the world would I get him? I hadn't been able to come up with the perfect gift yet. We were only a week away, but I wasn't going to get him just anything; my gift to Sam would have to mean something, though I didn't even really quite know what I wanted it to mean.

I laughed at myself. Allison would roll her eyes. She'd said many times lately, "You two are like teenagers experiencing their first love. You're cute and adorable and kind of annoying."

I pulled onto my gravel driveway and waved at Hobbit, who was sitting up on her pillow on the porch, her tail wagging and her short front legs anxious for the truck to stop so she could greet me properly. Once the truck was in park, she left the porch and met me halfway with a few kisses and some full-body wags.

"Hey, girl! Anyone bother you today?"

The house, barn, and grounds seemed undisturbed. Not long ago, I'd found them disturbed to the point that afterward I'd become concerned about leaving her alone. I still had surges of concern, but I was getting better. And Hobbit loved her home, her pillow, and her porch; although she enjoyed the people she'd been able to spend extra time with during her time away from the farm, she was pleased to have her routine back.

We walked around the property and did our daily inspection. There were no signs of the pumpkin plants, the vines having been pulled and composted in early November. The strawberry vines were there, dormant and waiting to bloom again in the spring, but they looked exactly how they were supposed to look, so there was no reason not to think another good crop was on its way.

A new habit I'd formed whenever I arrived at home was checking the door on the refurbished barn/kitchen just to make sure it was locked securely before I ventured inside the house. Today it was locked, and it looked like no one had tried to enter since I'd worked in there the night before. For part of the evening, Sam had helped me with jelly and cookies. He wasn't as skilled in the kitchen as he was at police work, but he was getting better. I didn't think canning or preserving or baking cookies for that matter would become one of his favorite or frequent activities, but his help had been appreciated.

"I've got lots of kitchen work today," I said to Hobbit. This caused her ears to first perk then sag. She wasn't allowed into the kitchen and though she was pretty patient about work I had to get done, she'd rather we just hung out together and ignored work altogether.

I laughed. "I'll try to hurry."

I grabbed the egg from the truck and took it inside, placing it safely in a bowl on the kitchen counter—the kitchen inside the house, which was used for personal meals and recipe experiments that weren't intended as sellable products. My aunt and uncle had left me the house, farm, and fancy barn kitchen. Uncle Stanley had originally planned to can jellies, jams, and preserves as a retirement activity. Neither of them had planned on being killed in a horrible car accident, but somehow Uncle Stanley must have known that he was creating something that someone would use.

Having paid bills and sorted through all the junk mail a few days ago, I'd cleared all the paper off the old, long dining table. It was now half-covered with jars and lids that were clean and ready, even though I would sterilize the jars in the barn before I filled them.

The dining room was bright with four big windows that faced the side of the property. Mostly, diners could look out to hilly countryside that backed into some thick woods, but in the fall, right before the pumpkins were harvested, you could see long green vines, big green leaves, and big orange gourds creeping over the hills. I hosted October family dinners just so everyone could enjoy the view.

I loaded the jars onto a tray to transport them to the barn. On the way out, I stopped at a big pot on the front porch and plucked some sprigs of fresh mint. I still had plenty and it was still growing well outside, though I thought I'd have to soon move it in to the back porch where it would get better winter sun.

More than anything, my short time in Arizona had taught me to be careful when working with jalapeño peppers. Once I was in the kitchen, I pulled on some disposable plastic gloves, grabbed a box of peppers from the refrigerator, cleaned them, and placed about ten on the worktable. Since I pureed the peppers it wasn't technically necessary to also slice them, but I liked the end texture better when I did. Once the stems were removed, I cut each pepper into three or four rings and then put the slices into a food processor. I poured a cup of apple cider vinegar in with the peppers and then pureed until only small bits of pepper remained.

Once that puree was poured into a pot on the stove, I added some lemon juice and sugar and brought the mixture to a boil before reducing the heat and simmering for five or so minutes. Then I added some pectin and brought it to another minute-long hard boil, took it off the heat, and added the mint sprigs and a small amount of peppermint essential oil—the real stuff, never imitation. Finally, I added a little green food coloring, which was probably the biggest reason the jelly had been so popular. It was eye-catching, and the bright green along with my simple red-bordered label had been an almost perfect magnet for those searching for gifts. Once I filled the jars, I hot-water processed them all. As the first batch hot-water processed, I started a new batch and so on. I had a number of processing pots, so there were times when it sounded like the entire kitchen was boiling. By the time Sam called, I'd made about fifty new jars of jelly but hadn't started on the cookies.

"So, you didn't arrest Brenton?" I said as I answered the phone.

"Hello to you, too," Sam said.

"Sorry. Hello, how was your day?"

Sam laughed. "I've had better days. Have you eaten?"

"Nope."

"I'll bring some sandwiches or something. Be there in a half hour."

A half hour gave me time to finish the last jars, setting them all carefully on the center worktable. They weren't supposed to be bothered for at least twenty-four hours, so these fifty wouldn't make it to Bailey's until the day after tomorrow. The jars Sam and I had made the night before would be tomorrow's inventory.

Inside the house, I stirred up a huge pitcher of iced tea. I'd always been a fan of the drink—being southern almost demanded that you like sweet iced tea—and it had become Sam's favorite, too. Apparently—or so he told me—after I'd served it to him the first time he'd come out to my farm to ask me questions regarding the murder of Matt Simonsen.

The times, they had definitely changed.

"No, I didn't arrest him. I probably could have, but I didn't want to," Sam said as he leaned back in the dining room chair. He'd changed into jeans and a white T-shirt, automatically transforming him into casual Sam. I liked both professional Sam and casual Sam, but casual Sam was my favorite, unless professional Sam happened to be my favorite that day. We'd finished off roast beef sandwiches and potato salad but were still enjoying the tea.

"I'm glad you didn't arrest him."

"I just wanted to get him out of there and away from Bailey's until he cooled off. He hadn't done much wrong, but he was on the verge of doing something potentially dangerous and something I was sure he would later regret. He's a good guy."

"He's a great guy. What happened to upset him?"

"He wouldn't tell me. He didn't have to. He asked if he needed an attorney. I told him I wasn't arresting him. I asked if there was anything going on that I could help him with."

"And he said no?"

Sam took a sip of tea. I wondered if he didn't know that I could sometimes see right through his avoidance. He wasn't totally under my control. There had been plenty of times in our short relationship that he'd informed me that he wasn't going to tell me something I really wanted to know. There'd been way too many murders in the Monson area recently, but we were typically a low-crime town, or so I'd thought. There was more going on in my community than I really knew, and I'd been surprised by some of the illegal activities Sam had told me about, though he hadn't always shared perpetrators' names.

"He said no," Sam said.

"He didn't. I can see he didn't. You don't want to tell me what he said, but can you give me a hint?"

"No."

"Let's see, he was accusing Denny Ridgeway of being the killer. Did it have something to do with the Ridgeways?" I said.

"Maybe," he said with a smile.

Now he was getting information out of me. We'd sometimes dance around something, trying to get information from each other. Usually both of us caved, or each of us offered enough to the conversation to make the entire story become clear.

I played along. "Because"—I smiled—"because Brenton had been acting strangely toward the Ridgeways since I saw him pull into the parking lot yesterday. He told you more about his relationship with the Ridgeways."

"Wait, why would he pull into the parking lot and not his loading/unloading area?" Sam asked. This was a legitimate question, not part of the game.

I shrugged. "Lots of reasons, but his stall isn't far from the front of the market. Maybe he prefers to go into the front."

"What would be some other reasons?"

"He'd unloaded and then left, took a break. It happens a lot. We have to leave to do something. Neighboring vendors take care of customers for us. Jeannine helps out Brenton all the time. . . ."

"What?"

"Well, normally Brenton helps out Jeannine, too, but she had to ask Barry to help her—that was today, so that's understandable, but I wonder if Brenton's been away from the market a lot lately. If so, that might mean something or nothing at all. Those busy times happen to us all, but remind me to show you something in a second."

"Okay."

"Anyway, sometimes we just unload our inventory and then move our vehicles to the front lot. If we need to get out of there quickly and if we think most of our inventory will be gone, the front lot's much easier to get out of than the back areas. I don't know if it's anything important, but your question about why he was coming in that way might be a really good one. You might want to find out if Brenton's been up to something away from the market."

"I will. What did you want to show me?"

"Wait, I still have more information to tell you. I should have told Vivienne, but I didn't want to."

"Becca, Vivienne's a great cop, and I'm not supposed to be questioning you at all. In fact, what we're doing now isn't the best of ideas. Tell me what you need to, but I'll probably have you tell her, too."

"The reason I didn't . . ." The reason I hadn't told Officer Norton was to protect Allison, but that didn't seem so necessary with Sam. "Anyway, that's not important. It's about the contracts between Bailey's and the tree farmers. I think Officer Norton knew a little something about them but not the details. Did Allison tell you anything?"

"No, but our time was cut short because of Brenton's behavior, and I know she also talked to Vivienne. She mentioned that she'd send me some paperwork that might be relevant, but I haven't seen it yet."

I was sure she meant the contracts. I told him about the odd similarities and differences between the two vendors' paperwork, about the fact that the Bailey's owners wouldn't have ever promised exclusivity to two vendors; that wasn't how they did business.

"That's great information, Becca. Thank you. I'll get on that first thing in the morning. I should have gone back to talk to Allison, but I got caught up doing other things."

I think Sam was still pleasantly surprised when I was so forthcoming with any information that I had. Keeping secrets from the police was another hard habit to break, but I was working on it.

"You're welcome."

"Okay, now what did you want to show me?"

"Hang on a second." I hurried to the kitchen and grabbed the decorated eggshell.

"I found this in my truck." I sat in the chair next to Sam instead of the one across the table as I handed him the ornament.

"What is it?"

"As far as I can tell, it's a decorated eggshell, made into

an ornament. It reminds me of elementary school presents we made for our parents."

"Who's it from?"

"I guess I have a secret admirer, a Secret Santa."

"Nah, I'm not a secret anymore." Sam smiled. "You really don't have any idea who put it in your truck?"

"No clue, but there is a little more to the story."

Sam nodded and I told him about Jeannine's alleged egg theft.

"Someone stole six eggs just so they could make you an ornament? That sounds . . ."

"Unreasonably far-fetched?"

"Yes."

"Maybe it was someone who bought eggs, maybe this egg has nothing to do with Jeannine's eggs, but I've tied the two stories together just because."

"It could be pure coincidence, but I don't know. Does 1987 mean anything to you? Is it secret code for something?"

"Not really. The thought crossed my mind that 1987 was the year that Ian was born, but that probably doesn't mean much." I bit my cheek. Sam and I had talked about Ian plenty, but it still made me somewhat uncomfortable.

Sam looked at me, a half smile pulling at his mouth. "That's possible, but I can't see Ian going to such measures, even if he is your secret admirer. He's much better artistically than this, too."

"That's what I thought."

"You care if I ask him about it, if I feel like I need to? That will only happen if I think it might lead to something more important. As it is, it's just a cute gift, but with the potential theft—small though it might be—and the murder . . . you never know."

"I'm okay with you talking to Ian about it."

"Good. I'll let you know."

"Thank you."

Sam sat the ornament on the table and said, "Let's look at it this way—we have our first ornament. Now we just need to get the tree."

"Sunday?"

"Definitely."

Hobbit barked her approval. We scratched behind her ears and then went to the barn to bake about ten dozen strawberry preserve–filled cookies.

Even solving a murder couldn't put off parade commitments.

Seven

Nothing's ever quite as perfect as we want it to be, no matter what it seems like from the outside looking in. Though I might have given the impression that my relationship with Sam was shiny and close to perfect, it's probably only fair to mention that there is a glitch—not a big one and not one that has me second-guessing our future, but a glitch nonetheless.

Sam moved to Monson from Chicago a few years ago. He'd been a police officer there, too, and though we've seen way too many murders in Monson recently, Chicago was worse, much worse. And more personal to Sam.

As I mentioned before, there'd been a fiancée. This is what I knew so far: her name was Clarissa and she was pretty, funny, and smart; that's all he'll tell me about her specifically—except for the really bad part, and I don't have all of those details, either. But what I do know is that

Clarissa was killed—tragically, brutally, and because Sam was a police officer. Those are the goriest details he'll share and they're pretty awful on their own. I can only imagine how truly heartbreaking the entire truth is. I'm sure that I'll learn it someday. I could research it myself; we're all connected to the world by keyboard, and terrible stories are usually the highest ranked on any search engine.

But there's a part of me that doesn't want to know the details until Sam wants to tell me. So, those nights when he's restless, or those nights when I wake up and find he's not beside me but usually somewhere outside, somewhere sitting and thinking and hopefully working through the pain, are nights that I sometimes either learn another small kernel of the truth or just remain silently supportive because there's just not much anyone can say.

"Hey," I said as I found him with Hobbit on the back patio. The night was cold, the clear sky bright with what I called a country quilt—you couldn't see that many stars from a well-lit city or town.

"Aw, sorry. We tried to stay quiet," Sam said, the light from the moon glimmering and making his eyes seem happy and jovial even though I knew they weren't.

"No problem." I sat in a chair next to him. "Nightmares?"

Sam huffed a small, non-funny laugh. "No, not this time. I just woke up. Nothing but my eyes opening."

"I guess that's good."

He was silent for a long beat, but then said, "It was as if I woke up because there were no nightmares this time."

I paused a moment, too. "Is that good?"

"I think it's probably very good. I'll never completely

get over what happened, Becca, but moving on is the goal. I want it and I know Clarissa would have wanted it, too."

"You might not believe this, but I'd love to know more about her. I'm okay if you want to talk about her. I'm okay even if you cared for her more than you could ever care for anyone else."

"Brooding me isn't the best me, but I still don't have much faith in my ability to tell the whole story. Someday. Maybe."

"You don't brood."

"You and she would have gotten along really well."

It was my turn to laugh. "Really? The two of us wouldn't have battled it out for you?"

"You would have been friends."

"I don't know. Did she like to can things? I mean, there's this whole group of people who think that canning preserves, jellies, jams, and whatever else is old-fashioned and silly. If she'd have thought that, I don't know." I wasn't sure I was handling this correctly, but it was the only way I knew how to handle it.

"I doubt Clarissa ever canned anything in her life. She was a city girl through and through. I actually wanted to move out to the suburbs, but she'd have none of that. She didn't like the idea of lawns or gardens, but I think she thought flowers were pretty. I also think she thought they only came from florists."

"I bet we could have taught each other a thing or two."

I heard Sam take a deep breath, and for a second I was concerned that I'd said something that caused him more pain.

"Well, that wasn't so bad," he finally said.

"Please tell me she was a dog person. If I'm beginning to like her, I don't want my affections to be false. If she didn't like dogs . . ."

"She loved them."

"Oh, good."

"And Becca?"

"Yes."

"I don't compare what I felt for her to what I feel for you. I don't think that would be fair—to her. I'm pretty sure you're the one for me. I knew it the second I had to question you regarding the first murder you were somehow involved in."

"That's kind of romantic."

Hobbit yawned with a dog throat-squeak and stood from where she was curled around Sam's feet. She'd adjusted well to Sam, though she still had loyalty to Ian.

"I think she's ready to head back to bed," Sam said.

"I can take her. You can stay out here if you want to."

"No, I think I'm good. I think I'm getting better all the time."

Hopefully, we all were.

Sam was gone by the time I woke a few hours later. His shift wasn't scheduled to start until 7 A.M., but he wanted to get a jump on investigating Reggie Stuckey's murder, so he'd left about 5 A.M. I was out of bed and ready to go by 6 A.M., which was unusually early for me and a shock to my system. Hobbit and I took our morning walk, but she was ready for the bed on the porch shortly afterward. We were both morning people, just not ridiculously early morning people.

I could get to Bailey's early, but unlike the enthusiastic summer crowds, which were there right at dawn to beat the heat, the December crowds meandered in around midmorning.

I could have baked more cookies, but I was now ahead of my originally planned schedule, so I had a few hours and enough curiosity to follow through on a couple tasks that were on my mind, and Hobbit could come with me.

I searched the Internet for the Stuckey Christmas Tree Farm. I knew that the Ridgeway Farm wasn't too far from Monson, about thirty minutes away, but it was a hilly and curvy drive that could take up to an hour in bad weather or with Christmas-week traffic. The drive itself had become a yearly tradition for many people. Apparently whatever the Ridgeways had done to market their farm had done wonders, because the Stuckey farm was much closer to town. Its location as well as the great condition of the trees I'd seen in the Stuckey truck made me doubly wonder why in the world I, and it seemed many others, had never even heard of the farm.

"Come on, girl," I said to Hobbit, "let's go check out some trees."

I loaded my inventory into the back of the truck, and Hobbit, suddenly wide awake again, climbed into the truck with her typical enthusiasm. Now, it didn't matter that it was early or that she normally had some time to herself in the mornings, she was just excited to be a part of the adventure. As I steered us down the highway toward town and the market, her tail wagged approvingly.

"Well, we're not going to the market, but we'll stop by later."

The tail continued to wag.

Monson was never too busy, but this predawn morning was particularly quiet. Downtown would be transformed by the parade soon, but I didn't think the decorating committee was supposed to begin until tomorrow. The semi-darkness and the few and far between strings of light had something to do with the peacefulness.

Through most of December, the upcoming parade made Monson look like Scrooge had moved in and taken over. It had become tradition not to do much to decorate until the parade, which was always the weekend before Christmas. We'd go from boring and bland to lit up like Vegas overnight, and then decorations would stay up through New Year's. As I skirted the edge of Main Street, I turned the radio off and left the window down a bit to enjoy the quiet, the cold air, and the scents of small town surrounded by farmland.

Once through town, I would turn onto the road that would lead me directly to the Stuckey farm, but first I pulled the truck into a parking spot and enjoyed the peace and the quiet morning.

"Look, girl, we get to live here," I said to Hobbit.

Hobbit leaned over me and peered out the window. Suddenly an orange tabby the size of a mountain lion darted across the road about a half block away.

Hobbit looked at me as if to ask if she could go play.

"No, we're working—investigating, to be more precise." She moved back to her side of the truck.

"Don't tell Sam," I added. "Don't tell anyone."

Her muzzle was sealed, I was sure, but even just asking my dog to keep a secret from Sam left me feeling suddenly uncomfortable. I'd tell him later, to alleviate the guilt I felt at not telling him beforehand. I was aware of my backward thinking, but I didn't dwell on it.

I was certain that Hobbit thought I was righteous and perfect, and she whined in agreement.

I put the truck back into drive and drove for about a mile until I came upon two dirt road turnoffs, one going each direction. From the map I'd found I was fairly certain I was supposed to turn left, but there was no signage to help with the decision.

"You'd think he'd want people to know about his farm," I said.

The sun was beginning to rise, so I could see a pretty good distance down the road. The area was wooded, but not thickly. I couldn't see any sign of a farm.

"Just a quick look." I pulled the truck onto the road and was pleasantly surprised to find it was much smoother than many other local dirt roads. I followed it into the sparse woods and then took a curve to the right and then another one to the left, and then I brought the truck to a dead, hard halt.

"Holy . . ." I said as I looked at the view in front of me.

Hobbit whined again.

"No, girl, I'm fine. It's just so . . . so amazing. I had no idea."

The Stuckey Tree Farm was a couple hundred yards straight ahead. The road I was on would lead me beside a smallish lot of trees and then to a spot in front of an old farmhouse. It was a farmhouse directly out of the early twentieth century; something that fit the small valley perfectly. The sun peeked out from behind a distant slope and had the house in its sights. The direct light should have highlighted any flaws, but I didn't see any.

The house was a tall two-story with a wraparound porch on the bottom level and a small corner porch on the top level. Opposite the top-level porch was a white spire with a decorative ball on its tip. There were pale-green shutters bordering all the windows, milky shears fluttering inside them. The whitewashed clapboard siding looked like it had recently been painted, which might have been the one thing about the extraordinary house that I didn't like. It was either an older house that had been refurbished or it was a new house built to look like something from the turn of the century; the century before the one we were currently in. It seemed like it should lean a little and perhaps be covered in chipped paint. But it was perfect.

The trees filling the land next to the left of the house were dark green, and the pine scent that found its way into the cab of my truck was just as intoxicating as the scents from the Ridgeway trees.

"There is just nothing like the real thing, is there?" I said.

There weren't as many pines as I thought there should be on a working tree farm, which probably explained the farm's almost anonymous existence. The trees I did see were of varying sizes, and I couldn't tell offhand where the ones that had been brought to the market had originally grown. Either the planted part of the land went back deeper than I could see or the stumps were well hidden.

"Stop!" a voice rang out from the middle of the tree patch. It took a second but I finally found the woman attached to it.

She wore a long, brown skirt and what I thought was a

beige muslin shirt. Her getup reminded me of Linda, who dressed the pioneer part. This woman was a lot older than Linda, though; her steel-gray hair had been pulled back into a bun at some point, but many pieces had come loose, giving her a wild and somewhat crazed look as she chased after an animal she was bound to never catch.

A goose—no, a huge goose—was running with quick, web-footed steps and intermittent flaps of its wings.

"Uh-oh," I said.

The goose had the serpentine move down pat. I had no idea that geese were so skilled at averting a chase. I wondered when it was just going to take off and fly.

"You stupid, stupid creature. Stop right this minute," the woman commanded. It did no good.

If I left at that moment, she'd notice my truck if she hadn't already. It was hard to miss. But I wanted to leave. In the span of a few seconds I predicted several potential outcomes, and none of them were appealing. The woman was either going to ask me to leave, ask me to come in and buy a tree, or ask me to help her catch the goose and if, by chance, it was a Christmas goose in the same vein as Dickens's, I wanted no part in the hunt.

I stalled a fraction of a second too long. The woman stopped, put her hands on her hips, and signaled in my direction.

"Could use your help," she yelled.

"Stay here," I said to Hobbit.

I got out of the truck and waved, hoping she'd see my small stature and think I wasn't up to the task. It didn't work.

"Just stop the damn creature. I'll chase him in your direction."

"How?"

She shrugged. "Any way you can. He's a stubborn old cuss, so you can't hurt him."

"Can he hurt me?" I knew the answer to this was yes. Geese could be wicked mean.

She shrugged again. "Just be careful."

"Okay," I said quietly.

I stepped away from the false security of the truck and walked a path that was ahead of both the goose and the woman.

The creature was pretty smart. It had quit running when she'd quit chasing it, but I was certain that its bill would be nipping and its wings would be flapping once she set everything in motion again.

"Good, yes, the other side of the driveway should work. Use your sidestepping abilities."

To my knowledge I didn't have any sidestepping abilities, but I nodded nonetheless and bent my knees in a wrestler stance.

"Well, you might want to look a little less intimidating. Try to look friendly, and then when he gets to you, grab him."

"Whatever you say," I muttered quietly but I stood upright.

The woman started running again, and so did the goose, sort of in my direction. I suddenly understood the need for sidestepping.

"You stupid bird!" she exclaimed.

I didn't take the time to point out that she was being intimidating with her words so I would have probably been okay with my stance.

I moved to my left, I moved to my right, back and forth

many times before the goose made it close enough that I could try to make some sort of move to catch it.

But how? I didn't want to hurt it, no matter how awful or stupid it might be. How does one reach for a big, flapping animal with a long neck and stop it without potentially breaking said neck? The way I chose was quickly proved wrong.

I pulled my head back and thrust my hands forward toward its body. Somehow, I didn't get my hands on any part of it, but it managed to take a nice bite out of my arm.

"Ow!" I said as pulled my injured arm back and let the goose pass by.

"Why'd you let it go?" the woman asked as I let her pass by, too.

I didn't answer.

Finally, probably having had enough of the whole situation, Hobbit stuck her nose in the open space at the top of the passenger window of the truck and barked. One quick but loud exclamation.

And the goose slid to a web-footed stop. It turned and looked at the other creature on the premises. Hobbit and the goose had a stare-down as the woman walked calmly up to the goose and pulled something from its bill. I wondered if it was some skin from my arm.

The woman walked back to me and held up a gold-chained necklace. "Took it from the kitchen counter. It'll be lucky if I don't finally cook it for dinner. Can I help you? You here for a tree?"

"Not really."

"Well, why then?"

"It's a long story. Maybe I could get this cleaned up?" The bite was bleeding enough that I didn't care if I was imposing.

"Sure, come on up to the house. You'll probably want to leave the dog in the truck. God bless him, though. I would've been chasing that wretched thing all day if he or she hadn't intervened."

"She. Am I at the Stuckey Christmas Tree Farm?" I was fairly sure I'd found the right spot, but the wayward goose made me wonder.

"Yes, you are. I'm afraid Mr. Stuckey has met with a tragic end recently, but I think there's someone here who can sell you a tree."

"Well, I don't really want a tree . . . it's still a long story. Are you family member?"

"Heavens, no; I'm a housekeeper, recently hired at that. Reggie was the only family member, really, but he has a couple workers to help him with the trees."

My list of questions was only growing.

"Any chance you'd have a minute to talk after I get this taken care of?" I said.

She squinted at me a long moment before she finally said, "I might, but you'll have to tell me more about who you are."

"Gladly."

"Deal. This way then."

Eight

Gellie (pronounced just like the stuff I made in my kitchen)
took me inside the house through the front door. The tan-
and-brown-toned entryway wasn't big but it didn't feel
cramped, either. Even with a bleeding arm, it was difficult
not to admire the staircase against the left wall. Its shiny
wood steps and carved banister were steep and led directly
to a small, railed walkway above. From my vantage point
below, it seemed that one could choose to go either right or
left and find places that begged to be discovered.

"Was this house redone, remodeled?" I asked as Gellie
led me down a hallway next to the stairs. We passed a couple of large rooms on our right but I didn't take the time to
look into them. Ahead was something that garnered most
of my attention—a huge aluminum table that I suspected to
be the center island for a kitchen. But if the size of the end
of the table I saw was any indication, the kitchen was enormous, probably bigger than the one in my converted barn.

"Yes, from top to bottom. Apparently, Mr. Stuckey, God rest that poor man's soul, only recently finished renovating. Barely any furniture is even in place."

"It's stunning."

"Yes. This way, this way."

Gellie stopped at a doorway that was located around a curve in the hallway, a curve that hid the tempting kitchen. I hesitated to follow her into the small bathroom that might have once been called a powder room, but she yanked me inside.

I wouldn't need stitches, but Gellie insisted on a good, soapy scrub, followed by some antibacterial cream and a Band-Aid or two to hold everything together tightly. She was rough but quick and efficient, and I felt like she'd killed any bacteria within a three-mile radius of the small bathroom.

"Come along, come into the kitchen. I hear that damn . . . excuse me, that goose, outside in the back. I'll have to let him in in a little bit."

"The goose comes into the house?" I asked as I enthusiastically followed her into a space that must have had its blueprint written from kitchen heaven.

"Yes, Batman—that's the goose's name—was Reggie's pet. I can't leave anything small and shiny anywhere. He loves to steal those sorts of things and take them to who knows where. I'm sure he has a stash worth a fortune somewhere."

"Wow!"

"I know, it's a weird thing, having a goose."

"Actually I was wow-ing about the kitchen."

I'd been correct—the space was huge, probably double the size of my barn, though they were the same square shape. A large, white porcelain two-tub sink took up the middle of the far wall and above it were three wide windows, which looked out onto a crop of green pine trees. The scene was a perfect model for snow globes. If only we could shake it just a little and fulfill the picture's potential.

I thought I'd heard about a new concrete countertop trend, and was impressed to see the thick, sturdy, gray substance all around. The cabinetry was white and simple with one raised inner border, and all the knobs were shiny chrome, which matched the center island.

There were two large appliances against the wall to our left. One was probably a refrigerator and the other a freezer. They were both light blue and enormous. I'd never seen the color on appliances before, and the doors were rounded at the edges, making them look like a pumped-up version of something from the 1960s.

"Are those custom made?" I said as I pointed to the light-blue doors.

"I believe so, but I can't remember what Mr. Stuckey told me."

"This must have been one successful tree farm," I muttered, though I hadn't truly meant to say the words aloud.

Gellie laughed. "No, not successful, not really. Mr. Stuckey just had money."

"I see."

"Have a seat. You like tea? Or I can make coffee. You like muffins?"

"Tea sounds great and I love muffins."

"Oh, good. I just made some cranberry–white chocolate muffins this morning. Habit, and Joel and Patricia are still out there with the trees—they're the ones who were helping Reggie. I'm still in shock about . . . everything, but I didn't know what else to do but come to work today. I suppose someone will come out of the woodwork and claim all this, but until then it feels wrong to leave the house, and of course Batman, unattended."

I scooted up to a stool next to the island.

"I'm so sorry for your loss," I said.

"That's the thing; it's not such a bad loss. I mean . . . I didn't know him well. I'm sorry about what happened and heartbroken just because it was a terrible way to go and it was undeserved, but I didn't have strong feelings for the man except that I thought he'd be a good boss. Am I callous? I don't mean to be."

"Not at all."

Gellie placed a matching china plate, cup, and saucer in front of me. The china's pattern was distinctly grandmotherly, delicate and beautiful. I suddenly decided that all tea should be drunk from such a cup and all muffins should be eaten from such a plate. The china's blue-and-yellow small floral pattern made everything taste better, I was sure.

Tea was poured and two enormous muffins were deposited on my plate. I knew I'd eat both of them, and I hoped I could keep my longing glances toward the serving plate in check when I was finished. *Two will be enough. Maybe.*

"So. You don't want a tree. Who are you and what are you doing here?"

I swallowed the heavenly first bite. "I'm Becca Robins and I work at the farmers' market where Reggie was killed."

"Oh. Well, that's . . . so why are you here?"

"I didn't know him. At all. I was curious about him. I'd never heard of him or his farm, and I just needed to see it for myself."

Gellie cocked her head and squinted. "Or you're the killer coming to hide or plant evidence or some such nonsense."

I took another bite. "I suppose that's a possibility, but you don't seem scared. You'd be more scared if you thought that was true."

Gellie looked at me even harder. "Nah, I don't need to be scared. I've got Batman."

I didn't want to because it would only break the banter, but I couldn't help it; I laughed. So did Gellie.

"You're just a curious person, I imagine," she said a moment later.

"That is true."

"All right then, ask me whatever you want to ask me. I don't know much, but I know a little about Mr. Stuckey."

"You said he had money. How?" I asked.

"Family money, but not from farming. This was just his hobby. He came from somewhere in Georgia originally. His family was in textiles, or some such thing, and I heard talk of politics."

"Politics? How?"

"Don't know the particulars, but it wasn't big politics— not governor, senator, or anything like that. Something smaller, but I'm not sure. He talked about it once and mentioned a different last name. I can't remember what the heck it was but it didn't sound familiar. I was only half listening. I'm not much into all that silliness, anyway. If I remember it, I'll let you know."

"Thanks. So, what about Reggie, though? No wife? Girl-friend? Ex-wife?"

"Not that I know of. I've got one of those exes myself. I talked to Reggie about him one day, but he didn't join in or offer anything about his own status. Just looked sad and stayed silent. I didn't know if he was sad because he'd never had one, or he'd had a bad one, or he still had someone somewhere that was making him miserable. I didn't ask."

"I've got two ex-husbands," I said. "It does seem like he would tell you if he had one or two or more. Sharing ex stories can be both therapeutic and bonding."

"Two? You've been busy for such a young lady."

I laughed again. "Not so young, but yes, I've made some unfortunate choices. I think I'm finally on track, though."

"Getting married for a third time?"

"Maybe." I paused and my eyes opened wide. A shot of adrenaline rattled my entire system. Was I really thinking about the idea of marriage? For a third time? Who does that? I took an extra-big bite of the second muffin to hide my panic and to keep my mouth from either groaning or saying words I'd later regret.

Gellie laughed again. "You're a funny little lady," she said. "I could see everything that just ran through your mind. You probably shouldn't play poker for much more of anything than popcorn. You've got no poker face."

She poured more tea into the pretty teacup, and I smiled around the bite of muffin.

"Do you know much about the people who work for Reggie? Who did you say—Patricia and Joel?" I asked after I swallowed authoritatively and then cleared my throat.

"A married couple. I'm not even sure if Reggie paid them legally. Maybe just with cash. I think I heard that they helped him out years ago and he was glad to have them back this year. I can't remember how long ago the original time was, but I'd be happy to introduce you to them."

"Did the police ask you about them?"

"Yes, but I couldn't tell them more than I told you. I think they all met."

"What about competition?"

"Reggie's? He didn't have any."

"Sure he did. The Ridgeway Farm, for example."

"No, what I'm saying is that Reggie didn't care enough to compete. He wasn't in this for the money, Becca. It was his fun. He sold some trees, but he did this for *fun*." She stood and turned toward the tray of muffins. "I'll tell you something you're going to find pretty interesting, though." She paused speaking to reload the serving plate. She was very formal about the steps it took for a muffin to get from point A to my plate. I'd probably limit myself to just one more.

"Okay."

"That name—Ridgeway—he said that name a couple times, said it as though he was just talking to himself."

"I don't understand," I said.

Gellie shrugged. "You're saying there's a Ridgeway Christmas tree farm. I've never heard of it."

"Really? It's famous."

"Not to this old lady. Nevertheless, I heard Reggie mutter the name a couple times. We weren't having a conversation; it was just him muttering. I don't think he knew I heard him, but I don't know for sure. If I happened to hear him and I haven't been here but for a couple weeks, imagine how often he must have said it."

I tried to imagine Reggie Stuckey walking around and muttering "Ridgeway." I couldn't picture anything but a befuddled and flighty man, which didn't fit with the person I'd met briefly in the Bailey's parking lot.

"Do you know the context? Was he angry, confused, laughing?"

Gellie thought a moment. "Matter-of-fact. He was simply matter-of-fact. It was like I heard blah, blah, blah, and Ridgeway."

"He must have felt comfortable around you."

"Everyone's comfortable around me, especially when I bake them muffins and serve them tea. I tend to blend into the woodwork, too." She lifted the serving plate toward me.

"Yes, thanks, I'd love another one. You ever do any office stuff for him, maybe fax papers or anything?"

Gellie laughed. "No, dear, I wouldn't know which way was up on a fax machine. Give me a coffeemaker or a blender and I can rule the world, but I'm not interested in becoming acquainted with a fax, a computer, an e-mail whachamhooie, or any of it."

I didn't learn much more from Gellie, except that she was from Smithfield and had a grown daughter who'd given her two of the most beautiful grandchildren in the world. She'd been a housekeeper and a cook all her life and she loved what she did even if geese were sometimes involved. Joel and Patricia Archer were nowhere to be found by the time we'd finished off the muffins and tea.

Hobbit and I were a little late, but we hurried to Bailey's. As I drove out of the small valley with the spectacular house that had an even more spectacular kitchen, a cook named Gellie, and a goose named Batman, I wondered if I'd imagined it all. I glanced in my rearview mirror and thought if I blinked and looked again, it might all be gone.

"Let's not find out," I said to Hobbit.

She agreed.

Nine

On the way to the market, I called Sam to tell him the details from my meeting with Gellie. I left out the goose bite. I'd had my sleeves pushed up when Batman bit me. I now had them rolled down, so I hoped the injury would go unnoticed, and I wasn't going to replay it over the phone.

Sam was genuinely pleased to have the new information, and said he'd tell me later if he found out more. In turn, I was genuinely pleased that he'd share with me.

This was working just fine.

The market was, not surprisingly, busy, and my late arrival put me in an immediate rush and made me unable to properly set up my stall. I started off behind and remained so until around noon, when things slowed a little and I could finally properly display what was left of my inventory, though it seemed a lame effort. Hobbit was patient in the back of the stall but I knew she'd rather be on her pillow on the porch. I wouldn't be able to leave for a couple more hours so I hurried to Brenton's stall, bought a couple of his home-made biscuits, and supplied Hobbit with treats and a big bowl of water. Brenton had been just as busy as the rest of us, so I didn't have an opportunity to ask him any questions. He seemed closer to the normal Brenton but still subdued.

When I'd left my stall for Brenton's, I'd asked Linda to keep an eye on Hobbit, which was an easy duty. Hobbit was comfortable and unbothered by my brief absence. But for the millionth time since she'd been the main part of my family, I wished she could talk in words and not just with facial expressions, because she was probably the only one to see whoever left the surprise on the back corner of my side table.

"Linda, did you by chance see who left this for me?" I held the item up as I leaned around the pole.

"No. What it is?"

"I think it's a Christmas tree ornament."

Specifically, it was an onion—a big, white, and almost perfectly round onion. But it was decorated with more care than had been taken on the eggshell. Instead of red and green markers, the artist had used ribbon. A green band of ribbon circled the top of the onion and a red one circled the bottom. Wire had been inserted through the bottom and came up through the top to form a hook. The onion was dense and heavy but the thick wire over a good, solid tree limb would hold it in place. That was, if I was so inclined to put an onion on my tree.

"Well, it's . . . kind of interesting," Linda said.

"Interesting is a good word."

"What's the circle in the middle?"

Glued to the middle spot in between the two colorful

bands was a round piece of thick paper that held a familiar design, though I couldn't place it at first.

"I'm not sure," I said. "But I think . . ." I held the onion closer. "I think maybe it's the South Carolina state seal or stamp, whatever they're called." I turned it and held the onion so Linda could inspect it more closely.

"I think you're right," she said.

The business lull was still in place, so Linda pulled out her fancy phone and did an Internet search.

She glanced at the phone's screen and then held it up next to the onion.

"Yep, that's it. It has Latin words. Hang on, I'm curious enough to know what it says." She moved her finger over the screen with a couple of expert swipes. "Huh, well there's more here than I expected to find; a full explanation. I've never paid a bit of attention, but it's kind of interesting. Here, read." She handed me the phone. The screen read:

The Great Seal of the State of South Carolina was adopted in 1776. The seal is made up of two elliptical areas, linked by branches of the palmetto tree. The image on the left is dominated by a tall palmetto tree and another tree, fallen and broken. This scene represents the battle fought on June 28, 1776, between defenders of the unfinished fort on Sullivan's Island, and the British Fleet. The standing tree represents the victorious defenders, and the fallen tree is the British Fleet. Banded together on the palmetto with the motto "Quis separabit?" ("Who will separate us?") are twelve spears that represent the first twelve states of the Union. Surrounding the image, at the top, is "South Carolina," and below, is "Animis Opibusque Parati," or "Prepared in Mind and Resources." The other image on the seal depicts a woman walking along a shore that is littered with weapons. The woman, symbolizing Hope, grasps a branch of laurel as the sun rises behind her. Below her image is the word "Spes," or "Hope," and over the image is the motto "Dum Spiro Spero," or "While I Breathe I Hope."

I looked up at Linda and said, "I would not have thought that learning that would ever be a priority, but it is interesting . . . in a high school history class sort of way. What in the world is it doing on an onion decorated as an ornament and then placed on a table in my stall? There was something else in my truck yesterday, too." I told her about the egg.

"Dunno. Maybe it's something Sam's doing? A . . . cute, but admittedly odd, way of celebrating your first Christmas together as a couple?"

"I don't think so, but maybe, I suppose." Sam wasn't the cutesy type, but as well as I thought I knew him, there was always the potential for surprises.

"Excuse me, Becs, I've got a customer. I'll try to think if I saw someone being sneaky, but I don't think I did." Linda patted my arm supportively, but then turned to the sudden line growing outside her stall.

I nodded absently and then turned my attention back to the onion.

"I don't know what to do except just ask people. I don't have a line at the moment. Shall we venture out?" I said to Hobbit, who agreed wholeheartedly. I knew this because she stood up, wagged her tail, and panted.

I put a sign on my table that I'd return shortly, and we stepped around it and made a quick beeline to Bo's onion stall.

He was currently the only onion vendor at the market. Because of the weather and his inordinately fertile land, he was able to grow and then, in turn, sell onions almost all year long.

Hobbit and I stayed back a couple steps as Bo finished with a young boy who held a piece of paper in his fist. I recognized what I was seeing: his parents had sent him in with a list. Bo double-checked the piece of paper and then smiled at me as he handed the boy some change. We'd become pretty good friends over the last few months, mostly because his mother and my mother had reignited their high school friendship, which had resulted in dinners and picnics that included both families, lots of laughter, and stories about our mother that Allison and I weren't sure we needed to know.

Bo was a big guy whose wardrobe choices were similar to mine. We both enjoyed overalls, though I'd never seen him in the short-pants variety.

"Hey, Becca; hey, Hobbit. How's your business? Mine's been pretty darn good, especially for December," he said happily when he was finished with the transaction.

"Great, really. It'll be one of our best Decembers ever, I think."

"What do you have there?" he asked as he looked at the odd onion I held.

"I found it in my stall. It looks like someone turned an onion into a Christmas ornament, doesn't it?"

"I'll be," he said as he took it from my hand. "I don't think I've ever seen such a thing. Can't say it's an attractive way to use an onion, but I do think it's creative. Who'd you say made it?"

"I don't know. It was on my side table. I'd like to find whoever did it, though. I'm curious."

Bo laughed. "You are the curious type." He handed me back the ornament. "It's a plain white onion. I've sold a number of them today. And yesterday, the day before, and so on. Sometimes I remember who I sell specific onions to, particularly if the customer is picky and they take their time going through them all, but this one, pre-decoration, doesn't stand out."

I turned the onion and tried to come up with another question, but I was blank.

"What's that circle?" Bo asked.

"It's South Carolina's state seal."

"Oh, sure, of course it is. You know . . ." he began. He rubbed his chin.

"What?"

"I've seen that recently, today or yesterday. I didn't realize it, but now that I see it again and know what it is, I'm sure I've seen it somewhere else."

"Here, at Bailey's?"

"I don't know. Shoot, I could have seen it on something official, something that it belongs on, but I didn't pay it any attention until now. I'll think about it and let you know if I remember. I'm kind of curious, too. I'd like to know who's so darn creative, particularly if it's with one of my onions."

"Thanks." I thought hard about what I could say that might help him remember more. "Has Sam bought any onions in the last couple days?"

"No." Bo shook his head.

"What about vendors? Who's bought from you today and yesterday, if you can remember?" Something told me my Secret Santa was someone I knew, someone who worked at Bailey's. Even a frequent customer didn't make much sense.

The personal touch, no matter what it might mean, might help me figure out if I knew the ornament artist.

"Gosh, let's see." Bo rubbed his chin again. "Brenton bought something—just one onion, but I can't remember if it was yellow or white. He buys onions one at a time all the time—though he switches up what kind. Allison bought a whole bunch of them, all kinds again. Oh, and that tree guy, the one who looks like Santa, bought a bunch of white ones. I think that's about it."

Brenton, Allison, and Denny. I didn't see any of them taking the time to create ornaments from eggs or onions, though they were all possible covert artists. But why? And, it was possible that the egg had been stolen from Jeannine's stall. If so, maybe the onion had been stolen, too.

"Bo, do you count your inventory every day?" I asked.

"Gosh, no, I do everything by weight and it's just an estimated weight at that. I haven't used a scale in years. I can pick up a bag of onions and know what it weighs. I'm pretty close to accurate."

I didn't keep a close inventory, either, but I knew how many jars fit into each box and it was pretty easy to have a good daily guesstimate. Neither Bo nor I was meticulous like Jeannine, and we never would be.

"Thanks, Bo. I'd love to know if you remember where else you saw the seal."

"Sure. I'll call you if it comes to me."

Hobbit and I walked away from Bo's stall with no real next destination in mind. When that happens, I usually just roam, which eventually leads me to my sister's office. I caught her in the aisle, just as she was hurrying back to it.

"Hey, sis. Hey, girl," she said as she reached down and

patted Hobbit's head. "I've got to make a quick call. Come with me."

I sat in the same chair I'd sat in the day before, and Hobbit found a space next to me that she could fit herself into. Allison's office was small, but today almost all the available extra space was taken up with boxes of flyers.

"They were supposed to go to the post office. They're our mail piece to announce the Ridgeway Farm trees. The printer messed up and sent them here. That's who I have to call. Give me just a few minutes."

Allison used her firm but friendly voice to inform the printer of their mistake. From the side of the conversation that I heard, I thought they might be trying to place the blame on her, but she managed to remind them of the initial agreement, an agreement that had been written and then signed. As was usual, she handled the problem perfectly.

When she hung up the phone, I held up the onion.

She blinked and said, "That's . . . interesting."

"I know. It's, as far as I know, the world's first onion Christmas ornament."

"Me, too. I have never seen another one like it. Did you make it?"

"No, someone left it in my stall today. Someone left an eggshell ornament in my truck yesterday, too, with the number 1987 written on it. I'm assuming it's the same person."

"Really? Who?"

"There's the mystery."

"Let me see."

I handed it to Allison and she turned it every direction. "It's the South Carolina state seal."

"It is."

"You have a proud South Carolinian admirer."

"Or something else."

"Like?"

"I think someone is trying to communicate something to me other than Season's Greetings. These are the pieces to some sort of puzzle."

"A puzzle to where the real gift is hidden, maybe? That's a cute idea."

"Or . . . well, there was a murder here."

"Clues to the killer?" Allison asked.

"That's pretty far-fetched, isn't it?"

"I think so. But maybe we can work to figure out the clues before we jump to conclusions. My interpretation is that something happened in South Carolina in 1987 and that something will lead you somewhere that's important to the ornaments, or their creator. That'll take some research."

"I'll look into it."

She handed me the onion. "Did you discuss this with Sam?"

"Not yet. He only knows about the egg."

"Talk to him. Maybe his police officer eyes and instincts will see things we aren't trained to see."

"I will."

Changing the subject, Allison said, "Sam released Brenton quickly yesterday. I tried to talk to Brenton again this morning, but he wasn't in the mood. He wasn't violent, but he also wasn't interested in talking to me."

I'd been trying to somehow tie the ornaments to Brenton, but I couldn't detect any real connection. Nevertheless, he was on my mind, too.

"Me, either. He's embarrassed. Sam said there was no real

reason to arrest him and once he cooled down a little and Sam told Brenton that he shouldn't behave the way he was behaving, Sam just wanted to let him go. He likes Brenton."

"Everyone likes Brenton. I wish I understood the history between him and the Ridgeways. I thought about asking Denny, but it feels like we as a market might have already been less-than-stellar hosts, and it might just be none of my business anyway," Allison said.

I'd thought about talking to Denny, too, but I'd been so busy that I hadn't yet made the effort.

"Did you know Brenton was once married?" I said.

"Sure. I know his ex-wife—not well, but as well as anyone, I suppose."

"Who is she?"

"You didn't know that Brenton was once married to Stephanie Frugit?" Allison said.

"As in Frugit Orchard, Stephanie Frugit?" I said as I sat up straight. How did I not know this?

"It was a long time ago, but yes, the one and only Stephanie Frugit is Brenton's ex-wife. She's the one who told Brenton he should sell his dog biscuits here at Bailey's. Of course, that was after she laughed at the idea of her orchard having a stall here."

The Frugit Orchard issue had occurred about ten years earlier. I remembered Allison's anger at the way she felt she'd been treated by Stephanie when Allison suggested that a Frugit Orchard apple stall at the then up-and-coming Bailey's would benefit everyone involved. Stephanie Frugit had laughed at the idea and had even been quoted as saying *That little Monson market would never be able to handle the popularity of a Frugit Orchard apple stand"* to a newspaper reporter who was writing a story on Monson businesses.

The worst part of the entire episode was that the apples were delicious, probably some of the best I'd ever eaten. I knew that Linda only purchased Frugit Orchard apples. They were easy to find; they were sold in most South Carolina grocery stores, and they were the number-one apple brand sold by all the local produce wholesalers. They were almost everywhere, except at Bailey's. Over the years as Bailey's had grown, I'd sometimes wondered if Stephanie Frugit might reconsider and set up at stall at the market. But knowing what I knew of her stubborn and way-too-proud reputation, I thought it unlikely.

"No matter how hard I try to create that picture in my mind, I can't imagine Brenton married to Stephanie Frugit. In fact, from what I know about them both, I can't even imagine them liking each other," I said.

"Their marriage ended badly, I hear." Allison winced; she didn't like to gossip.

"When Brenton was freaking out yesterday, Barry said he was going to call Brenton's ex-wife," I said, as I wondered if Barry truly had made that call and what the result had been.

Allison shrugged. "Sometimes time passing can help. You and Scott seemed to get along fine recently."

The Scott she was speaking of was my second ex-husband. The other had been named Scott as well. I'd run into Scott the Second at a local fair and festival.

"Well, mostly," I said. I sat back again. "What do you know about Reggie Stuckey?"

"Until a couple days ago, I didn't know anything about

him. His arrival was a mystery, his death a tragic mystery. I'd never heard of him or his trees until they both showed up here this week."

I told her about my time with Gellie and the new information I'd gleaned.

"But Allison, the one big thing I came away from Gellie with was this: Remember when Reggie said he was going to call his 'gal' and have her fax over the contract?"

"Sure. It arrived shortly thereafter."

"There were no 'gals,' no office personnel. There was Gellie and someone named Patricia Archer, who helped with the trees. Gellie didn't know anything about sending a fax to you or anyone else, for that matter. I didn't meet Patricia Archer, but Gellie said she'd never seen her come into the house."

"That could mean nothing. Maybe he just used the word *gal* because it sounded right to him. Maybe he didn't want to say that he'd have his 'guy' fax over the contract. Some people are funny about those sorts of things."

"But the only guy is Patricia's husband, Joel, and he helps with the trees, too. I doubt it, but I suppose it's possible." I wished I'd thought to ask Gellie if Reggie had an office in the house and if I could look at it.

"The mystery of Reggie Stuckey only continues to grow," Allison said.

I sighed, but had nothing more to add, so Hobbit, the onion, and I headed back to my stall and watched for suspicious-looking people bearing strange homemade farmers' market ornaments.

No one stood out.

Ten

Mid-afternoon, I put my again-empty boxes and Hobbit into the truck and rode the bumpy back load/unload path out of the market and toward the highway. There had been no new ornaments to add to the collection, either in my stall or my truck. Linda said she didn't think she had seen anyone acting strangely or suspiciously around my stall, though it had been so busy she couldn't be certain.

I pulled the truck around to the front parking lot and stopped on the edge of the lot between Allison's office and the Ridgeway setup. The Stuckey truck had been removed earlier though I hadn't witnessed its departure.

Denny was tending to some of his corralled trees—it looked like he was fanning their limbs and making sure none of them were being unduly crushed. His tree adjustments reminded me of my pumpkin adjustments. It was important to move growing pumpkins and their vines every now and then so the gourds wouldn't end up with a flat side or some other misshape.

Billie and Ned were closer to the truck than the tree corral and were sitting in facing chairs, but they acted as if they weren't aware of each other. Billie concentrated on one of her fingernails and Ned was leaning forward with his elbows on his knees as he thumbed something on his phone.

"Stay here, girl," I said to Hobbit as I put the truck into park and turned off the engine. I had a sudden desire to see if I could get some questions answered.

"Becca, hello!" Denny said happily as I walked toward the corral. The two seated siblings sat up a little straighter and returned my smile and wave.

"Hi," I said as Denny remained behind the low rope of the corral. "How are you all doing? Comfortable?"

"I think we're fine. We've already sold more trees than I anticipated," Denny said. "The Stuckey tragedy didn't disrupt Bailey's business much, if at all."

Gone was the tenderness I thought I'd witnessed when we found Reggie's body and shortly thereafter, but Denny was correct. Bailey's business hadn't suffered. Briefly, I wondered what would have happened if the legendary Denny had been the murder victim instead of the much-lesser-known Reggie.

"No, it didn't. I didn't know much about Reggie. Did he have a family?"

"Not that I'm aware of," Denny said, but a twitch pulled at the corner of his mouth. I knew this because the twitch stretched through his beard.

"You must have known each other a little, being in the same business and all."

"We did. We hadn't had many dealings for the last few years, but there was a time . . . oh, I suppose that's not important now."

"You were close?"

Denny waved off the question.

"Well," I said, "then I'm sorry for your loss."

"Anyone's death creates a loss, and one that was so brutal . . . well, it's tragic, just tragic."

The December sunlight was tinged with gray; I liked December sunlight and its subtle promise of the season. It was comforting, but today it only seemed to discolor Denny's normally ruddy skin. I wondered if it was my imagination.

"Denny, can I ask you another question? It's one of those none-of-my-business questions, but I'd really like to ask."

Denny crossed his arms in front of himself. I didn't think he was aware of how loudly his body language spoke. He briefly glanced over at Billie and Ned, who pretended not to be interested in Denny and me, and said, "Sure. Can't promise I can answer, but ask away."

"What's between you and your family"—I looked at Billie and Ned and then back at Denny—"and Brenton Jones?"

"I don't guess I know what you mean. I don't even know who you mean."

I looked at him a long moment. He might have been lying, but it was hard to tell. He was stoic, and I sensed that the wall he'd put up with his crossed arms was impenetrable because he'd had practice building it before. On the other hand, he emanated such a natural honesty that he was either truly honest, or really, really good at lying.

I continued, "I've known Brenton for as long as I've worked at Bailey's, which is just about eight years. He's never once been anything but friendly and kind. When he pulled into the parking lot the other day, I thought his eyes might burn right out of their sockets with the look he was giving your truck. He's been agitated since the day you arrived. There's something between you all. I know it's no one's business but yours, but I'm curious, very curious, and I was hoping you'd tell me at least a little something about your issues."

"I think you're asking the wrong person, Becca. I don't have a problem with this fella you're talking about. You might want to ask him."

"I have."

"What does he say?"

"Nothing."

It was Denny's turn to study me. He did, his eyes suddenly focused and slanted. It never occurred to me that the mere act of me asking these questions could somehow make him suspicious of me, but that's what I was sensing—he suddenly didn't trust me.

Instantly, I wanted to do or say something trustworthy. My "want to be liked" part wanted to be stroked. Had I just done or said something that might make Denny like me less? Denny Ridgeway and I didn't really know each other. Just because we'd had a couple friendly conversations in the parking lot and had found a dead body together didn't give either of us the right to expect full disclosure—in either direction. It was an interesting, eye-opening moment.

But maybe it was okay not to be trusted. I'd ride it and see where it went. I let him study me without saying anything.

I wasn't demure; I probably couldn't do that one even if I tried, and I wasn't as stoic as he was, either. The corner of my mouth wanted to twitch, but I think I held it still.

Finally, his features relaxed a bit, he looked away, and he said, "I wish I could help you, Becca, but I can't."

"What about Billie and Ned?" I looked their direction.

"What about them?"

"That day I met all of you, Billie was just as upset as Brenton when she came out of the market after rounding up some drinks."

"She was?"

I nodded.

"Let's go ask her."

Denny stepped over the low rope and took long strides toward his siblings. They both stood and smiled and I was struck by Denny's position of power within the family. I'd briefly noticed it the first time I'd met the three of them. Denny was in charge, and they "snapped to" when he approached.

"Billie, Ned, you both remember Becca?" Denny said.

They both muttered, "Sure," as they smiled and nodded.

"Billie, Becca says you were upset a couple days ago, the day we all met. When you came out of the market with our drinks?"

"I was?"

"Yes," I said. "You went into the market to get some soft drinks and seemed . . . shaken when you came back out."

Billie shook her head slowly. "I don't think so. No, I don't remember being upset."

Unlike Denny, Billie wasn't gifted with either an honest aura or the ability to lie well. She shifted her weight from one foot to the other and rubbed her finger under her nose as she avoided eye contact with everyone.

"There you have it. She wasn't upset," Denny said.

I squinted at him, but he hid any indication that he was seeing the same act I was seeing. He was good.

"Well, that's good to hear. I'm glad," I said. "Of course, if anything isn't up to par, let Allison know. She always wants to make sure all vendors are well taken care of."

"Thank you for that, Becca. Thank you," Denny said. "And now, you'll have to excuse us, but we need to get back to work."

They had no immediate customers, but I just smiled, thanked them for their time, and made my way back to Hobbit.

"I don't know if they're killers," I said to her as she greeted me with a friendly nose nudge to my thigh, "but I bet you a pound of Brenton's dog biscuits they're keeping secrets. I bet you ten more that those secrets just might lead us to Reggie's killer." I thought a moment. "Okay, well, I can't be sure of the last part, of course, but I'd really like to know their secrets."

She sniffed as if to tell me she'd like to know, too.

I opened the glove box and searched for something to write a note with. I found an old receipt and a nubby pencil and wrote:

1. Why did Reggie have so much money? Textiles? Politics?
2. Why did Brenton dislike the Ridgeways?
3. What happened in South Carolina in 1987?
4. How in the world was Brenton married to Stephanie Frugit???
5. What are the Ridgeways hiding?

"I know it's been a long day, girl, but I have one more stop before we go home. You okay with that?"

Of course she was. I stuffed the list into one of my overalls pockets and turned the truck around. As I pulled out of the parking lot, I happened to glance back toward the market; more specifically, toward the back of the Ridgeway truck. When I'd been writing the note, this area had been hidden from my view, and it turned out to be the area in which the three Ridgeway siblings had congregated. They didn't see that I was watching what looked to be a heated discussion, or perhaps just a heated lecture from Denny. His face was back to a ruddy red and he was emphasizing his words with air-pounding hands.

I was moving the truck so slowly that someone behind me honked, which caused the Ridgeways to look my direction.

"Shoot," I said, not because I was caught, but rather because I wished I were better at understanding what I'd done or asked to cause the ruckus.

Maybe I'd have to find a way to spy . . . I mean, investigate, later.

anie Frugit was on a rung comparable to the biggest Hollywood stars. And even I had to admit she played the role well. She wore the right clothes, said the right things, and had created her own successful blog: "Apple Woman of South Carolina," which received a ridiculous amount of hits every single day. Somehow Stephanie had a lot to say about apples and about being a single woman in the business world. Until today, I had no idea that she hadn't always been single, and I wondered how many of her loyal readers knew. The fact that bigger-than-life Stephanie Frugit had once been married to mild-mannered Brenton was so hard to believe, however, I wondered if Allison had been mistaken.

There was at least one way to find out.

I turned down the "secret" road and steered the truck stealthily forward and through the woods. The air coming through the slightly lowered windows felt suddenly colder as the trees and their canopy of thick leafless branches got thicker. It was the perfect fairy-tale-like drive that always led to the perfect fairyland, particularly when the trees were in their full summer greenery, but even today there was a sense of entering a storybook.

The orchard was huge, bigger than any farm I was accustomed to. This was beyond a farmers' market farm, beyond a roadside stand farm, and much more expansive than Reggie Stuckey's farm, which was tiny compared to Stephanie's behemoth. Though Frugit Orchard was beautiful, it had a distinctly industrial feel to it; it was so large and so pristine, I could easily imagine robots shining fence posts and steering tractors. There was just no way this place could look the way it looked by using mere human labor.

But there were no robots in sight as I exited the woods and arrived onto the orchard's wide, deep front lawn.

Back a ways and in the middle of a valley that was mostly apple trees was Southfork—or at least that's what my mother called it, because it looked so much like the mansion from the *Dallas* television show. It was necessary that the house be big; anything smaller would have been dwarfed by the rest of the orchard. Since Stephanie was—or claimed to be—single, unless she had a lot of company, the house must have a constant noise of her echoed footsteps.

Precise rows of apple trees fanned out over the rest of the visible land, seemingly into eternity. There was a barn behind the house, but it was hardly noticeable.

Every time the sun rose, it did so from behind the property, glorifying each inch of acreage. I'd seen the place at sunup; it was stunning.

It had been a few years since I'd ventured out to have a look at Frugit (our nickname for the entire orchard) and I couldn't remember why I'd made the trip. I'd never once before seen Stephanie working outside, but today was different. She was at the edge of the house and the north orchards, standing on a fence slat and looking toward the trees. She was dressed in tight jeans and a red-and-green button-down shirt. I wondered if she'd been doing some sort of holiday photo shoot. Her long, strawberry-blonde hair was loose and evenly wavy. She glanced in my direction and even from a distance of about fifty yards I could see her wrinkle her nose at my old orange truck.

"Be extra well-behaved while I go talk to the tall, intimidating lady with the great hair, okay?" I said to Hobbit.

Hobbit whined, but it was in the affirmative.

Stephanie didn't hesitate, but stepped off the fence and walked purposefully toward me. I knew she was somewhere in her early fifties, but she seemed ageless. She was perfect: not only her hair, but her body, her clothing choices. I guessed she sported a precise pedicure under those tan leather cowboy boots. I steered the truck up the driveway and met her at the edge of the property.

My door decided to protest a little more loudly than usual as I pushed it open. I plopped myself off the seat and onto the ground.

"Good girl," I said to Hobbit when I'd closed the door.

"Can I help you?" Stephanie said as she shaded her eyes with one hand and put the other on a hip. In that pose, she belonged on a postcard.

"I hope so," I said as I walked toward her. She'd stopped moving, so I thought one of us should close the space. "My name is Becca Robins and I work at Bailey's Farmers' Market." I extended a hand.

I truly thought she'd ignore my gesture, but she surprised me and reached out. "Okay, well, what can I do for you?"

"I . . . well, I was wondering about something."

Stephanie squinted and began to look impatient. "I'm not setting up a stall at a farmers' market. My business is too big for that. My apples are too good. Seriously, I'd kill the other apple growers' business. Not my style. I figure there's room for us all."

I paused. *Wait, what? She's being altruistic?* I was completely caught off guard.

When my pause went on too long, she smiled quickly and then said, "So, have a nice day."

I spoke just as she turned to walk away. "Wait, no, I don't want to talk to you about putting a stall in Bailey's. I want to talk to you about your ex-husband, Brenton Jones."

I had her attention again. "Is he okay?"

"Yes, he's fine."

"What about him do you want to discuss?"

"Well, first, I wondered if the two of you had been married, but you just confirmed that, so thank you."

Stephanie Frugit drew her eyebrows together but then relaxed them back to normal an instant later. She smiled. "You might be the first person I've ever met in a long time who thinks it's okay to be so direct. You might not know this, but I'm a little like that myself," she said.

"I've heard."

Stephanie laughed. It was a loud, ringing laugh that made me want to laugh, too.

"Come in, Becca Robins from Bailey's Farmers' Market. I can pour you either an iced tea or a whiskey. You want something stronger or weaker, you'll have to go elsewhere." She turned, leaving me on my own to figure out the latch on the closed gate before I could trail behind.

I got the latch on the third try and waved at Hobbit as I closed the gate behind me. She lifted her nose in the air to cheer me on, her version of a fist pump.

Even though we'd shaken hands, I hadn't noticed Stephanie had been wearing gloves; but she was removing the second one, one finger at a time, when I joined her in the front entryway.

Stephanie was tall with killer posture and shoulders that were so wide they'd be masculine on anyone else. I'd noticed that she walked smoothly but with such long strides that I'd have to jog if we ever decided to hang out at a mall together. She had the sharpest, most judgmental green eyes I'd ever seen.

I felt downright frumpy just breathing the same air.

"In there." She nodded with her head. "Have a seat. I'll go place our drink order. It's whiskey for me. You?"

"Iced tea would be great," I said. Even if she'd wanted someone to drink with, I was driving and not a frequent drinker, and I was dating a cop. Even Stephanie couldn't intimidate me quite that far.

"Excellent," she said. "I'll be back momentarily. Make yourself at home."

The thought of throwing off my shoes and putting my feet up on something did cross my mind, but only as a semi-amusing idea. I ventured into the room she'd nodded toward and was pleasantly surprised again.

It was big and full of expensive furniture, but it was all comfortable furniture: contemporary but homey. Chairs, couches, and tables were all well placed for entertaining. It looked like a room in which you could choose to read a book quietly, play a game of cards with a large group, or chat easily with a roomful of guests. In fact, it was so big that all of those could be done at once and everyone would still have some privacy. I took a seat on a chair that flanked the predictably large fireplace. I tried sitting forward on the edge, and back with my ankles crossed. Finally, I chose something that was in between.

A large portrait of Stephanie hung above the fireplace. She was dressed in a white, off-the-shoulder evening gown. The painter had exaggerated the lines of her collarbones and, again, I realized that the look would have been decidedly masculine on anyone else, but it wasn't on her. On her, it was strong and feminine and somewhat ferocious.

"Here we are," Stephanie said as she came into the room carrying a tray with our drinks. She set the tray on the table next to me and asked how I took my iced tea.

After the appropriate amount of sugar had been stirred in, she sat on a chair and faced me. "Are you dating Brenton or something?"

"Oh, no, nothing like that. He and I have known each other for years. We've been friends."

"Great. So, why do you want to know about his marriage to me?"

"Well, at first I wanted to confirm that the two of you had been married." She nodded. I continued, "You know, he's pretty soft-spoken. I'm trying to . . ."

Stephanie laughed. "Imagine him with me?"

"That sounds awful, but yes." She'd mentioned that she liked direct.

"Not really. I understand. It's been a long time since I've truly talked about Brenton." She smiled and looked back into the past for a moment. "We had a great time for a long time. We were young—really young, though."

"Too young?"

Stephanie shrugged. "I don't know. Perhaps, but only in the way our ambitions changed. When we divorced we still loved each other, it was just that neither of us could imagine living the kind of life that the other one wanted." Her eyes opened wide and then she took a sip of her whiskey. "Wow, I can't believe I just shared that with a virtual stranger. You'd better share something with me quickly before I resent inviting you in."

"I've been divorced twice and I didn't like or love either of my husbands when we parted. I've reconnected with one, but only as a friend and that's been fun, but I'm very jealous that you and Brenton were able to do what you did. I still hate the horrible feelings I had during my divorces."

She took another sip. "That was a good and fair share. But, hell, Becca, divorce is ugly no matter how 'amicable' it is."

"That's probably true."

"Brenton still selling dog biscuits?" she asked.

"Oh, yes, very successfully. He has a big Internet business, too."

"I'll have to look it up."

"You two don't talk at all?"

"No, not for years."

"But . . ."

"What?"

"A fellow vendor, Barry, said he was going to call you."

"I talk to Barry all the time. He tried to call me two days ago, but he didn't leave a message. I tried to call him back but I have yet to hear from him. Was he calling me about Brenton?" Concern creased her barely wrinkled forehead, but I was certain it would flatten out again quickly.

"You and Barry talk, but not you and Brenton?"

"Barry's my uncle. What's up with Brenton?"

"Oh. I see. You heard about Reggie Stuckey?"

"I did. Becca, what does this have to do with Brenton?"

"I don't think Reggie's murder has anything to do with Brenton, but many things happened at once and . . . well, do you know if Brenton has had a conflict with the Ridgeway family?"

Stephanie hid it well, but I was fairly certain I saw a shadow of surprise darken her green eyes.

"The Christmas tree family?"

"Yes."

"Not that I'm aware of."

I was 93.3 percent sure she was lying, but I didn't want to call her on it. Just knowing she was lying might eventually tell me something important anyway.

"Did you or Brenton know Reggie Stuckey?" I said.

"The guy who was killed?"

"Yes."

She took a smooth sip of her drink. Even the ice in her glass clinked in key.

I assumed that Stephanie Frugit didn't get rattled, but her behavior had already surprised me. The woman I was sitting across from might be powerful and direct, but there was something warm about her, something she didn't show easily. I'd caught her either on a good day or a bad day— only she knew which it was.

And she was momentarily shaken. She didn't want me to see it, but her pale skin went a shade of gray, and tears pooled in her eyes, if only briefly. She normalized quickly.

"He was a nice man," she said.

"I didn't know him. I feel like I missed out. He didn't advertise his tree farm well at all."

"No." Stephanie laughed. "Reggie Stuckey had loads of money. He only ran the farm for fun. He'd end up giving away more trees than he sold."

"How did he get his money?"

"His family, textiles or something."

"I'd heard politics, too."

Stephanie shrugged and put the glass to her lips again.

"Do you know if Brenton knew him?"

"You'll have to ask him." She put her glass on a table next to her chair. "Now, tell me, Becca, why are you asking me all these questions? I deserve to know."

I thought about it and then I did something I rarely did when I was snooping into places I had no business snooping into: I told her the truth. She listened intently as I told her about how sweet and wonderful her ex-husband was, but how he uncharacteristically fumed with what I'd interpreted as anger when he saw the Ridgeways and their truck at Bailey's. I told her how he was happy that Reggie might have had a conflicting contract with Bailey's, and how he had behaved almost violently. I told her about his trip to the police station and his quick release.

She listened with her focused green eyes. A couple of times I wondered if she ever blinked. When I was finished she simply said, "That's too bad. I'm sorry for whatever is bothering Brenton. I'm sorry if he worried you and your sister, but I can assure you he won't hurt anyone. It's just not in him."

"I didn't think so, either," I said. "But isn't anyone capable of violence if they're pushed?"

She shook her head and pulled her green eyes away from my less spectacular blue ones. "No, not Brenton. He's kind to the core."

I had the urge to say again that I thought so, too, but I held back, and that proved to be a wise choice.

"Look, Becca." She turned her gaze back to me again. "People aren't always who they seem to be. You just need to know that, and that's all I can tell you."

"I do," I said. "We all have our 'other selves,' I suppose."

"No, I mean this literally, people aren't always who they say they are."

"Say they are" is different than "seem to be," I thought.

"Are you talking about Brenton or someone else?" I said.

"I'd feel like I was being disloyal if I told you anything more. Besides, if you're nosy enough—and I do think you are—you'll figure it out pretty quickly."

"Any chance you'd share another small hint?"

She laughed her deep, ringing laugh and I once again had the urge to laugh with her. I just smiled instead.

"No, but I've had a great time with this—whatever sort of word volley this was. You ask good questions."

"Not good enough or I'd have the answers."

Stephanie reached for her glass and took one last gulp of the whiskey and said, "You might be closer than you think."

Twelve

I discussed with Hobbit the conversation between Stephanie and me. Mostly, it was just so I could replay everything in my own head. I had an inkling that Stephanie Frugit had answered every question I'd had—and more. I just didn't know how to decipher her code.

By the time we made it home, Hobbit was fast asleep, her nose nudged against my thigh and one of her back paws high on the passenger-side door. It was a shame to have to wake her, but wake her I did, and with urgency when I spied something unexpected on my front porch.

I'd had plenty of packages left on the porch, and lots of deliveries occurred when I was away from the house. But this item wasn't a box or a container.

I pulled the truck along the driveway and parked as close to the porch as possible.

I thought about calling Sam but that seemed premature.

I'd take a closer look first. Just in case, I made sure I knew which pocket my phone was in.

From the truck, it looked like a handmade doll. Chills ran up and down my spine and then made my teeth chatter. I'd seen enough horror movies to have witnessed dolls transforming from children's toys to something menacing and deadly. But this one wasn't opening its eyes, or pulling itself up to a standing position.

"Come on," I said to Hobbit. "It's just a stupid doll. I think."

I got less spooked as we moved closer. When I realized the doll was adorned in red and green ribbon, I became more curious than concerned. It looked like my ornament collection was gaining a new addition.

The doll was about eight inches tall and crudely made of cornhusks, ribbon, and string. Barry of Barry Good Corn didn't sell corn in December, but he still hung out at the market. A couple years earlier, he'd started selling dried cornhusks in the off season. Crafters used them, so he figured adding the product made sense. The husks wouldn't ever make him rich, but they were an addition that gave him an excuse to be at the market even when he didn't have produce to sell. I guessed that like the other ornament items, these cornhusks had come from Bailey's, and they might have been stolen.

I knew it was a girl doll because it had a cornhusk skirt, the waist of which was tied with both a green and a red ribbon. The waist-length hair was made with a cut piece of husk, its multiple tips curling in all directions. It occurred to me that it must have taken a lot of time just to make the hair. The face was drawn in with black dot eyes and a simple black *L* nose, but the perfectly shaped lips were bright red, giving her a whole Christmas-elf-floozy persona. A paper clip had been stretched, bent, and again used for the hook.

I inspected it from top to bottom but there was no other clue to lead me to its creator. There were no years noted and no state seals. She was just a cornhusk Christmas doll ornament and one, I had to admit, I thought was cute. It was the first market-product ornament I'd received that I would consider putting on a tree.

I looked up and around the property. Nothing had been disturbed, but someone had secretly dropped it off, probably knowing that I wasn't home, although that wasn't ever much of a mystery. My orange truck was pretty good at giving away my location.

There was no harm done, but it was still creepy. If I'd just found it and not the others before it, I might not have felt uncomfortable, but I did. I didn't like the fact that someone had easily traipsed around my property and *could* have caused more harm without being noticed. I really didn't like the idea that Hobbit could have once again been exposed to someone up to no good.

I looked at my dog. She was also inspecting the property with her eyes and her lifted nose.

"We might have to get some cameras, girl."

She agreed.

I carried the doll into the house and checked every room and every closet, just in case. Nothing had been disturbed. Nothing was out of place. No one had tried to come in through a window, and the back sliding door was still locked, its glass intact. Simply, someone had come onto my property and left a doll ornament. Someone who had stocked up on Bailey's products or shopped there frequently was stretching his or her creative skills.

After a full inspection of the premises, I called Sam, but he didn't answer. I debated leaving a detailed message about the newest ornament but decided just to let him see it when he came over later that evening. I had plenty of cookies to bake to keep me busy.

I transitioned easily into baking mode. My mind was so busy thinking about ornaments, Stephanie Frugit's words, and murder that I finished the cookies without really noticing that I'd started.

When the last batch was cooling and Sam still hadn't arrived, I was anxious to do something else productive, so I switched on my old laptop. Once it finally warmed up, I began searching. I started with "1987 South Carolina" and was overwhelmed by the large amount of available links. On October 3, the South Carolina Gamecocks football team had played the number-two ranked Nebraska Cornhuskers. South Carolina lost 21–30. And 1987 was the inaugural year for former governor Carroll Ashmore Campbell Jr.

As enjoyable as I found the glimpse into the past, I wasn't interested enough in any of the listings to pay them close attention. I skimmed, searching for something that might ring a relevant bell. As my eyes moved over the screen, I hoped to find the name "Stuckey" or "Ridgeway," but nothing stood out.

I typed in "Ridgeway South Carolina 1987" and found a number of items regarding Monson and a couple of listings about the Christmas tree farm but nothing that seemed important to the murder of Reggie Stuckey, or at least nothing that I could interpret as being important.

I felt like a hamster on a wheel, getting nowhere quickly. Out of frustration, I just typed "Reggie Stuckey wife" into the browser and finally found something that might prove to be helpful—a chunk of information that might at least lead somewhere.

The first link listed was to a Wikipedia page for South Carolina state senator Evelyn Rasmussen Stuckey, who served from 1985 until 1987. The dates at the top of the page, of course, caught my attention immediately. I wasn't politically savvy but I knew that state senators served four-year terms. I glanced at Evelyn's picture and noted that she was an attractive blonde before I continued to read the entry.

Evelyn Rasmussen was born in Charleston, South Carolina, in 1958. She remained there until she'd completed her education, graduating from the University of South Carolina law school summa cum laude. Upon receiving her law degree, she escaped the city for the country life with a man she'd met at a small town gas station when she was on a road trip through the state. Evelyn married Reggie Stuckey in 1984 and settled outside the small town of Monson, South Carolina, but her ambition was bigger than any small town, and she ran for and won a local race for the state senate.

Though a seat with the state senate is usually one of the lesser-known political positions, Evelyn Stuckey was an immediate force to be reckoned with. Her intelligence, quick wit, physical height, and her loud, deep voice garnered attention from any reporter looking for something interesting and perhaps unique to cover.

And then, suddenly, in the spring of 1987, she disappeared. She stepped down from her senate seat, divorced her husband, and disappeared off the South Carolina political radar—any radar, maybe. Many have speculated why she took such a sudden turn, but no one has been able to obtain the real answer.

Following the entry, there was also a note added later, dated last December. It read: "It is believed that Evelyn Rasmussen has been living Smithfield, South Carolina. She hasn't practiced law for some time, but there are rumors that she raises chickens and sells farm fresh eggs at area grocery stores and the local farmers' market."

"No!" I exclaimed when I read the additional note. Hobbit had been resting on my feet and she jumped to attention. "Sorry, girl." I petted her head, easing her back to a reclining position.

I read the entire entry again and searched for any other sites that would shed more light on Evelyn, and then debated if I would call Mamma Maria and ask her about her potential fellow vendor tonight or wait until tomorrow.

I wanted to call someone, I wanted to jump up and down and exclaim that I'd figured it out! I'd really figured it out! But, what, really had become clear? Not much, I realized.

The 1987 egg, the state seal onion, the pretty blondeish girl doll: Were they all pointing at Evelyn Stuckey? Why? Had she killed her ex-husband? Or, maybe she just knew who the killer was. I'd wondered why I was the recipient of the ornaments, and I now thought I better understood. It was all tied together with the farmers' market connection.

If Evelyn Stuckey did work at the Smithfield Market, my secret ornament giver was trying to use the market connection to make sure I was able to find her. It was genius.

The sound of tires on my driveway pulled me off the chair and quickly over to the front door. I couldn't wait to tell Sam everything.

But it wasn't Sam pulling in; it was Allison, and she was alone. I was immediately concerned.

"Everything okay?" I said as I opened the door.

"Sure. Can't one fraternal twin sister stop by and visit the other one?"

"Not when one of the twins has a family, it's later than a normal visit, and she didn't call first."

Allison laughed and then pulled a piece of paper out of her pocket. "I brought your orders. The form you left on your table filled up quickly. I thought you should have it."

I took the paper but continued to look at Allison. "You could have just called with a total number."

"Yes, you're right," Allison said. "I was actually hoping to catch both you and Sam. Is he coming over this evening?"

"I think so."

"Well, then you get the news first."

"Is it something really good?"

"It's interesting, but I'm not sure if it's good or helpful to solving the murder. I didn't want to talk about it"—she looked around—"well, anywhere but here or at Sam's house. I gambled that you were here. I don't want other market vendors or other police officers to hear what I have to say. Yet."

"Really?" I said, still standing in the open doorway with Hobbit. "This must be good."

"May I come in?"

I stepped back and welcomed her inside.

"Mel called this evening, right before I was packing up to leave. He doesn't typically work late, so I was surprised to hear from him," Allison said.

"And he was upset?" I said as I handed her a glass of water.

Sam had arrived only about a minute after Allison had come into the house. The two of them sat on stools on the outside of the kitchen island counter as I gathered drinks and snacks.

"Yes, at himself. I think he waited until everyone else in the office went home before calling me because he felt so bad," Allison said.

"Mel's one of the market owners?" Sam asked as he set his glass on the counter. He'd had a long day, but still looked police-officer fresh and crisp.

"No, he works for the owners. He does whatever they need done, including filing and typing. He's young and . . . well, as far as I can tell, he's a pretty good guy. Anyway, he said that last week a woman from Reggie Stuckey's office called and asked about selling trees at Bailey's. Mel told them that could probably be arranged but he'd have to check with the owners first."

"Sounds reasonable," I said.

"Yes, well, he jumped the gun. He offered to send over a contract so that Reggie could look it over while he checked with the owners."

"Oh," I said. "That explains why Reggie had a contract."

Allison shook her head. "No, not really. Remember that the contract was a doctored version of the Ridgeway contract. When the woman said she'd prefer a fax, he said that he printed out a new, blank copy right then and there and then sent the fax, but apparently it never went through."

"A bogus number?" I asked.

"He thinks so."

"Does Mel have the fax number he used?" Sam asked.

"Yes. I tried it. It goes to a disconnected number," Allison said.

"I'm not sure why he was upset."

"He thinks he should have told someone about the call and the incorrect number."

"Hindsight and all. I'll go talk to him tomorrow, but I don't think he did anything wrong. If he doesn't want the owners to know that he attempted to send Reggie a contract, he won't be happy to see me, but I don't think he needs to be worried," Sam said.

"I know. I told him I was going to talk to you this evening, but that you'd have to be involved officially. He's upset because he thinks that he shouldn't have even tried to send the contract until he'd received approval from the owners, which he never did."

"I doubt any of it is really his fault, but we need to get to the bottom of it. I'll work on phone records, etc."

"There's no woman," I said.

"What's that?" Allison said.

"There's no office person or assistant. Reggie was set up with a skeleton crew. I was at his place today. Well, he had a female housekeeper and a woman who's part of a married couple that help with the trees but no assistant or secretary. It would be nice to know who the woman who called Mel is."

I gave them both a brief overview of my visit with Gellie and Batman, even though Sam had heard the details earlier. Some other officers had been out to the Stuckey farm, so I suspected that he was now comparing my experience to theirs, but he only listened without adding to the conversation.

"I don't have any idea who called then," Allison said.

"I'll track her down," Sam said.

Allison's new information might have felt big, but I could tell she was a little deflated after sharing the details. I knew what it was like to have something be bigger in my mind than in reality. I didn't want to upstage her, but I really wanted to share what I'd discovered, too. "I've got more information." I said when it seemed like Allison was finished.

"What?" Allison and Sam said together.

"I know who Reggie Stuckey was once married to."

Sam sat up straighter. "I'd like to know."

"Evelyn Rasmussen Stuckey was her married name. She went back down to Evelyn Rasmussen when she and Reggie divorced in the late eighties. She was a state senator."

"Senator Stuckey?" Allison said. "I don't recall the State of South Carolina electing a senator of that name."

"Not a big senator, just a state representative senator."

"Oh."

"I couldn't name a current state senator if my life depended on it," I said. "They're not the most well-known politicians, but I guess Evelyn was a force to be reckoned with, at least until she mysteriously stepped down from her position and she and Reggie divorced."

"Okay?" Sam said, prompting me to continue.

"I bet that whatever it was that happened to cause her to step down, it happened around 1987." The egg and onion ornaments were on the far counter. I picked them up and put them down in front of Sam and Allison. "Someone knows who the killer is, and I bet you a dozen of Jeannine's eggs that they're using these ornaments to try to tell us who it is. And somehow, Evelyn is involved, even if she isn't the killer."

"That's a pretty big theory," Sam said. "Tell me more."

"We've got one more clue." I gathered the doll, which was hidden from their view in a space next to the refrigerator. I was about the drama now. I placed the doll next to the onion and the egg. "Evelyn didn't really look like this doll, but she was pretty and blonde." I'd printed out a picture of her and I placed it next to the doll. "However, I think this doll is supposed to be her. I think all these are about her."

I showed them what I'd found. They were both surprised by the fact that Evelyn now worked at the Smithfield Market, and they were only lukewarm to the idea that I was the recipient of the ornaments because I worked at a farmers' market, too.

"But lots of us work at Bailey's," Allison said.

I shrugged. "I'm just the lucky one, that's all," I said.

Sam's eyes were stern and thoughtful, but he didn't agree or disagree.

"Why wouldn't this person just tell the police who the killer is? What's with the clues?" Allison said.

"I thought about that, too," I said. "Sam, what do you think—the person sending the ornaments isn't 100 percent sure?"

"I think it's that. Partially. There's more—maybe he or she likes the game. Maybe the killer is the one sending them to throw the investigation off track. There's also the other option—maybe these are just gifts and have nothing at all to do with the murder."

I looked at the strange group of ornaments and, though Sam could be correct, I strongly sensed that these were clues to something, hopefully that would lead to the killer.

"You know," Sam said, "the doll reminds me more of your friend, the one at the Smithfield Market who sells pies, than the Internet picture of Evelyn Rasmussen Stuckey."

"Mamma Maria?" I asked as I picked up the doll again. He was right. There was something overdone about the doll—well, as overdone as a cornhusk doll could be.

"She's coming to Bailey's," Allison said. "I mean, she's going to have a stall at Bailey's, at least part-time."

"I heard," I said distractedly. I'd fallen into thought, but was jolted out again by both Sam's and Allison's chuckles.

"You are so transparent, little sister."

"What?"

"You're going to Smithfield tomorrow, right? You'd go tonight if the market were open," Sam added.

I smiled. They knew me too well.

Thirteen

The evening ended with me sharing the details of my visit with Stephanie Frugit, but neither Sam nor Allison thought that part of my day was nearly as interesting as the other parts. Allison had known that Brenton was once married to Stephanie, and Sam didn't think the long-ago marriage mattered, though he would stop by and talk to Stephanie himself just to see if there might be something pertinent to the current murder.

In case my concern about Hobbit being home alone had been rekindled because of the appearance of the doll ornament, Allison said she'd take Hobbit while I ventured to the Smithfield Market. Sam offered to let her stay at his house, though he had to work. I also knew that both Ian and George would welcome her at the lavender farm. It was wonderful to have options.

Ultimately, I knew she'd be happiest at home for the few

hours I would be away, so I instructed her once again on the ins and outs of the doggie door. She seemed just fine with the solution and happily sent me away as she curled up on the porch. She liked her routine, and I'd switched it up enough the day before.

I didn't like that I thought it was necessary, but I was pretty sure I would soon be installing a security camera.

There was a slightly deeper chill to the air this morning. In addition to donning my long overalls, I pulled a sweater over my long-sleeved T-shirt and kept the windows rolled up as I drove the thirty minutes to Smithfield.

The trip through the South Carolina countryside wasn't meant to be done speedily. The two-lane highway had been built to accommodate the random, slow-moving tractor or trucks older than my own that couldn't quite make it over fifty miles per hour anymore. There wasn't a large amount of traffic to contend with, but sometimes you had to let a few vehicles pass the other direction before you passed something moving slowly in front of you. Doing so without a friendly wave was unheard of.

From this stretch of road it seemed that the entire world was made up of farms, one right next to the other, one crop suddenly becoming a different crop. Crops weren't flourishing this time of year, of course, but that didn't make the drive less interesting; it just changed where you looked.

December was the time to notice the handiwork that had gone into houses, barns, fences, and even mailboxes. I didn't know where or when the tradition had begun, but at some point someone must have created such an interesting mailbox that it prompted others to follow along.

By the time I made it halfway through the trip, I'd enjoyed

almost a full cup of Maytabee's coffee, the sun had risen up over the small slopes of hilly countryside, and I'd noticed a variety of interesting mailboxes: a chicken, a pig, a horse, and a surprisingly odd, giant, silver dollar shape. There were others, but those were the ones that stood out the most, the ones that looked as if they'd recently seen some new paint.

I was always pretty sure there was no other place in the world I'd rather live; the drive this morning only reinforced my opinion.

The Smithfield Market's parking lot was mostly empty, but a few trucks, similar in age and wear to mine, sat close to the entrance. Like Bailey's, this market had a back unload/load area, so the vendors' vehicles wouldn't be in plain sight. It hadn't occurred to me that I might be too early for vendors, but as I noticed the sparse turnout, I remembered that Smithfield typically opened a little later in the day in December.

I debated searching the town for another cup of coffee, but decided to go ahead and explore the quiet market grounds anyway. Again, like Bailey's, the space was open, even if all the stalls weren't set up and ready to sell yet. I might not see much, but I could walk around and at least enjoy the peacefulness before the customers started crowding the aisles.

While Bailey's was set up in a U-shape, Smithfield was set up closer to a W-shape, with three aisles spreading out from the entrance and short aisles deeper inside connecting the three larger ones. I'd met the market's manager, but I didn't know where his office was located or if there was even one on the premises. Allison's was in a small though visible front building; there were no such buildings at the Smithfield entrance.

The tent stalls at Bailey's were protected by an aluminum topper, a ceiling of sorts. Smithfield vendors had only the cover of their individual tents; the set-up contributed to the open yet disjointed feeling of the market. It was a good market though, with a good, strong vendor list, just not as perfectly wonderful as Bailey's—at least in my opinion.

As I stood inside the opening, I realized that either I wasn't as early as I thought I was or there were a large number of early bird vendors who'd parked in their hidden-from-view load areas.

"Excuse me?" a voice said.

I turned toward the low drawl. The farmer who greeted me wasn't much taller than me, and his overalls and long, red T-shirt made us look like we might make good twins for some sort of Grant Wood portrait. He was bald, his perfect oval head matching his peach-colored complexion, and his gray eyes were both steely obvious and quietly inconspicuous. He was somewhere between my age and my parents' age but it was impossible to know exactly which one he was closer to.

"Hi," I said.

"Hi. Can I help you find something?"

"Sure. I'm here to visit Mamma Maria and I know where her stall is, but I'd also like to purchase some eggs. I've heard that someone named Evelyn has an egg stall here but I'm not sure where it's located."

The man's interesting eyes opened wide before straightening to a tight squint. "You mean Evie?"

I shrugged. "I was told Evelyn, but that might be her."

He looked around, down two of the three main aisles. He

shifted his weight from one boot-clad foot to the other as he rubbed his chin. "Evie's down that way." He pointed to the left aisle. "But she doesn't sell many eggs anymore."

His comment begged the question, so I asked, "Why not?"

He blinked and then shook his head. "It doesn't matter, but if she doesn't have any to sell or if you'd rather not buy them, we have another stall down that way." He pointed to the right aisle. "Rebecca always has a good supply of fresh, *fresh* eggs."

"Thanks."

"You're welcome." The man tipped an invisible hat and then hurried down the left aisle.

I didn't know if he was odd, I was odd, or Evelyn—Evie—was odd, but the short interaction was disquieting. I shook it off.

"Mamma Maria first," I mumbled before I set off down the middle aisle.

Though there weren't many customers yet, the temperature had warmed a little from when I'd first set out in my truck. But I still needed the sweater, and market traffic might start building any minute just because warming weather sometimes caused the crowds to suddenly come out in force.

Mamma Maria's stall was different than it had been the last time I'd visited her. There'd been a tall, refrigerated display case in the back corner that turned slowly and showed off her pies in all their glory—and glorious was a good description for her creations—but the display case was now MIA. The reason probably had something to do with her move to Bailey's.

"Becca?" she said as she threaded her head and neck

through the opening in her back wall. She balanced three pie boxes precariously, as the tent flap didn't seem to want to open all the way. I hurried around to help her.

"It's great to see you again, but I'm surprised. What're you doing here?" she said as I took two boxes and set them on the front table.

"It's great to see you, too," I said. "Here, let me help you unload and then I'll tell you why I'm here."

"Great. I'll take the help."

We made quick duty of unloading the thirty-three pies she'd brought. Except for five of them, all had been presold, and most were her beloved pumpkin cream. She once told me that she sold more pumpkin cream pies between the middle of October and the end of December than she did her other pies the rest of the year.

"People get in the mood for pumpkin and they just stay in the mood until almost the new year," she'd once said.

I understood completely and had her put aside one of the extras for me.

Once set up, she said again, "What're you doing here, Becca? You're up to something."

"My reputation precedes me," I said.

"Something like that." Mamma laughed. "Ask me whatever you'd like to ask. I'm intrigued and interested that you want to talk to me."

"Thanks." The man with the gray eyes had made me wary, so I stepped a little closer to her and said, "Does someone named Evelyn sell eggs here?"

"You mean Evil Evie?" Mamma gasped and put her hand over her mouth. "I can't believe I just said that. That was so rude. Forgive me. You're a friend and I lost my sense of professionalism for a moment." She cleared her throat. "There's a woman named Evie who sells eggs over in the far aisle, but she's strange, frankly. Not evil. Probably. Though that's the nickname she's been given—Evil Evie. It has a nice ring, I guess, and—oh, goodness, it's just plain awful that that's what she's called, but unfortunately, it is." Mamma sighed and rubbed her knuckle over her forehead.

"How is she strange?" I said.

"She's abrupt, not friendly. She used to sell lots of eggs, but she brings in less and less inventory all the time. She's withdrawn." Mamma's eyes pinched. "It's actually quite sad, but anytime any of us attempt to befriend her, we're met with biting, sarcastic remarks."

I thought about whether or not to tell Mamma who I thought Evil Evie really was. It didn't seem to matter much if I was wrong, so I said, "Is there any chance she's Evelyn Rasmussen Stuckey, who was once a state senator and married to the man who was recently killed in the Bailey's parking lot?"

Mamma blinked and then laughed. "Oh, Becca, I have no idea, but leave it up to you to find such a connection. Hang on a second, I know someone who might be able to help." She stepped back, sat in folding chair, and pulled out her cell phone.

As I waited, I wondered if she still had a supply of plastic forks somewhere in her stall. The pumpkin cream pie that now had my name on it was beckoning to me more loudly than the conspiracy theories I had rumbling around in my head. I peered under tables and into whatever other areas that looked like a storage space.

There were no forks under the table and the spaces were

mostly empty, emphasizing that her partial move was well on its way. I was suddenly excited about the reality of having Mamma around Bailey's more often. I was friendly with almost everyone at my market, but Linda and I had become very good friends. Linda would welcome Mamma, too. A mental picture of the three of us formed in my mind: me in my overalls, Linda in her pioneer garb, and Mamma with her cleavage. We'd make a fun trio, I mused silently. I slipped a reminder to the back of my mind to ask Allison where she'd placed Mamma's stall.

"Here he comes now," Mamma said as she appeared next to me. "Addy's been around a long time. He knows everything about everybody, though he might not give up the information easily."

Addy was my overalled bald twin with the strange eyes. He was stepping quickly in our direction.

"Mamma, how are you today?" he asked as they hugged over the front table. It was purely a friendly hug. I was continually surprised by Mamma's ability to make friends with men and somehow keep it simply friendly. She was knock-out gorgeous with a perfect body, topped off by the cleavage I'd just been thinking about, but once most men got to know her and knew she was in a committed relationship, those men were able to keep their eyes up and their hands to themselves, at least as far as I'd seen.

"Great. Addy, this is my friend Becca Robins. She's from the Bailey's market."

Addy smiled and shook my hand. "We sort of met earlier."

"I didn't ask Addy for details, but I did ask him about someone named Evelyn who sold eggs," I said to Mamma.

"Oh, well, I think Becca has a more in-depth question regarding Evie. Becca's a good friend, Addy, but we both understand if you don't want to gossip about our fellow vendor."

"What's the question?"

I looked around again, feeling silly about my need to know, but not silly enough to miss the opportunity.

"Addy, any chance Evie is Evelyn Rasmussen Stuckey? Maybe she was a state senator back in the eighties?"

Addy blinked his crazy eyes. I tried not to stare, tried not to count until he blinked again.

"I don't know all the details, but I do know her last name is Rasmussen. She doesn't tell anyone, but I overheard her on the phone one day. I wasn't eavesdropping, really I wasn't. I just happened to hear her and I filed the information away. What else do you know?"

I told Mamma and Addy what I'd learned about the former senator and that she had at one time been married to a man who'd recently been murdered. Both of them were fascinated by the story, but unfortunately Addy had nothing else to contribute. I thought he had more questions for me, but he was called off to attend to something else, his quick departure reminding me of Allison's continual pull from many different directions.

"Is he a new manager?" I said.

"No, he just helps out Jack, the market's main manager. Addy can get you whatever you or your stall might need. He's been wonderful."

"His eyes are . . ."

Mamma laughed. "You get used to them, but they are kind of different."

"Yeah."

"Look, Becca, just go talk to her. She's surly but she won't hurt you. I don't think." Mamma's eyebrows came together. "No, she won't hurt anyone. I don't think she has in all the years I've been here, and if Jack thought she was dangerous, he wouldn't let her stay. I don't think."

It was my turn to laugh. "Your confidence is inspiring."

"You'll be fine. The worst she can do is tell you to go away, though I doubt she'd use pleasant words."

"I'll take that challenge."

Mamma pointed me in the right direction. I set off down the main aisle and then took the second, narrower offshoot aisle and wove my way around a small curve.

And there she was. She didn't look evil at all. She was smiling, maybe laughing, as she read something on a notebook she was holding.

Evie didn't resemble the pictures of the dynamic Evelyn I'd seen online, except that her long, crossed legs meant she was probably tall. Evie had short, silver-gray hair, thick glasses, and an age spot–covered face. If she truly was Evelyn, she was only in her early fifties, but she looked much older. I couldn't help but silently compare her to the other early-fifties woman I'd recently met. Stephanie Frugit looked as though she'd found a fountain of youth compared to Evie. As Evie laughed, she didn't look the least bit unpleasant, but her demeanor changed quickly when she noticed I was smiling in her direction. Her smile flipped into a frown and her previously endearing age spots sagged heavily as her eyes squinted unhappily.

"Help you?" she said, though it was clear she didn't mean it.

"Evelyn? Evelyn Rasmussen?" I said. I hadn't had much of a plan, so jumping right in was the only option that came to mind.

Her sour face soured more. "Who's asking?"

My non-plan went forward as I extended a hand. "I'm Becca Robins. I work at Bailey's Farmers' Market in Monson. I believe your ex-husband was Reggie Stuckey?" I waited, but she didn't move; I wondered if she breathed.

"I'm afraid I have some bad news if you are that Evelyn." I cleared my throat. "Reggie was killed. In his tree truck. In the Bailey's lot."

I'd never seen a smile come to life more slowly. It was sinister and made me hold my own breath, but once it was formed, Evelyn's face transformed again—not back to its friendly happy version, but to something appropriately fitting her "evil" nickname.

"And you think that's bad news?" she said.

I gulped.

Fourteen

Evie stood, her frame unfolding as I'd predicted: she was very tall. As a short person I made it a rule not to allow some- one's height intimidate me. I stuck out my chin and looked up at the woman as she stepped closer. She leaned over her display table—which displayed nothing at all—and sig- naled to me with one single pull of her finger.

"Becca Robins from Bailey's Farmers' Market. Come closer."

Like a stupid fly to a spider, I went.

She leaned over and put her mouth to my ear. I figured there was only a small chance she'd bite it off, so I leaned in, too.

"I used to be that Evelyn, but that was a long, long time ago. I haven't been her for many years—decades. I didn't like her so I got rid of her and became someone I could better tolerate. I haven't been married to Reggie Stuckey since I've become that better person. This will sound heart-less, but I just don't care that he was killed. I'm not the least bit sorry. I hated him when we parted ways, but thankfully that hate has turned into a quiet buzz of disinterest—thus, and I repeat, I do not care. If I still hated him I would care more, because I would be elated at the news. I'm not. I'm nothing at the news. Understand?"

I nodded, not pointing out that her previous smile had looked close to elation, or strong happiness, at least. "I do, but I wonder if I could buy you a coffee and ask you some more questions."

Evie stood tall and I was sure her lifted eyebrows raised her entire height a couple inches; she'd become gigantic. "You are too gutsy for your own good, Becca Robins."

I smiled. "So I've heard. You know, you might not be Evelyn Rasmussen Stuckey any longer, but you were prob-ably accused of being too gutsy for your own good a few times, too, back then. Even now, you don't strike me as afraid of anything."

I stood my ground. I wasn't afraid. Evil Evie wasn't evil at all, but she wanted people to think she was because then they would leave her alone. I knew enough about people who came to work at a market every day to know that she still *needed* to be around people—perhaps at a distance, but she wasn't ready to completely let go of human contact. It was either that or she didn't want to give up her nicely placed corner stall space so someone else could get it. I gam-bled on my first idea.

"I can't leave," she said. "I'm running a business here. You should know about that."

I leaned a little to my left and peered around her long, thin body. "Doesn't look like you've got much to sell."

As I was leaning and looking, a shot of surprise rattled in my chest. I was proud that I swallowed it before it could jump up and make a noise. There were items lined up on a small table at the back of the stall that caught my full attention, but I didn't want Evil Evie to know I was bothered.

She laughed again. "You're probably right."

She'd changed. When I hadn't backed down, she'd relaxed and become much less scary, which only reinforced the idea that she was putting on one big act. I'd known an Evil Evie or two.

I nodded and smiled.

"All right, Becca, you may buy me a cup of coffee and I will answer some of your questions, but do not ask me why Reggie and I divorced. I won't answer that one, and it would be intrusive and rude of you anyway."

I nodded. Why she and Reggie divorced was, of course, my main question, but she was probably correct: reasons behind divorce are no one else's business. That, however, didn't stop my second ex-husband from sharing the gory details of our divorce with the world, but that was just the way Scott did things.

"This way," Evie said, her long legs leading us away from her stall.

As I followed behind, I ventured one more look at the back table. I'd seen what I thought I'd seen: decorated eggshells were lined up along the length of the table. They were crafted in a more professional manner than the egg I'd found in my truck, but there was no question that they were meant to be Christmas tree ornaments, or just decorations maybe; green, red, gold, and silver made up the combined color scheme. I didn't think they were intended to be for sale; they were back and away from the few boxes of eggs placed in a pathetic display on a side table. I felt sorry for the poor eggs—the ones for sale, not the decorated ones.

It was only by chance that my eyes also skimmed the notebook that Evie had been looking at when I'd approached. She'd dropped it on the ground next to her chair. She must have forgotten about what she was looking at because if she'd remembered she would have at least flipped it over to hide the article.

I guessed it was a Smithfield paper but I didn't take the time to look at the masthead. Instead, my attention was grabbed by the front-page headline: "Monson Christmas Tree Farmer Murdered in His Own Truck."

So, Evie didn't care? She'd been laughing as she'd been reading, she smiled when I first mentioned the murder; her behavior didn't quite live up to the nonchalant attitude she claimed to have. I looked back toward her just as she turned to make sure I was close behind.

I smiled; she grimaced, but I didn't think she'd seen me looking at the paper. She continued to lead the way.

Bailey's was well-outfitted with food carts, food stations, and a large, open tent with tables where people could eat. But I had to give it to Smithfield; they'd created a central food-court-like space that made it easy to peruse all the offerings at once, make a choice, and then enjoy your food and drinks in a space away from all other market traffic. I knew Allison wished for such a setup, but it would take some maneuvering of stalls whose vendors didn't want to move, so our food stations were still more spread out than she'd like. Maybe someday, she'd said a number of times.

Evie marched to a coffee/tea cart, ordered two large black coffees, and then directed me to a table away from everyone else.

The crowd had already grown and since it was still morning, the coffee cart was one of the more popular offerings. I watched people watch Evie. Market customers didn't pay her much attention, but fellow vendors did. Some squinted at her from afar, some purposefully looked away from her, and others scowled. I couldn't imagine having such a horrible relationship with so many people I worked with and came in contact with. A spat or a disagreement here and there was normal, but such blatant dislike was alarming.

"Oh, look, we're getting in the spirit. Finally," Evie said as she set a cup of coffee on the table in front of me and handed me a green-and-red coffee stirrer. "It's not much, but at least it's something."

"Some people start decorating for Christmas before Halloween."

"That's not the way it's done, either. You're supposed to clean up the dishes, get the turkey carcass from Thanksgiving ready for soup stock, and *then* pull out the decorations."

I smiled. "You like Christmas."

"Yes, I do."

I would have reached a whole new level of rude if I'd pointed out how strange it was that this woman whose nickname began with "Evil" didn't seem like the Christmas spirit type.

"Have you always?" I asked, making the best small talk I could.

"Yes, actually, I have." Evie scowled. "Oh, I think it's too commercial, and kids are bratty and awful about it, but I still just love it. Aw, shoot, it probably has something to do with the fact that I once owned—well, my husband did, anyway—a Christmas tree farm. I'll admit that, I suppose. There was nothing like the smells, nothing like when it finally got cool enough that it felt like it might just snow a little. And when it did snow, and . . . oh, well, it was what it was, I suppose." Evie looked down and then took a sip of her coffee.

And I suddenly felt sorry for her.

"When you two were married, did you live at the same farm he owned when he was killed?"

"Yes."

"I stopped by there the other day. It's beautiful."

"Yes." Another sip.

I tried to put myself in her shoes, but the view still wasn't clear. I switched gears.

"You were a pretty successful politician."

Evie harrumphed. "No, I was a state senator. The one other person I ran against was clearly an idiot. It wasn't a difficult race to win."

"But you did. And you garnered a lot of attention. And I've seen an idiot or two get elected."

"This might surprise you, but I had a big mouth."

"And you were . . . are smart."

"Yes."

"And, correct me if I'm wrong, you played it very well. You used your height, your loud voice, and your smarts, and people paid attention. A number of articles from that time mention that you were destined to go places."

"And look where I ended up." But there was no bitterness or sadness in her voice, just a calm acceptance.

"But you're here because of decisions only you made. You stepped down. Why?"

"I didn't want to do it anymore."

Clearly, that was her oft-used answer. "How did it go from something you thrived at to something you didn't want to do any longer?"

"Things happened."

"What things?" It was like pulling teeth, but I was willing to keep trying.

"Life."

"Reggie did something to you," I said. I had no idea why I said it. Perhaps I wanted to say something that would cause her to react enough that she'd quit giving me rehearsed answers.

"No."

But her eyes flashed this time. I'd hit a nerve. It was a deep nerve, one she'd buried, but I'd grazed it a little.

"Yes, he did! Reggie hurt you in some way, so you left politics. That's what it was. Was he physically abusive?"

"No, he never laid a hand on me. He was a gentle man, though he might not have been considered a gentleman."

She liked puzzles.

"The only other reason would be an affair. Reggie had an affair—no, that wouldn't make sense. Why would you quit politics if your husband had an affair? That probably happens all the time. You must have had the affair."

For a long instant, I thought she was going to confirm

my suspicion. I could see the affirmation flash in her eyes and pull at the corners of her mouth. But, instead, she said, "Look, Becca, I'm not going to tell you what happened in my marriage. It's none of your business. I quit politics. Why does the reason have to be something big? Maybe I just didn't like it. Maybe I just didn't like Reggie so I divorced him. Reasons don't always have to be big and ugly."

"They why don't you want to talk about them? Why the mystery?"

"You must have missed the part where I said it was none of your business. But the other part is that it was a long, long time ago. A different life, a different time. Who gives a hoo-haw what happened back then anyway?"

"Well, since Reggie was murdered, don't you think it's natural to look at his past? And when someone finds someone like you and your interesting history in that past . . . well, how could it not be explored?"

"By Becca who works at a farmers' market? Or by the police?"

I sipped my coffee. "Good point."

Evie smiled, genuinely this time. "What you don't realize is that I've talked more to you about my past than I have to anyone in a long time. I would probably tell the police to . . . well, to leave me alone, and I promise I wouldn't talk to anyone here."

"Okay. Then why me?"

"I'm not really sure. You're kind of obnoxious, but in a persistent, confident, and cute way." She rolled her eyes. "Perhaps you remind me of someone, though you're awful teeny. Your nosiness would work well on someone tall." She sat up straight.

"Don't I wish."

Evie laughed.

"Hey, can I ask about the ornaments? The eggshells in your stall?"

Evie shrugged. "I just enjoy crafting them. No one buys many of my eggs anymore. I don't have many to sell. It's something to do to pass the time in December."

"You enjoy being at the market, don't you?"

Evie looked around and then leaned forward. "I do, but don't tell anyone. No one here knows who I am—or if they do, they keep it to themselves. I hope they never find out. I can be here, be outside—that was one of my favorite parts about the tree farm, all the time outside—be around people, but I don't have to talk to many if I don't want to. It's a good spot for me."

I made a mental note to ask Mamma not to spread the word that Evie used to be Evelyn. I'd ask her to talk to Addy about it, too, but something told me he wasn't telling anyone.

"I wouldn't know what to do with myself if I wasn't outside most of the time," I said.

"Tell me about your market business."

I told Evie about my farm and my products. She was fascinated, mostly by the strawberries. She'd never been able to grow a successful crop. I gave her a few pointers, which she seemed to appreciate.

And when she was done, she was done. She stood abruptly and told me she had to get back to her stall, but it had been good to talk to me. She wasn't necessarily friendly but she wasn't evil.

I sat at the table a moment and thought about the conversation Evie and I had had, and then I weaved my way through

the market and back to Mamma and asked her to keep our
new secret. She agreed, and I left Smithfield with a pumpkin
cream pie and only a few more pieces to the Reggie puzzle.
I felt strongly that an affair had been part of the reason
behind Evelyn and Reggie's divorce and her move away
from politics, but who had had the affair? I understood that
infidelity could be devastating, but if it had occurred, it had
demolished everything. A marriage and promising career,
both gone.

Whatever had happened, clearly it had seemed like there
was no way to salvage what Reggie and Evelyn had worked
hard to create.

Was there anyone who could give me more answers?

Of course there was, but I just had to figure out who.
And how to get them to tell me.

Fifteen

My cell phone buzzed only a few minutes after I pulled out of the now-crowded Smithfield Market parking lot.

"Hey, Sam," I said.

"Are you still in Smithfield?"

"Just leaving. Would you like to hear what I learned with my crack-detective questioning skills?"

"Yes." I heard the smile in his voice. "But I wondered if you wanted to do some tag-team detective work. You can tell me in person."

"Oh yes," I said. I wasn't sure exactly what he meant. He could have just been flirting, but all options were appealing.

"Meet me at Reggie Stuckey's farm. Officers have been out to the house, and they talked to the same housekeeper you talked to. But after your intel, I'd like to get my own take."

"And I'm invited?"

"There are some perks to dating a cop, you know."

"Well, yeah, but . . ."

Sam laughed. "If it was a crime scene, you wouldn't be invited, but since you've already been there and I'd like this to be casual . . ."

"Wait. You're using me as an in? You want me to ease the way for you?"

"Of course. Why wouldn't I use my connections?"

"Indeed." I smiled and hoped he heard it. "See you in about twenty."

The trip back to the Stuckey farm was much quicker than I anticipated. I wasn't slowed by tractors or pockets of traffic. Sam was at the spot off the main road that led down the other road to the farm. He'd parked his cruiser and was standing next to a recently placed "For Sale" sign as he typed something into his phone. He was in full cop mode, his uniform crisp and his hair smoothly slicked back.

He turned, smiled, and waved as I pulled my truck next to his car.

"Hey," I said as I joined him by the sign.

"Hey," he said as he finished typing. "Did you know the farm was for sale?"

"I didn't see the sign here yesterday, but Ian told me he looked at this farm before he bought the land he now owns." I looked at the Realtor's name. I didn't recognize it. "It must have been put up after I left yesterday."

"I'm curious as to when the property really was put on the market and who made the decision to do so."

"I have no idea." I shrugged.

Sam punched a button on his phone and held the device up to his ear.

"Vivienne, call this Realtor and ask her for details regarding the Stuckey farm being listed for sale. Ask who put it on the market and when." He recited the Realtor's name and phone number that was written on the sign. "And has anyone checked if Stuckey had a life insurance policy or a will or something that would make someone a decision-maker regarding the sale of the farm? Uh-huh. Good. Well, check again, deeper maybe. Check with the bank just to be sure. We're missing a connection that needs to be found. Thanks. Yeah, call me back. Thanks again." He closed his phone and then peered down the road and fell into thought.

"Sam, should we get in there and see Gellie and Batman?"

"Batman?"

"The goose."

"That's right. You mentioned the goose. I think we should. Let's leave your truck here. You can ride in the police car and tell me about your meeting with Evelyn."

"Can I drive?"

"No."

"Someday, I'm sure you'll let me. I guess you have to get really serious about someone to let them drive your police car."

I'd heard that Sam had taken charge of the Monson police motor pool, small though it might be, and he required all officers to pass annual refresher courses before he allowed them to drive. I'd overheard some of them groan good-naturedly about his strict rules and his protectiveness over the department's vehicles.

His blue eyes looked hard into mine as he seemed to think for a beat or two. He wasn't bothered by my teasing, but there was something about the intensity of his stare that made me stand still and stare back.

A second later, he half smiled. "I take my police department–issued vehicles very seriously. I'll get your door, though."

"Thank you," I said as I looked away. I tried not to let him see that he'd once again taken my breath away and made my heartbeat race almost to the point of discomfort.

For some reason I didn't want him to know how often he upped my blood pressure. I was a bit too old and too often divorced for such silliness.

Sam held open the passenger-side door and I climbed in. The smirk on his face and the subtle roll of his eyes told me he'd seen my teenager-ish reaction.

"Don't forget, Becca, it's really okay to have strong feelings for someone you're in a relationship with. I don't know much, but I'm pretty sure I know that."

"Damn," I said as he closed the door.

"Now, tell me about Evelyn," he said as he got in the driver's side and started the car.

Since I'd only just left Smithfield, it was easy to remember the details of our conversation. I quickly told Sam the specifics as he guided the cruiser down the again surprisingly smooth dirt road that led to the Stuckey farm.

He listened attentively, but even he couldn't maintain his stern cop attitude when we entered the valley and became part of the beautiful snow-globe-like scene.

"Wow," he said. "This is amazing. I can't believe Reggie Stuckey ever set foot outside his property. This is something."

"I got the impression he didn't leave much. He never pushed his tree business like he could have. Gellie said he had customers, but not many."

"I almost wouldn't want any. I'd want to leave the trees as they are."

"I agree, but there must be need for some rotation, some need to harvest and plant. I don't know a thing about pine trees, so don't quote me."

"We could pick one up here," Sam said.

"Tempting, but I already told Denny we'd come up to his place and cut one down up there. Speaking of Denny . . . you saw Brenton's behavior toward the Ridgeways. Even though Brenton didn't tell you anything, have you talked to the Ridgeways?"

"I have, and I don't know one thing more. They were all very quiet."

"I know. I asked Billie why she was upset the first day they were there. She came out of the market and looked panicked. Since Brenton had already shown signs of irritation, I chalked up her behavior to maybe seeing him. She claimed she hadn't been upset at all, and that I was misinterpreting."

"Huh, didn't know that part. I'll look at it closer," Sam said.

A Santa hat–clad person stepped out from the main copse of trees and waved in our direction, interrupting the conversation. It took a second for me to recognize Gellie. She was dressed in jeans and a sweatshirt, and even though the large hat struck me as being in better condition than Jeannine's, it folded forward and covered part of her face.

"There. That's Gellie."

Sam pulled the cruiser next to the spot from which Gellie had emerged.

"Oh, hi!" she said. "You're Becca from yesterday, right? Come back for more muffins?"

I smiled. "They were delicious, but I wanted to show Sam the farm. It's beautiful."

In fact, I didn't think that Sam was using me as an in. He could handle that on his own, but it suddenly seemed like a good idea so I went with it.

"Sam, hi," Gellie said as she walked to him and extended her hand. "You two . . ."

"We're dating," Sam said. He sent me another amused look.

"Oh, the police have already been here. I just wondered."

"It's nice to meet you, Gellie. This place is amazing," Sam said.

"It is, isn't it? I haven't worked here long, but I'm sure going to miss being here."

"Maybe the new owner will want a housekeeper?" I said.

"That would be great, but I can't count on it."

"What're you doing out here with a Santa hat?" I said.

"Someone has to come out to greet the few customers we have. I sold two trees about an hour ago. I had to catch the people before they drove away. The Archers should be here shortly, but I didn't want people to go without their trees."

"Gellie, do you know who put up the 'For Sale' sign?" Sam asked.

"I do. Right after Becca left yesterday, a Realtor stopped by and said she was hired to put the house on the market right away."

"Did she say who she was hired by?" Sam asked.

"See, I asked the same question, but she wouldn't tell me. I thought it was sneaky, but I'm not sure if I'm supposed to still be showing up here, so who am I to question what anyone is doing? I have her card inside. You want it?"

"Yes, thanks."

The now-familiar quack of a goose pulled our attention across to the other side of the property.

"That's Batman," I said to Sam. "What's he doing?" I said to Gellie.

She shook her head. "I have no idea. Stupid animal just likes to run and hear himself talk. I hope he hasn't stolen something again."

I wondered who'd take care of Batman when Gellie wasn't around. She read my mind.

"I'll make sure he doesn't get forgotten. I've been feeding him, and I will until someone tells me to go away."

It was evident that she liked him more than she wanted to let on.

Gellie looked at Sam. "You think you should tell me to go away?"

"No, ma'am, in fact, I'm glad you've stuck around. It would be sad to see this place quickly fall apart because no one paid attention to it."

"Good. Well then, you two want to come in? I'll get the card and you can look around the place? Oh, don't give me that surprised look. I wasn't born yesterday. I know you're a cop, and you're looking very cop-like. You're probably truly friendly, too, but you want to take a look around the place, don't you?"

Sam smiled. "Yes, I do."

"You too, huh?" she said to me.

"Yes."

"Come on in."

From the outside, the house looked like it should be the focal point of famous artists' paintings. From the inside, it was almost as perfect as a house could get. Each room on the first floor was comfortably and traditionally furnished. Each space was big enough not to feel crowded and yet not so big that a person felt lost. Even though the space wasn't open, the rooms flowed nicely. I'd been so focused on the kitchen the day before that I hadn't really noticed everything else.

"Did Reggie have an office in the house?" Sam asked Gellie after she gave him the Realtor's card.

"Yes, upstairs. The other officers looked around up there, but go ahead and do whatever you need to do. I hope you find a clue to the killer."

Sam's main intention had been to take a close look at things like paperwork in drawers and other things cops look for to give them clues, so after Gellie's first floor tour, he and I took the stairs up to the second floor.

The office was one of the longer rooms, located at the back of the house. French doors led to a small balcony, which overlooked a stretch of South Carolina countryside that was mostly hidden from the rest of the world. It was pristine and almost untouched, and I hoped it stayed that way for a long time.

In the short few minutes I'd known Reggie, I hadn't thought he leaned toward sophisticated tastes that included tobacco pipes and rich, dark woodwork, but his office told me differently.

The floor and wall-to-wall bookshelves were crafted from a dark cherrywood that shone as though Gellie had just dusted and oiled everything in sight. The large desk matched the other woodwork, and the two leather chairs and couch were tanned and subtle against their background. A small, glass-topped table flanked one of the chairs. Atop it sat a pipe and a bag of tobacco, both seemingly unused, even though a rich tobacco scent hung in the air.

"I wonder if the new owners would let me rent just this room from them," I said.

Sam, all business, was peering into the desk's drawers. "You could ask."

"I wouldn't get any work done. I'd just sit here, read, and sniff."

Sam didn't respond, so I looked up.

"Find anything?" I asked as I joined him.

"Not a thing. The file drawer is empty. Completely."

We looked through the other drawers and found only a few pens, pencils, and one unused notebook.

"No computer, no files, no fax machine. Nothing," I said.

"I'm beginning to think he had an office somewhere else. Let's ask Gellie if she knows."

Sam determined there wasn't anything else to see in the office, so we continued the rest of the tour.

"This house is comfortable but not lived in, not really," Sam commented as we looked into a seemingly unused bathroom. "It's obvious that Reggie spent time in his bedroom and the family room and kitchen downstairs, but everywhere else is so . . . not touched. Even the pipe scent in the office isn't smoky; it's more tobacco than smoke. He didn't spend a lot of time in there."

"Gellie said it was recently remodeled. The Realtor won't have to do a thing. She could have an open house right this second and the place would probably sell quickly," I said.

Sam's eyebrows came together but he didn't say anything as he turned and opened a linen closet in the hallway.

"You don't suppose he not only had an office somewhere else, but another house, too?" I said as we both looked at the perfectly folded towels and washcloths.

"Let's go find Gellie," Sam said.

"Well, I haven't been here all that long, but he was around most of the time," Gellie said. She served us cookies, something she called gingerbread biscuits, and I was trying to figure out how to take the entire plate when she wasn't looking. I'd already considered the idea of putting them down the front flap of my overalls. Maybe I could blame Batman.

"What did he do when he was here?" Sam asked.

Gellie shrugged. "Mostly he worked outside. I'm not here in the evenings. Well, I wasn't; now I stay a little later to make sure Batman isn't in trouble. What am I going to do with that goose?" She looked at Sam.

"I'd say call animal control. They might be able to find him a good home, but I bet that's not what you want to do," he said.

"No, I'm not ready to do that. I'll just keep trying to figure it out."

"Gellie, I saw a small shed outside, but I'm not sure how far back and over the hills the property extends. Is there any chance there's another building somewhere?"

Gellie shook her head, the ball from the Santa hat bouncing off her cheek. "I'm not really sure, but I don't think it goes far. Oh, wait, of course! I bet you didn't look in the garage. I bet the other officers didn't, either."

"No." Sam stood. I eyed the cookies first and then stood, too.

"I didn't even think about it. He stored that big truck . . . the one he was . . . well, he stored it right around the side of the house, kind of behind the garage. He had an office of sorts . . . well a desk at least, set up in the garage. I've been so flustered, I didn't even think to see if anyone looked out there. I'm so sorry."

"No problem, we'll look now."

Gellie led the way. "I'm getting to be too old for my own good. I really should have said something earlier."

"It's okay." But it wasn't okay. Sam wasn't happy that he hadn't already thought to search the garage and that the other Monson officers might not have, either.

He followed Gellie and I followed him as we weaved down a back hallway behind the kitchen. It was the first hint I'd had that this house was old. I quietly tapped the wall and thought it was made of lath and plaster. And the old, wood floor was scratched and dull. This part of the house hadn't been given a remodel.

"Reggie wasn't secretive at all. A little odd and mumbly but not really secretive," Gellie said from the front of our line. I'd already told Sam about his Ridgeway mumbles. "But a couple times he just appeared in the kitchen when I wasn't expecting him. He showed me this back hallway and explained that this is the easiest way back into the house from the garage. I wondered why he needed to come in through the garage if he never went anywhere; that's when he told me that he had tools and a desk back here. I never even came out to see what he was talking about. Maybe that's why I didn't remember."

"Why do you suppose he did that? He had a great office in this great house."

"Not sure, except that . . . well, this sounds stupid, but I think he liked to hang out with Batman and he couldn't do that inside for long stretches of time. Oh, sometimes he could, but do you know how much a goose poops?"

"No," I said.

"Lots. That creature gets into the house all the time, but I try to shoo it out before it causes too much damage."

"I see," I said.

Gellie pushed through a door that opened to a spacious garage. My second ex-husband, Scott, would have used the space to create a fully equipped car-shop garage, but Reggie must not have been into fixing things.

Except for the far wall, there wasn't much to see. There was no vehicle, which Sam noted. Reggie did have a truck other than his large delivery truck registered in his name. Sam wanted to know where it had gone.

The shelves against the far wall were full, however—full of the things you might expect to find at a Christmas tree farm. There were boxes of sharp implements similar to what I'd seen in Reggie's chest. I shivered when I saw the cold, casually stored spikes. Two axes made an *X* as they leaned against one of the bottom shelves.

"What's that?" I pointed to a gun-like trigger mechanism that was stored on a shelf with a full supply of cans with yellow labels. The mechanism had a long tube that was in a loose circle on the floor, and it was attached to a generator.

"I believe it's a flocking gun. You attach the can and shoot the contents at a tree," Sam said.

I looked at him with raised eyebrows.

"White stuff to flock a tree, make it look like it has snow on it."

"Oh."

The shelves were full of other, less interesting things like hammers and a couple wrenches. It was a poorly stocked garage, tool wise, but a desk in a back corner proved to be much more interesting.

"What a mess," Gellie said as the three of us stood in a half circle around the paper-and-file piles.

"I'm going to have someone come out and process the items on the desk, Gellie, but I'll take a quick look first. You okay with that?"

Gellie shrugged. "Don't think it matters one way or another if I care, but I don't. If it helps you find Reggie's killer, all's the better. I'm going back inside, though. You two don't need my help."

Sam flipped a switch, which illuminated the garage with a healthy supply of yellow-fluorescent light. I would have preferred to open the garage door, but I knew we shouldn't do something that might disrupt the evidence, if there was, in fact, evidence.

"At least he's somewhat normal," I said. "He really did have a computer and a printer; the printer's also a fax machine. He's not as strange as his gorgeous but uptight house makes him seem."

"Uh-huh," Sam said distractedly as he looked at the items on the desk and then pushed buttons on the printer/fax. "I'd like to find the fax number or a sent and received log, but I think I'll let the crime scene people figure it out."

From what I could see, Reggie's organization resembled

how my dining room table sometimes looked, though my paperwork messes were usually in stacks more than they were just papers everywhere.

"Sam, this is weirder than I thought—maybe *not* normal," I said, though it was more me thinking aloud than to get his attention.

"How do you mean?"

"It's messy, really messy. Even messy people—myself included—have a system to their mess. This looks like someone rifled through it, maybe looking for something."

"And if they found it, we'll never know what *it* was." Sam pulled out his phone and started snapping pictures.

"Do you really think the other officers didn't look out here?" I asked.

"They said there was no computer, but this isn't a crime scene so there's a chance they weren't as thorough as we all should be. We asked Gellie about Reggie's activities. If they didn't ask, they might not have thought about a desk being in the garage." Sam stopped snapping pictures, looked through the ones he'd taken, and said, "Okay, let's see if we can see anything interesting."

The usual paperwork suspects were everywhere—invoices, statements, supplies bought, and trees sold. The most curious thing about the mountain of papers was that some pieces were old, from as far back as ten years ago. The file drawers were full to overflowing, presumably with even older paperwork, but there was neither rhyme nor reason to the filing system.

"Hmm," Sam said as he opened a file he'd wrangled out of one of the packed drawers.

"What'd you find?" I asked.

"It's all about the Ridgeways," he said as he held it so I could look, too.

There were articles and pictures of Denny, Billie, and Ned Ridgeway from over the years. Mostly there were articles that highlighted the Ridgeway farm, but there were also articles about social events that one or some of the Ridgeways had attended. The dates on the articles went back as far as 1991.

"I suppose it would be okay to keep a file about your competition," I said as I glanced at the pages, which Sam was quickly flipping through. "The Ridgeways were much more successful than Reggie ever was. Maybe he was jealous."

Sam rubbed his chin. "Maybe, but everyone keeps telling us that he didn't have a Christmas tree farm to be successful, and that's becoming more and more obvious. We haven't figured out where all his money came from yet, but we're working on it—family money, textiles, probably nothing surprising. He could have done more to find more customers. Shoot, just a picture of the setting around here in some sort of advertisement would have garnered a bunch of attention. I'll take this one with us." He closed the file, stuck it under his arm, and then sat down on the creaky office chair.

He pushed the power button on the old dusty computer and we waited patiently while its technologically ancient innards warmed up.

"No password, that's a good start," Sam said as he pulled the chair closer to the desk and started moving the mouse. "Simple, non-password-protected e-mail, too; not the best way to protect your privacy, but helpful to us, at least."

As nosy as I was, looking at someone's e-mail was a new level of intrusive. I got over it quickly, though, when Sam said, "Well, now we might be getting somewhere."

"What?"

"Looks like Reggie had an admirer. Read this one, it's from someone called 'Old Girl.'"

"That's not a very flattering name," I said. "At least Old-But-I-Still-Got-It Girl would be a little better."

Sam smiled.

I read aloud: "But I've missed you for so long. There has to be a way for us to meet again. No one has to know."

"I'd like to know who Old Girl is," Sam said. "We have ways of tracking that down, though they aren't as quick as I would like."

"What was Reggie's response? Or what did he write that prompted her to say what she said?" I said.

A couple clicks of the mouse later, and the text on the screen read, "No, not possible. We hurt too many people. They're just beginning to heal; maybe some will never heal. We can't. We just can't. I'm sorry, desperately sorry."

"I'll have someone put together the entire conversation," Sam said.

"Yeah," I said, "you need to find out who this is. This could be talking about the affair I sensed when I was talking to Evie. Affairs are good motives for murder."

"Possibly, but we'd better at least track Old Girl down and talk to her. I didn't think Evelyn was all that important, but now I'm beginning to think she needs an official visit."

"So, you're saying I might have uncovered something

important to your case?" A swell of excitement built in my chest.

Sam stood from the chair and looked at me with my favorite version of his eyes. "That's exactly what I'm saying. Good job."

I doubted very much that he ever complimented any of his coworkers with those eyes and then that hug, and most definitely not with the kiss that came next. In fact, he was usually so darn professional that I was caught off guard by his reaction. Thrilled, but still caught off guard.

"Here, help me unhook this hard drive from the monitor. I'll take it in and have it looked at thoroughly," he said when he released me. I wondered if he'd even noticed what he'd done. Surely a piece of his slicked hair should protest the unprofessional kiss, but it all remained neatly in place. Maybe a wrinkle in his uniform would show. Nope, no such luck. How did he do that?

Sam searched the rest of the garage just in case we'd missed something. We scanned the area right outside but didn't find anything of interest there, either. Then we gathered the computer and told Gellie we were taking it and the file. As the police car rolled along the long driveway, Batman stood beside the house and watched us leave. I looked back and saw Gellie talking to the goose but she didn't wield a butcher knife and Batman didn't run away, so I figured they might be working on a temporary truce.

Our movement was halted by an incoming newer model truck. It veered around us as though it had done the maneuver a time or two before.

Of all the things to notice about the truck and the people inside, the thing that garnered the biggest chunk of my interest was the color and length of the passenger's hair. A long, blonde ponytail trailed out from her thin winter cap.

"Sam, she might be the cornhusk doll," I said without really thinking about what I was saying.

Sam didn't need further explanation. He turned the cruiser around and we went to talk to whoever was in the truck.

Sixteen

Patricia and Joel Archer were not happy that a police officer wanted to talk to them, which only made Sam more persistent with his questions.

"We just worked for Reggie out here," Joel said. "We just helped him harvest trees. I don't think we ever spent much time in the house."

Patricia's long, blonde ponytail was only the first reason I was interested in knowing more about her. The rest of her reminded me of a farm worker version of Mamma Maria. Mamma was younger than Patricia, but both women were fond of heavy eye makeup and red lipstick. They were also tall and thin, and, even though Patricia wore what amounted to a flannel jacket, I guessed that her curves could rival Mamma's.

Those facts, along with what Gellie had told me the day before about the Archers returning to help Reggie after they hadn't been around for some time and Patricia's resemblance to the cornhusk ornament, made me quickly think her, and maybe her husband's, activities around the time of Reggie's murder needed to be looked at closely. Before we'd gotten back out of the cruiser, though, Sam had warned me about jumping to any conclusions without having real evidence.

Still.

"When's the last time either of you saw Reggie?" Sam asked.

The Archers looked at each other, and both of them shrugged lightly. We were standing outside the copse of pine trees, but I was paying such close attention to what the Archers had to say that I didn't have time to appreciate the strong pine scent.

"I guess the day before he was killed. We helped him load up the truck to take it to the farmers' market," Joel said.

"What did you know about his plans to sell at Bailey's?"

"It was something that had only come together last week," Joel said confidently. "He was excited about it. He said that he'd been working with a woman from the market, and that it was a good market, and that it would be good to get more of his trees out to the world."

I watched Patricia as Joel spoke. I was certain she looked down and blushed a tiny bit when Joel mentioned the "woman from the market," but those actions didn't tell me anything, particularly when she looked back up quickly and I realized that the blush could have been attributed to the cool air.

"Did either of you ever go into his office, the one in the house or the one in the garage?"

"No," Joel said, but Patricia wasn't so quick to speak.

"Well," she finally said, her voice soft and tense.

"Go on," Sam said.

"He sent me in the garage for some spikes the day before . . . the day before we loaded up for the market."

I didn't know if the police had released to the press that Reggie had been killed with a Christmas tree spike, so I remained quiet.

Joel didn't say anything but his eyebrows came together in a tight knit as he looked at his wife.

"I thought . . . never mind," Joel said.

Sam and I looked at each other before he turned to Joel. "Never mind what, Mr. Archer?"

"It's nothing really. I just thought Reggie told us the garage was off-limits, that we weren't ever to go in there, but he must have made an exception for Patricia."

"It was just that one time," she was quick to add. "Just that one time."

"And you retrieved a spike, just one?" Sam said.

Patricia nodded. "I did. I'm sure he would have asked Joel to get it for him, but Joel was helping to deliver a tree."

I didn't know what Joel had been doing but the nervous twitches around his eyes told me that he probably hadn't been delivering a tree.

"Did you ever fax anything for Reggie, or gather a fax, or help with any sort of paperwork at all?" Sam asked.

"No," Patricia said.

"Where did you take the tree?" Sam asked Joel, pen and paper at the ready to write down an address.

"Uh, well . . . I just met someone on the corner of Main Street and Pomegranate. They met me there with their truck. They were from . . . Smithfield and we just met there."

"Do you have any other information? Names, the kind of truck?"

"No, I'm afraid not."

"What about that truck?" Sam nodded to the mint-condition, shiny, blue truck they'd been riding in.

"That's . . . that's Reggie's," Joel said, clearly embarrassed. "We don't have a vehicle, so we were using that one. We didn't think there would be any harm in doing so. Reggie always drove us around."

"He ever let you drive it without him?"

"Uh. Oh. No, not that I remember," Joel said.

"But he would have," Patricia added. "We were sort of friends."

"Friends, but the garage was off-limits?" Sam said as he used the pen to scratch at a spot above his ear.

"Well, we'd all known each other before," Patricia said.

"Friends from way back?" I said. "When was way back?"

"Oh, we were kids, in our early twenties at least. It was back in the mid-to-late eighties. We helped with the trees back then, too."

"So you probably knew Reggie's wife?" Sam said.

"Sure. Evelyn. We knew her well," Patricia said, but I thought I caught another look Joel sent in her direction. She caught it, too, and pinched her mouth closed.

"Tell me, what do you remember about their divorce?" Sam asked. I was surprised by his abruptness, but I liked it.

"Nothing," Joel said before his wife could speak again.

"Really? Evelyn, a person you knew very well, gave up her political position and divorced her husband and you don't remember anything about it," Sam said.

"No, sir," Joel said.

If I was reading the look on her face correctly, Patricia might never speak again.

"You two going to stick around now that Reggie's gone?" Sam asked.

"We thought we'd help with the trees until we're shut down or told to leave."

"Why?"

"Like I said, we knew each other. Reggie was a friend. Sort of."

"You care if we look in the shed?" Sam said as he started walking that direction. I followed behind.

"Sure. Go ahead."

Joel and Patricia followed behind me.

The shed was almost empty. There were two axes locked in place with a cross bar against a wall and one flocking gun, loaded (as far as I could tell, given my limited understanding of flocking guns) with a can of flocking spray. Two short stools were against a side wall, but those few items were all that was there. Sam gave the small space a quick once-over and I silently wondered why we hadn't looked in it earlier.

Sam wrote down the address that Joel gave him for where they were staying but Joel added that they truly wouldn't be around for long. I suspected that was a recent decision. Sam didn't tell them not to leave town, but to stay in touch if they did, just in case he had more questions about their "friendship" with Reggie Stuckey.

They were thrilled and relieved to see us go, though they both tried to hide it.

As we drove away again, I said, "Why didn't we check the shed earlier?"

"I knew what was in there a couple days ago. The other

officers looked inside and included an item inventory in their report. I should have taken another look on my own probably, but the reason I asked Joel was simply to see his reaction. He didn't seem to mind us looking, which made me think he hadn't hidden anything in there."

"Like what?"

"I have no idea."

"What do you think of them?"

"I think they're up to no good, but I'm not sure murder is a part of that 'no good.' They're staying around so they can make some money. It's a cash business, I'm assuming, and without Reggie around, their cut of the cash just got bigger."

"They're stealing. Sort of?"

"No doubt in my mind. I also think Patricia's been in Reggie's garage more than she admitted to, though I don't know why or who she didn't want to know she'd been there—us or her husband."

"Could she be the mystery 'girl' who was working for Reggie?"

"Maybe. I really need to better analyze the phone and fax records. I also need to know more about the Archers. I'll do some research. Also, I suppose that will be one of the questions I ask Evelyn."

"Oh yeah, the lead I fleshed out for you."

Sam laughed. "Yes, that one."

He dropped me at my truck, but offered to take me with him to talk to the real estate agent, which is where he was planning to go after he dropped the computer and the file at the station.

I wanted to go with him, but farmers' market duty called. I had customers who'd be looking for their orders and other customers who'd be looking for me and my other jams and jellies.

I did manage to get one more kiss out of him before we parted ways, though.

I liked it when he multitasked.

Seventeen

"You are popular today," Linda said as she peered around our common tent wall when I came through the back. "You should leave me some jars. I'm happy to take care of customers if you're busy."

We all looked after each other's businesses; it wasn't a burden. Usually. But I felt like I'd stretched everyone's goodwill over the last year or so. Linda especially would never say I was taking advantage, but I wanted to be sensitive to it.

"Thanks. I think I can catch up today and we'll see where it goes from there. I'm still a little surprised by how well everything's selling."

Linda smiled. "Me, too, and I love it. Believe it or not, my pie sales have gone way up. People are coming to Bailey's just for the jalapeño-mint jelly, Becca; I got the juicy spot next to you. My cranberry cream pie is flying out of here. So thanks."

Leave it to Linda to know exactly what to say to make me feel better.

"I didn't know you had cranberry cream pie! I'll be buying one of those today."

"Deal. I'll put your name on one."

Pumpkin cream and cranberry cream. Sam and I would be set for dessert for the next few days.

Sam and I. The growing line of customers outside my stall didn't give me much time to ponder how quickly I'd begun thinking in terms of "Sam and I" or "me and Sam." But I knew it had happened quickly, and the concept was continually gaining favor in my mind.

Sheesh, maybe the holiday spirit's getting to me, I thought.

I came up for air many jars of jelly, jam, and preserves later. Just as I blew my bangs out of my eyes, a familiar face appeared outside my stall.

"Ian! Hello again," I said. "How's it going?"

"Busy. I can't believe how many people want to give yard art as gifts this year."

"It's good to be busy," I said, having just gone through one of the busiest rushes I thought I'd ever been through, and was luckily to still be alive to talk about it.

"It is." Ian smiled. I could see him building courage for something. I waited patiently. "Hey, I'm going to send you and Sam an invitation to a New Year's gathering. You okay with that?"

"Of course. Sounds like fun."

"Good." Ian paused.

"What?"

"George and Gypsy will be there, but so will someone else. I wanted to you know beforehand."

"I've heard. You and Betsy?"

"Yeah."

"You happy?"

"I am, but does that seem weird to hear?"

"Not even a little bit. I'm happy you're happy." I was.

"She's not as awful as you might have thought she was before you and I broke up."

Betsy had tried to intervene in our relationship by forcing our breakup. She'd seen something early on that the rest of us had taken a little longer to recognize: that Ian and I weren't meant to be long-term and Sam and I (there it was again, *Sam and I*) were meant to be together. She'd been obnoxious in the way she'd handled her revelation, but I could probably forgive her. Eventually.

"She just saw someone she liked and went after him," I said. "She has great taste. I know."

"She's assured me she doesn't make a habit of doing such things and she really wants to have a good heart-to-heart with you, and she asked me specifically not to tell you that. But I thought me stepping over that small boundary might help even things out."

I laughed. "I'm good with even. I look forward to the New Year's gathering. I'm sure Sam will, too."

"Good to hear. Okay, well, I'm out of here again. More orders just today. It's a good thing I can't do much with the farm right now."

"See you later, Ian."

"You two are so civilized," Linda said as she looked around our common wall again. Maybe we should just take that wall down.

"It's awkward every now and then," I said. "But doable."

"Sam and Ian seem to get along just fine, too."

I shrugged. "They do. There are times I wonder if the two of them plotted the whole thing—me falling for one so I could see the other one more clearly."

Linda laughed. "No, Becca, that's not what happened. I'm just impressed by y'all's maturity."

"Me, too, frankly."

I stepped closer to Linda with the goal of peering around the wall to see how much inventory she had left. I thought about offering to cover her stall for the rest of the day just so I wouldn't feel bad about asking her to do the same for me sometime down the road, build up the favor bank a little, at least.

But I was stopped when my toe ran into something. I looked down, but I must have propelled whatever it was to a spot under my front table. I crouched down.

"What's up?" Linda said.

The object I'd kicked under the table was alarming, even though I didn't think it was meant to be. I reached for it and stood.

"Is that a tree?" Linda asked.

"I think so."

It was a crude design, made of metal, and only just resembling a pine tree. It was simply a flat piece of metal with scooped branches. The branches spread wider as they moved down the small tree. A hole had been carved or cut through the top of the tree, and a paper clip was once again used as the ornament hanger.

I pulled out my cell phone and called Ian.

"Hey," he said. "You change your mind about the party?"

"No. Where are you?"

"On the way home. What can I do for you?"

"Did you drop a Christmas tree ornament by my stall?"

"No. I didn't have one to drop."

"By chance, have any pieces of your metal gone missing from your stall?"

Ian was silent a second. "Well, I don't really have the raw materials at the market but one of my smaller pieces went missing yesterday. I thought it had either gone missing or I'd just forgotten that I hadn't brought it."

"Any chance it was made of thin metal, maybe with about a seven- or eight-inch flat part?"

"Yes. It was a small piece for a garden. It was a simple wind fan, short, not meant to be tall. Did you find it?"

"I might have found part of it."

"Should I come back?"

"Only if you want to. I'll show it to Allison. I think that the wind fan has been disassembled and used to make a Christmas tree ornament."

"That's strange."

"I know." I thought about telling him about the other ornaments, but I decided that Allison and Sam should know about this one first.

"I'll follow up tomorrow. Just have Allison call me if she wants me to come back in. I didn't mention the missing piece to her because I wasn't sure if it was missing or I was just too busy to remember everything."

"I understand. I'll let her know. Talk to you later." I clicked off the call.

"Becca, what's the deal with the ornaments? It's getting a little creepy," Linda said.

"I agree. And, I don't know." I looked around the market and then at my stall. There were plenty of shoppers, but the crowd had lessened a little, and I didn't have very many jars left to sell. "Uh, I need to find Allison. Do you mind . . . ?"

"Not at all. Go. Get this ornament thing figured out."

Somehow I quickly zoned in on Allison. I happened to call her right at the moment she was stepping out of her office. My call sent her back inside, and I met her there a minute later.

"Uh, that's interesting," Allison said as she looked at the ornament. "And you're 100 percent positive that this wasn't from Ian? Just a friendly gesture?"

"I'm sure. He could tell by the tone of my voice that I needed to know the truth."

"Becca, I don't have any idea what's going on, but it's kind of harmless."

"In a somewhat disturbing way. I really do think someone's leaving clues as to who the killer is. I'm feeling it even more after my conversation with Evelyn, and Sam's and my search of Reggie's house. There's something with the Ridgeways, Reggie Stuckey, and Brenton, maybe their pasts."

"Brenton is the anomaly," Allison said. "Reggie's murder could have something to do with Christmas tree farming, but how does Brenton fit in?"

"I think we should ask him again. Just you and me. Let's try."

"I'd love to, but he called me this morning. He won't be back at the market until the new year. We'll be quiet tomorrow because of the parade, but he's taking some extended time off. He claims that his Internet orders are getting backed up and he needs to get them taken care of. He left some flyers on his display table yesterday before he left."

Though I'd been preparing the cookies for the parade,

the fact that the town preparations would begin tomorrow caught me off guard. I felt like I'd misplaced a day or two somewhere. I didn't admit as much to Allison. "Brenton's ex-wife mentioned something that might apply to him— that maybe he's not who he said he is. How do we find out more about Brenton Jones without asking him?" I said.

"Sounds like a job for the police. Sam and the other officers have access to public records and such. They can track him, see what he's been up to. They're probably working on it already."

"As far as I know, Brenton has been around Monson forever," I said.

"He's worked at the market almost since its inception in 1990. Oh, wait, hang on." Allison reached to the file drawer on the side of her desk and opened it. She quickly found the file she was looking for, pulled it out, and placed it on the top of her desk. "Shoot. I guess he's been archived. I forget who has and who hasn't. This is Brenton's file, but he's been here so long that I sent his original application to the market's archives. All the file has now is copies of his equipment request forms and a new phone and e-mail contact sheet. I can request the application be faxed over."

Without waiting for me to comment, Allison picked up the handset of her phone and punched a number. "I have to leave a message. No one's answering." She left the message and then hung up the phone.

"I gotta say, sis, I feel weird about thinking that Brenton has anything at all to do with a murder," I said. "He's a friend. I feel disloyal, and I don't like it."

"Me, either," Allison agreed. "I still don't think he's a killer, but his behavior has been so strange, so different. It bears looking at more closely. I don't think he's having some sort of mental breakdown or anything like that. I think he's angry about the Ridgeways, plain and simple. I think he has some connection to them and that connection is either the reason Reggie Stuckey was murdered or a clue to who the killer is."

"Really?"

"I'm not sure, Becs, but a look at his application just to see if there's anything there won't hurt anyone."

"Why wouldn't he just tell the police about the connection, particularly if he's not directly involved?" I said.

"You well know that people's motives for doing or not doing something can be personal and sometimes muddled."

"True," I said.

"What? You're thinking about something else," Allison said.

"Kind of. If Brenton's ex-wife won't tell me more about him, maybe someone else will."

"Like?"

"Fellow market vendors."

"I suppose you could try." She looked at her watch. "But you'd better hurry. After today, most everyone will be involved with the parade for a couple days, and then there's Christmas. I suspect vendors will be making their way out of here soon, if they haven't already, and will be hard to find for a while."

With that, we both stood. Still holding the tree ornament, I turned one way down an aisle while Allison turned the other. I'd interrupted her original plan but she didn't miss a beat and was back on track to her market duties.

My first plan, my only one really, was to find Barry. He'd been the one to tell me about Brenton's ex-wife in the first place. Stephanie was his niece, so he probably knew more about Brenton. But I was sidetracked along the way; I was so close to the Bailey's entrance that I had a perfect view of the Ridgeway setup. I didn't see Ned, but Denny and Billie were both there; Denny working with a tree, Billie sitting on a lawn chair again, but looking at some papers this time. They didn't look busy, so I took advantage of the lull and hurried over to try to talk to Denny.

"Becca, how are you?" he said as though he didn't remember the discomfort from our last conversation.

"Hi, Becca," Billie said but she remained seated.

"Hi. Wow, you've sold some trees. That's great!"

"Yes, we're doing well," Denny said.

"Mind if I ask how you are all keeping up at your farm? You have some employees?"

"A few, but right now Ned is there. It'll slow down here tomorrow, but we'll all deliver the trees to the parade and another employee will man the fort down here."

I nodded.

"What's that?" Denny said as he pointed to the metal tree I was still holding.

"That, I believe, is a Christmas tree ornament. I have a Secret Santa."

Denny laughed and Billie glanced over briefly, but returned her attention back to the papers a second later.

I was still bothered that Denny didn't ho-ho-ho.

"You and your fella will have something to put on your tree now. You still planning on coming up on Sunday?" Denny said.

"Yes, we're looking forward to it."

"Good, can't wait to have you up there."

"Denny, can I ask you another question that's probably too personal to ask?" I said, waiting for him to cross him arms again, like the last time I'd asked if I could snoop more deeply than was probably acceptable.

But he didn't cross his arms this time. He didn't protest. Instead, his eyes actually twinkled. I liked that. "I get the sense that's never stopped you before. Sure—I won't promise that I'll answer, but let's have a seat." He guided me away from Billie to the other end of the tree corral. There were no chairs, so I just assumed he wanted to move away from his sister if someone was going to ask him a potentially too-personal question.

"Look, I know you said you don't know Brenton. What if I just ask if there's some sort of connection between the two of you, but not what that connection is. It's just you and me, Denny, and I'd really like to know."

Denny thought a long, long time before he answered, but I steeled myself silent for as long as it took.

"Gosh, Becca, I don't know . . . I don't feel like I should tell you. It's not my place, if you know what I mean."

"So there is a connection?"

Denny put his finger next to his nose, a gesture that made me smile. He was almost the spitting image of the Santa from a book my parents read every year to Allison and me when we were little; the all-time classic and favorite, *The Night Before Christmas*.

But Denny didn't magically disappear back up a chimney to his waiting sleigh and reindeer like the Santa in the book did. His eyes even stopped twinkling. "Yes, Becca, there is a connection."

Again, I was struck by his choice of words. *Yes, Virginia, there is a Santa Claus.* I wondered if he was doing it on purpose.

"It's from a long time ago," he continued, "but I'll be 100 percent honest with you, my dear; I'm certain that Brenton had nothing to do with Reggie Stuckey's murder. I think we have an odd and surprising coincidence regarding Brenton's behavior and Reggie's death."

I wasn't even going to go there, but I thought his journey from point A to point B was interesting.

"Do you know Brenton's ex-wife?"

"Stephanie Frugit? Yes."

He hadn't missed a beat. I hadn't meant to be tricky. It was just a question, but he'd answered so quickly. Somehow, some way, he and Brenton's pasts *were* tied together much more tightly than he wanted to indicate. They'd known each other, and very well, if I was reading him right.

"I see," I said.

Denny smiled and his eyes found their twinkle again. "You know, sometimes we say things on accident, but sometimes they're on purpose."

"You wanted me to know that you and Brenton had a close connection in your pasts? You didn't want to say anything in front of your sister, though?"

Denny shrugged.

"Then why won't you just tell me what the connection is? She can't hear us over here."

"Not my place, Becca, not my place. Excuse me, I have work to do. If people want pretty places to put all those ornaments"—he pointed to the tree I still held—"then I'd better make sure all the branches are in good condition."

As Denny disappeared into his man-made copse of trees,

I turned back toward the market. That was one of the most frustrating conversations I could remember having in a long time—at least since the one with the Archers earlier that morning. I debated going over to talk to Billie, but I looked back to see that Denny was still watching me. I was sure he shook his head ever so slightly. If I wanted to talk to her, I'd have to find a way to catch her alone. I smiled and she and I waved at each other as I hurried away.

How was I going to find the connection? Denny said that he was sure that Brenton wasn't the killer. Great, so then give up the rest of the information. *Not his place, not his place.* I didn't think anyone had taken Brenton's angry parking lot accusation that Denny had killed Reggie seriously, but despite that, it seemed Denny wasn't retaliating. In fact, he seemed protective of Brenton's reputation.

He was keeping the secret, whatever it was. Brenton wasn't telling. His ex-wife wasn't telling. Maybe I could get someone else to give it up. Who?

My head was swimming from questions and looking for clues, but I still wanted to talk to Barry before he left for the day.

Barry of Barry Good Corn had been growing and selling corn for longer than I'd been alive. He'd been in the corn business for almost forty years, and he often told stories from the "old days." Those stories frequently mentioned fellow market workers, but at that moment I couldn't remember one story he'd told that included Brenton. I wished I could.

"Becca, what's new?" Barry said as I approached his stall. His bulk put a strain on the plastic folding chair he was sitting in. He held a magazine with a picture of a tractor on the cover, but I didn't catch the name before he placed it on his knee.

"Can I come in?" I asked.

"Sure." Barry stood and moved the chair. "Here, have a seat."

"No, thanks, I'm okay. I'll just be a minute."

Barry had had a successful marriage for almost fifty years, and a good amount of its success was probably due to the fact that he wasn't home all the time, even when he didn't have much more to do than sit in his market stall and read a magazine just in case someone wanted to buy a cornhusk.

"All righty."

"Stephanie Frugit's your niece?" I jumped in.

"Yes, ma'am. I had an older brother who's left this world now, but Stephanie is his little girl. She's amazing."

"I know. I met her."

"You know her reputation and her level of fame, right?"

"Sure."

"Everyone knows who she is. We're very proud of all she's accomplished."

"No wonder you know Brenton so well."

"Yes, but they haven't been married for a long, long time."

"When did they divorce?"

"Oh, shoot, they were still pretty young. Let's see, they were both about twenty-five, so 1989 or so. I can't remember exactly."

Well, it wasn't 1987. "This is personal, but do you know why they divorced?"

"That *is* personal, Becca, but I think they just decided that neither of them wanted the life the other wanted."

Stephanie had said something similar.

I squinted and then sighed. "Barry, what's the connection between Brenton and the Ridgeways?"

"Oh." Barry shifted his weight to his other foot and then he shifted back again. "I don't rightly know."

"His ex-wife is your niece, you've known Brenton forever, but you don't know his connection to the Ridgeways?"

"Becca, I don't know the Ridgeways. They've had that tree farm forever, but they've always stayed to themselves. Their farm's in the hills and this is the first year they've been at Bailey's. I don't know them."

He wasn't lying, at least not about not knowing them. He was keeping something else from me and to himself, though, but I wasn't sure exactly what.

"How in the world can I find the connection?"

Barry shrugged. "Ask the parties involved."

"They aren't telling."

"Then maybe it's none of your business, Miss Nosy." Barry smirked playfully.

He was correct. It probably was none of my business, but I just couldn't help but think that we were so close to knowing who the killer was because of that connection.

I'd gotten ideas in my head before, though, ideas that were off base and ended up leading to nowhere at all, or leading me straight into more trouble. Maybe that's what this one was.

But, maybe not.

Eighteen

Downtown Monson was suddenly decked out. Whoever had been in charge of this year's decorations had gone far above and beyond. I parked my truck at the end of the street and spent a few moments just admiring the currently unlit colorful lights wrapped around the streetlight poles, and the array of trees, some already starting to be decorated, that lined the entire three-block-long drag. Come sundown, Monson would be so bright we might attract passing UFOs.

I was glad to finally get out of bed and have something to do. I'd spent the night tossing and turning and trying to figure out why or how some people might be connected to other people. I'd replayed conversations over and over again, trying to glean something new, something that might help lead the police to a killer.

Sam had had to work late, though oddly not on anything related to Reggie Stuckey's murder; he'd stayed at his own house so he wouldn't disturb me. In fact, I hadn't slept anyway, and I would have welcomed the disturbance even just to have someone to talk to. He hadn't seen the new ornament. Since he'd been so busy with other police work, I hadn't even told him about it yet. My decision to keep it to myself seemed wrong as the sun had risen, and I hoped to drop off some cookies at the parade site and then find Sam at the police station to let him know about the tree.

For the moment, though, I enjoyed the line of perfect, or at least almost perfect, real trees. It seemed like the entries only improved every year, and this year's artists would have some beautiful palettes to work with. I didn't see the Ridgeways anywhere, but they had outdone themselves. I thought the trees they brought to Bailey's were wonderful, but these were even better: greener and fuller. From my vantage point, even though they were mostly not decorated yet, I had no doubt this year's would easily outdo all the ones from previous years.

"Becca! Come help me with this."

I tried to find the person attached to the voice. It took a second, but I finally saw my dad perched high on a ladder against a wall of the library.

"Dad?" I said as I hurried out of the truck.

"Here, I don't feel secure enough up here to let go and get this string in place. If you'd just hold the ladder a second, I'd be fine."

I gripped both sides of the ladder and held it tightly. "What are you doing up there?"

"This is the job of the VP of decoration's husband. I'm to string lights. I've been stringing lights since about three this morning and will probably be stringing them into the night."

"Mom's the one in charge of decorations? I didn't know. What about her allergy?"

"She's taken pills of some sort. And she didn't know about her job until this morning."

"What happened?"

"Got a call from Vivienne Norton last night. Officer Norton said that the decorator dumped the job. Vivienne knew your mom knew her way around a sewing machine and some knitting needles; she figured that those skills somehow put her in the running for the position."

"Does Allison know? You should have called me earlier."

"We decided not to tell either of you girls. You'd both dump whatever you were doing to help us out. You have jobs and people to attend to. Polly and I have time for a decorating emergency."

"Well, I'm here now at least. We can get those lights strung and then do whatever else you've been assigned to do."

"Deal."

My plans to find Sam were diverted—all day. After the string of blinking white lights was hung across the front of the library and numerous strings in other places were attended to, we helped a couple of early artists with their tree prep. I had never paid attention to the amount of tinsel the town used for the parade, but I wondered if we should call Guinness World Records.

Though Bailey's wasn't closed, the first day of the parade was never a shopping day. Almost everyone who lived in and around Monson was somehow involved in the parade festivities: cooking, baking, decorating, or just family time in preparation for attending the first evening's kickoff. It was Monson's moment to shine, and everyone wanted to be a part of the elbow grease that created the shine.

After Main Street was decorated to the hilt, I helped with the food. Instead of one area for people to grab a snack or a hot or cold drink, we set up stations. Everyone donated everything, and money donation jars were also put out on each station. People paid what they could or what they wanted to donate to the charity for cookies, candy, soda, and hot chocolate. The stations always reminded me of Charlie Brown's Lucy and her psychiatry stand. Every station was well stocked by late afternoon, with all remaining food and drink products stored in the library's basement. Teenagers were recruited to check and restock the stations throughout the evening.

One of the yearly tree artists was Wanda Neil. I saw her unload boxes of decorations and asked if I could help her transport them to her tree. As evening approached, I ended up assisting her with decorating her goldfish tree. It was a theme she began a few years ago and it had given Wanda legend status. Throughout the year, Wanda purchased anything goldfish related she could find. She'd also taken to crafting them. Papier-mâché, woodwork, and origami were only the beginnings of what she used to create goldfish. By the time she was done placing all the ornaments on her tree, it was almost impossible to see any green for all the orange and black.

Wanda was probably about my age and had, like me, somehow acquired an inheritance, though no one understood quite where it had come from or how much it was. There were continual rumors as to the amount. I'd heard it was millions, and I'd also heard that she was almost broke and had been seen stealing food from a Dumpster behind a restaurant—I didn't think that one was true.

Wanda looked like a delicate beauty but behaved like a strong farm woman. She had long, straight chocolate-brown hair that she always pulled back into a smooth ponytail. I'd never seen her flawless, white skin show one sign that it had seen either sun or exertion, but I knew it had seen plenty of both. Her eyes and long eyelashes matched her hair color perfectly and her small features were precise. She reminded me of an old-fashioned porcelain doll, except that she didn't wear dresses, and I was certain lace would never cross her mind. She always wore old, faded, ripped jeans and T-shirts that had seen better days.

She had a good-sized parcel of land only a few miles from mine and though she had a plentiful garden, she didn't sell what she grew. She did lots of canning and preserving though—pickling, too.

She worked her garden and land by herself. She weeded, watered, planted, and picked everything on her own. She also kept her old, large farmhouse immaculate, except for the kitchen. She kept her kitchen clean, but it was always in use. Something was always being chopped, cooked, or baked. It wasn't possible that she could eat everything she prepared but whenever asked where it all went, she'd just shrug and avoid the answer. There were rumors about that, too. Some said she took all the food to homeless shelters. Others said she would secretly, under cover of night, deliver food to the poorer families in the community. I believed both of those were possible.

Wanda was also strange, weird, and odd. This was not just my opinion, but though she was eccentric, she was wonderful to be around if you didn't try too hard to figure out what she was really talking about.

"Love this one," she said as she held out a small, stuffed goldfish for my approval.

"It's cute."

"No, Becca, it isn't cute. It has much more to contribute to the world. It is helping to make our space more pleasant," she said adamantly.

See, not just my opinion.

"Of course," I said. When Sam had met her, he'd commented on how it was a good thing she'd inherited money and property because she'd have a difficult time keeping a job.

Wanda sighed as she placed the toy on a branch. "There are some that are more difficult to part with than others."

"I understand."

She smiled and looked pointedly at me. It was a look she'd given me a number of times, and I always wondered if it was her way of telling me that she was just one big act, that she knew people thought she was slightly off-kilter and she liked it that way.

Sam had told me that the police would check on her frequently just to make sure she was okay. She always was, and he said that some officers, Vivienne in particular, mentioned that they and Wanda carried on easy and coherent conversations.

"How much do you think my tree will go for this year?" she asked.

"Gosh, I don't know. If I remember correctly, your trees have always been some of the most popular."

It was true. The sheer overload of goldfish of every kind was enough for the tree to gain attention. Everyone was also convinced that if they became the proud owner of a gold-fish tree, they'd probably be the only ones in the world to be so lucky.

"I know, but look around. Did you see the fairy tree? I might have to buy that one myself."

I'd also heard that Wanda had purchased a number of trees over the years, though it was a mystery as to where they ended up.

"I missed it," I said as I craned to look around Wanda and down the row.

"It's spectacular," she said as she clapped her hands together. "Spectacular."

"I'll have to find it."

"Hi, Becca, what a wonderful tree!"

I had to look around the other side of the tree to see that Billie had approached and was taking the spirit of the event very seriously. She was dressed as either Santa's helper or an elf. She wore a short, tight green dress and red leggings. She'd topped off the look with a green floppy hat and had painted on rosy cheeks. The flannel shirts and jeans I'd seen her in had hidden her great figure. I'd already thought she was probably in her early fifties, but she rocked the elf look like a pro. I didn't see Denny close by, so I hoped for a chance to slip in a few questions for her.

"It's perfect," Wanda said. "Oh, are you one of the Ridge-ways?"

"I am. Billie Ridgeway." Billie extended her hand, but Wanda only cocked her head and started tapping a finger on her lips.

"Hey, Billie, this is great. Thanks for donating so many trees," I said.

Since the Ridgeways weren't located directly in Monson, they might not know or know of Wanda, but I couldn't figure out a polite way to explain the unusual behavior.

"Oh, you're welcome," she said. She smiled uncomfortably at Wanda and then turned back to me. "Do you need anything else?"

"No, I think we're good, but thanks. Actually, do you have a few minutes? I'd love to talk to you. I'll buy you a cookie," I said.

"Oh. Well, thank you, Becca, but maybe later. Denny wants me to check on this row of trees."

I tried to think of something to keep her from leaving, but it seemed like she wanted to turn away. Then she became captivated by something on the tree. She zoned in so strongly on an ornament that both Wanda and I were compelled to move around the tree to see what had captured her attention.

"That's lovely," Billie said as she pointed at a goldfish that stood out from the others around it. This ornament in particular was made of the same material that my recently acquired tree was made out of—some sort of thin, flat metal. Unlike the stuffed and sewn ornaments that framed it, this one wasn't orange and black, but just the tarnished brown of the metal.

"It's quite wonderful, isn't it?" Wanda said.

"Where did you get that one?" I asked.

"I seldom remember, unless I make and name them myself. I just don't remember where I get them."

Billie smiled at Wanda and then at me. "Well, it's a great tree, very unique. Good luck with the bids."

"Thank you, Billie Ridgeway," Wanda said before she skipped back around the tree to continue decorating.

"When you're available, I'd love to visit a little," I said.

"Sure. I'll find you," she said. I didn't think she would.

Billie turned and continued down toward the next tree, the bells on her pointy-toed shoes jingling as she walked.

I looked at the metal fish one more time and shook off the unwelcome sense of coincidence that was creeping in on me. Was this something that I needed to pay attention to, or was it just pure chance that this ornament was so similar to the tree, and there was nothing I should sense as strange about it? Hairs rose on the back of my neck. I turned and looked around.

The sun had set, the chill in the air had grown chillier, and the crowd was quickly beginning to grow. Last-minute decorations were still being placed on most trees, but onlookers were already browsing, some drinking hot chocolate, some eating Christmas cookies.

The only person who noticed me looking around was Denny, who was across the street, inspecting a tree as Billie had inspected Wanda's. He was dressed in a bright-red sweater and black jeans, which made him look even more like Santa. He happened to look up as I looked over. He smiled and waved. I did the same. Maybe that's why Billie hadn't wanted to talk; maybe she'd seen Denny. He certainly seemed to rule the Ridgeway family roost.

"All this Christmas stuff and not a mistletoe in sight." A voice pulled me back to reality.

"Hi," I said to Sam. He was dressed in jeans and a long-sleeved red T-shirt with a Santa iron-on over his chest. I bit the insides of my cheeks to contain a laugh. I didn't think I'd ever seen him look so casual, or in something so "cute" even when he was trying to be casual. "You're not working?"

"Oh, I'm working. This"—he pointed to the Santa— "was Vivienne's idea. She asked if some of us would look a little less cop-like for the event."

"And you agreed?"

"I drew the short stir stick."

"You look adorable."

"Why, thank you."

"You're Officer Brion," Wanda said. This time, she extended her hand to him.

"I am. Nice to see you, Wanda."

"You, too. You know," she said with a high lilt, "those Ridgeway people aren't to be trusted."

"Oh, I don't know. They donated the trees," Sam said after shooting me a quick glance.

"Yes, that's very kind, but that woman, the one that was just here talking to me and Becca, she's up to no good."

"How? Why?"

"I can't remember. I just can't remember."

"Something happened before?" Sam asked.

"Yes, I believe so. Many years ago."

"Sometime in the eighties?" I couldn't resist.

"Yes, actually, I think that's correct."

"Can you remember what it was?" I said, now suddenly truly interested.

Wanda shook her head slowly. "No, I don't think I can. Maybe it will come to me later."

Sam took a business card out of his back pocket. "If you remember, would you give me a call?"

"Of course." Wanda took the card and then turned her

attention back to the tree. "I'm okay now, Becca. Thanks for your help, but you should go play with your boyfriend."

"Uh, okay, well, the tree looks spectacular," I said.

"I know."

"Any chance that's an act?" I said when we were out of her earshot.

"Partially. I think she plays everyone; she likes to. That itself, though, is a form of mental instability, but we make sure she's okay. I've talked to doctors, and she's perfectly capable of caring for herself. Don't worry; if she needs help, we'll make sure she gets it."

I stopped walking and looked up at Sam. "I had no idea you were that in tune with all of this."

He laughed. "This is my home. I'm a police officer, and even though I more closely resemble a child going to sing in a holiday show this evening, I do take my job seriously."

"I know, but . . . well, good job, that's all."

"Thank you."

I'd lost track of my parents and still hadn't seen Allison or anyone else from the market, but I wanted to tell Sam about my newest ornament, so I directed him to one of the snack stations. We placed our order, dropped some money into the jar, and then sat on the curb away from the crowd, where he could keep watch for problems and I could tell him about the ornament without anyone hearing.

"You're sure it wasn't Ian?" Sam asked.

"I'm sure. I think he heard the concern in my voice. He knew that if it was some sort of joke or something for fun, it was time for the fun to end."

"Any chance I could dust it for fingerprints?"

"Oh, geez, Sam, that never occurred to me. I'm sure I

ruined any chance for that. See, you haven't taught me all the professional ins and outs yet."

"Right. Well, it most likely wouldn't do much good anyway. It was outside. Any prints we found might not lead us anywhere or mean much of anything anyway." He took a sip of hot chocolate, leaving a dot of whipped cream on his nose. I wiped it with my thumb.

"Do you still think it might be a Secret Santa?" I asked.

"No, I don't. I think it's exactly what you think it is, some sort of trail of clues, though I'm hesitant to say they lead to a killer. It's probably something much more harmless. I hope it is, and I hope they tie together at some point, but right now it feels like a bunch of unconnected pieces of information."

"What about the Realtor? How'd that go?"

"Reggie's farm has been available to purchase for a long time, which is why Ian looked at it, I guess. But it wasn't 'officially' put up for sale until Reggie died. The Realtor received instructions to put it on the market the day after Reggie's demise. This and some other information that Vivienne dug up led me right back to Evelyn Rasmussen. Evelyn was Reggie's beneficiary as well as the executor of his will."

"Beneficiary? She's getting money?"

"Yep. Twenty thousand dollars."

"Well, that's a good sum of money, but hardly enough to kill for, I would think, and hardly enough to say Reggie was well off."

"Reggie was worth three million dollars."

I choked on my hot chocolate. "What?"

"Yes, we've heard it was old family money. According to Reggie's attorney, Reggie wanted to leave everything to

Evelyn but she insisted on only the twenty thousand. The rest of the money will go to animal charities."

"I'm stunned."

"There's more. You know your affair angle?"

"Yes."

"I do believe Reggie is the one who had the affair," Sam said.

"Oh! With who?"

"That I don't know, but I sensed that Reggie wanted to leave all that money to his ex-wife because he felt guilty."

"And the attorney confirmed this?"

"No, not confirmed, just hinted."

"Oh, I wish I'd been there to see you work."

"Hey, I invited you."

"I know."

"Hey, do you suppose we could just enjoy the rest of the evening? I mean, I'll have to be on the alert, but it's the Christmas parade, it's our first year together. I'd like to look at trees, maybe bid on a couple—though I still want our own tree."

"You mean we should just try to be a couple, no murder investigation involved?"

"Yes, if you wouldn't mind."

"I wouldn't mind a bit."

The trees were amazing. My favorite had been threaded with a toy train track, a small train engine somehow quietly chugging its way around the winding track. We placed a bid on it, but there wasn't much chance we'd win; everyone was bidding on the train tree. I overdosed on cookies and Sam overdosed on hot chocolate.

My mother managed a brief hello but she had enough to do to keep her on the move. Allison, her husband, Tom, and her son, Mathis, walked with us for as long as Mathis allowed, but the parents had to cater to Mathis's desire to move more quickly than our relaxing pace.

The evening was perfect, and we managed to keep far away from the subject of murder and investigation. Until it was time to go home.

Though he would be over later that night, Sam walked me to my truck. I was glad he did, because I would have had to find him again quickly once I saw what was inside, sitting in the same spot I'd found the egg.

On the passenger seat was a new ornament to add to my collection.

It was the metallic goldfish. There was no doubt in my mind that it was the same one that had been on Wanda's tree, but the mystery of who put it there was just that: a mystery.

At least this time I thought about potential fingerprints.

Nineteen

Saturday morning started way too early and with way too much excitement. But that was mostly because the evening before had ended far too late.

Sam and I hurried the ornament to Gus, our local crime scene guy who was set up to handle technologically easy crime scene things like fingerprints, and then I went home to Hobbit. Sam spent most of the rest of the night working. Though Monson was still small and the outside world didn't intrude too much, a couple of the downtown businesses had done exactly what I'd been thinking of doing—they'd installed security cameras. Between attempting to obtain any of the footage they might have captured that included the goldfish tree, questioning parade participants and attendees, and, as he put it, "some general investigation," Sam again went to his own home to grab a couple hours' sleep instead of joining Hobbit and me at my farm. I was tired enough to sleep better than the night before, but I was still dragging when the phone sounded.

Since the parade was already set up and ready to welcome the world again that evening, I planned to work at Bailey's during the day. It was typical, though, that this Saturday's market business would be similar to yesterday's pace—slow. I'd decided to bake a few dozen more cookies for the parade before going to Bailey's, so I planned on getting up early, but I was awakened even earlier I'd expected.

"Sis?" I said as I answered my cell. "You okay?"

"Fine; I thought I'd let you know what I found, though. I think it's important. I already called Sam."

"Okay."

"The main office faxed me a copy of Brenton's original market application, and I think it explains some of why he reacted the way he did toward the Ridgeways."

"I'm ready."

"It's literally what his ex-wife was trying to tell you. Brenton changed his identity. Well, his last name, though he didn't do it secretly."

"I don't understand."

"Brenton used to be Brenton Ridgeway."

"That's crazy. How do you know?"

"He wrote a note on his original application. In case we did background checks, he wanted to give us full disclosure."

Even if Brenton was a Ridgeway, and I thought it might take a few hours and a couple pots of coffee for me to accept such news, I still couldn't fathom what that might mean when it came to Reggie's murder. Or maybe I just didn't want to. I now hoped that one had absolutely nothing to do with the other, and that my intuition about the importance of the connection had been plain wrong.

"How are they related? I mean, how is he a Ridgeway?" I asked.

"I don't know, but I suspect he's a sibling."

"What did Sam say?"

"That he was going to talk to Brenton and see what the reason is for all the secrecy."

"Does he think Brenton's lie somehow makes him the killer?"

"Don't know. You'll have to call him. I bet he'll tell you more than he told me."

"Thank you."

I'd somehow made it into my kitchen. I looked around. I was surprised—shocked, even—at the news. Brenton being a Ridgeway and not Brenton Jones wasn't something I could hear and automatically accept.

For a long moment I thought about calling Sam. The cookie ingredients were ready to be used, but I was certain that if I attempted to follow through with my plan to bake, I'd only end up with a disaster. More than I wanted to call Sam, I wanted to talk to Brenton in person. I had to.

There was a chance, though, that Sam wouldn't want me visiting Brenton. There was a chance Sam was already on his way and we'd run into each other, which would be awkward, at the very least.

When Sam and I had gone from a friendship to a romantic relationship, I'd tried to make a silent deal with myself that I wouldn't take advantage of his law enforcement position to satisfy my own curiosity. Before we'd crossed over into romantic territory, I hadn't minded asking him questions that I had no real right to ask. I'd even scaled the ledge of the building that housed the police department just to see if I could find out who he or his fellow officers were questioning.

But now I thought I should work to conduct myself with more decorum, be less nosy, more mind-my-own-business.

But I really, really wanted to talk to Brenton. In person.

Another plan took shape. I wasn't going to risk the chance of running into Sam at Brenton's house, but I knew where the secret turnoff to Stephanie Frugit's orchard was located and I'd already made her acquaintance.

"She's not here," the man said. He took off his cowboy hat and swiped back his short, black hair as he looked out at the expanse of the apple orchard. "Well, she's out there somewhere."

"Out in the orchard?"

"Yes, ma'am." Elias was probably about my age. He worked at the orchard but I wasn't sure if he held a management position or was just one of the farmhands. He didn't converse easily. He was short and wide, but in a muscular way that gave the impression that he could pull an apple tree out of the ground with one big tug. His tanned face made me think he sometimes forgot the cowboy hat.

"Point me in the right direction. I'll head out and talk to her."

"No, that's not wise. It's a big orchard."

"I don't think I'll get lost." I peered around him and out to the lines of trees. They were without leaves, but there were so many that just their bare limbs created dense rows. "I can find my way back."

"No, Ms. Frugit would be angry if I let you go."

I put my hands on my hips and looked at Elias. "Then I guess I'll just have to wait for her."

"It might be a while. She's inspecting the trees. It's what she does."

"I understand. I can wait."

"Suit yourself." Elias turned to leave me alone to stand by the entrance of the orchard. He must not have been worried that I would, indeed, make my way into the trees and search for Stephanie. He was probably right. I didn't think I'd get lost but I was sure I could spend a lot of time searching and still not find her. We could easily cross rows and miss each other completely, maybe more than once.

But Elias turned back to face me again. "How about I give you a lift?"

"You want to drive me into the orchard?"

"Yes, but not in my truck. I have a four-wheeler. It'll be quicker that way."

I appreciated the accommodating attitude switch.

"Great! Thanks!"

If I hadn't had a mission in mind, I might have enjoyed the ride on the back of the four-wheeler as Elias steered us though rows of apple trees. I'd walked through a number of orchards in my day. I'd picked fruit, both from low-hanging branches and from top rungs of ladders, but there was something magically different about Frugit Orchard. I'd never quite experienced anything like the alternating shades of light and shadow, the cool breeze that had somehow found its way into the trees. There was something special about the light and the shadow, as if it was touched by something unreal, something from a fairy-tale forest where castles were located. There were no apples on the trees, but I was certain I could smell their sweetness anyway.

Elias drove us up a ridge and then down a hill, and then turned the four-wheeler to the left. He stopped, flipped on a brake, and rose to stand on the footrests as he looked around.

"See her?" I asked, raising my voice over the noise of the engine.

"Maybe." Elias sat down again and I wrapped my arms around his waist as he turned the accelerator handle.

After another few minutes up the path, we turned right and suddenly came upon Stephanie Frugit.

Stephanie lived up to her reputation even when she was alone and inspecting her orchard. She sat on a beautiful sable horse, and wore chaps, a Western blouse, and a feminine cowboy hat. Out from under the hat, her long hair shone in the sunshine and framed her shoulders perfectly as the breeze blew it just enough to make the highlights glimmer.

After Elias turned the key on the vehicle, she said, "That was a noisy arrival."

"Sorry, Ms. Frugit, but she wasn't going to leave."

"I understand, Elias. I knew she'd be back again soon anyway," Stephanie said.

"How did you know?" I said.

"Because I sensed you would figure out some of what I couldn't tell you. You'd want to talk to me, and I wanted to talk to you again, too. So, tell me, did you figure it out?"

I looked at Elias.

"It's okay; Elias has worked for me for years. He knows many of my secrets."

"Brenton used to be a Ridgeway."

Stephanie smiled and then dismounted the horse. "That's

right. Very good. How did you figure it out? Old public records? Maybe our divorce papers? Did my uncle tell you?"

"No, I didn't even think about looking at your divorce papers, and your uncle might be one of the best liars I've ever known; I got nothing from Barry. Were you a Ridgeway, too?"

"Only by marriage, and only briefly."

"I found out from his original Bailey's application. He noted the recent name change."

Stephanie laughed. "Of course. The answer was right there all the time. Isn't that usually the way it is?"

I shrugged. It wasn't my experience that answers were usually that close at hand, but maybe life's questions had been easier for her than me.

"Here, Elias, take Applewood. Becca and I will walk a little. We'll come back here, so we won't go far, and we won't be gone long."

Stephanie led the way to the next row and we began walking slowly under the arch of branches.

"When Brenton and I were married, he was a Ridgeway. Our divorce records mention his last name. That's why I wondered about the public records," she repeated.

I still didn't know for sure if Brenton was a sibling to the three other Ridgeways I'd met, but I thought I'd act as if that's what I'd discovered, and start with a more general question. "What happened, Stephanie—why did he change his name and leave his family?"

"They did something that he thought was the reason for their father's death, something that caused great stress to the family. He blamed them, Denny, Ned, and Billie equally."

Definitely siblings. "You aren't going to tell me what it was, are you?"

"I can't, but not because of any loyalty to Brenton. My only promise to him was that I wouldn't be forthcoming to anyone about his identity. It was legal, you know, the way he changed his name. He wasn't hiding from anyone. Brenton never would hide. It wasn't his style. But he hoped that time and distance between him and the Ridgeway name would grow until no one knew or remembered."

"It must have been ugly."

"Yes, very. You told me Brenton behaved strangely around the Ridgeways. I'm not surprised. He will never be able to forgive them. Never. They've all been able to keep their distance from each other. I imagine Brenton seeing the Ridgeways at Bailey's was akin to people he despised moving into his house. He would have felt angry, hurt, and betrayed."

"That's how he acted."

"Well, the Ridgeways knew where he worked; they shouldn't have ever come to the market. I talked to my uncle and he told me that your sister would never have allowed the Ridgeways to sell their trees there if she'd known what had happened."

I stopped walking.

"Tell me what happened and I'll tell you how Allison would have reacted," I said.

Stephanie just looked at me with raised eyebrows and then looked away.

"I can't find anything juicy on the Internet, which means it was a story that was kept very quiet. I didn't see anything about the Ridgeway patriarch, I don't know who he was or how he died. I keep I thinking that someone had an affair," I said. "Is there anything to that idea?"

"Yes, someone had an affair," she said easily, as if she was glad I'd asked.

It was a start. "Who?" I said.

"See, that's the part I can't tell you. It would be wrong and gossipy."

"And the affair somehow killed their father?"

"Sort of."

I sighed. "That's pretty frustrating to hear."

"I know, but . . . well, I can tell you this much. I shouldn't tell you, but I will. The affair was in the news. Nothing's a secret anymore, Becca. Search the Internet a little deeper, you'll find it. You have to understand that times were different. Yes, reporters wanted a scoop, a great story, but they were also a little kinder back then. The affair was reported, but when certain parties asked them to stop reporting, they listened to those certain parties' requests."

"It seems like the press loved Evelyn Rasmussen Stuckey. Everyone *still* loves the Ridgeways."

"You'll find it."

"Will this lead to a killer?"

"I don't know, but you know that Brenton didn't kill anyone, don't you?"

"No, I don't. I hope he didn't, but I have no way of knowing much of anything, especially since people like you are being so secretive."

"Well, Brenton didn't kill anyone. Trust me."

I sighed again. "I suppose that if I sent the police out here to talk to you, you still wouldn't answer these questions."

Stephanie thought for a long time before she answered. "That's the thing, Becca: the police won't come out here to ask those questions, because there's no reason to. The fact that I was once married to Brenton is something from a long time ago. How could our marriage possibly be relevant to a murder that just occurred? The police wouldn't waste their time. You're just a civilian. No one's heard a word about what you and I have discussed today. It's your word against mine. It doesn't matter anyway."

I wondered if I should break my silent promise to myself and try to persuade Sam to cross the line a little. Probably not.

"Now, tell me about the parade. I haven't been in years. Too many people want to talk to me. I don't like to interrupt festivities."

It was true, I never saw Stephanie anywhere around town. Many people thought she was snooty because of her success. I might have thought that a time or two myself. I suddenly felt a little sorry for Stephanie Frugit. Her cagey non-answers still irritated me, but the thread of sympathy made me think twice. Even her minor celebrity status dictated some of her choices and decisions; I couldn't imagine how debilitating a big dose of celebrity would be.

I described some of the trees, talked about the massive amounts of other decorations and the good-sized crowd, and promised her I'd e-mail her my jelly-filled cookie recipe.

By the time we'd returned to Elias, we were laughing about an incident that had occurred during last year's parade and made statewide South Carolina news. A tree, one with lots of lights and strung with popcorn, had spontaneously burst into flame. No one had been hurt and the only damage done was the demise of the poor tree and its ornaments, but the reaction to the fire had been so quick and efficient that five different fire extinguishers had come quickly to the rescue. Rules against using flammable string with too many lights had been put into place for this year's festivities.

Finally, Stephanie's dismissal was friendly. It wasn't that we'd become friends; we'd never meet for coffee, and she'd never have a booth at Bailey's. In fact, she'd probably never shop there. But our short time together had changed my opinion regarding her reputation, and she knew that if she ever did want to visit Bailey's, she'd now know a stall vendor other than her ex-husband.

Elias escorted me back to my truck on his four-wheeler, but as I hung on to him with one arm, I turned back to see Stephanie Frugit remount her horse. Once she was aboard, she sat tall in the saddle and a gentle wind blew her hair again. The sun bounced perfectly off the trees and leaves around her and she looked the part of the legendary status she'd become. We waved to each other.

I drove away from Frugit Orchard with little more knowledge than I'd had when I arrived, but a sense of satisfaction boosted my confidence nonetheless.

Someone in the Ridgeway family had had an affair. Did that have anything to do with the murder? I could only guess that it did and that the ornament clues I'd received somehow told the story. At least one of the two divorces—Reggie and Evelyn's or Brenton and Stephanie's—must have been the result of the affair. Had Reggie and Stephanie been a secret couple? Or maybe Brenton and Evelyn? I even had to consider that Reggie and Brenton or Stephanie and Evelyn had been the couple, but I truly didn't think so. It seemed even less likely that Reggie and Stephanie had ever had any interest in each other. And Brenton and Evelyn? I couldn't be sure.

Truly, I could not imagine the recoupling that I was trying so hard to picture. Nothing fit, nothing worked.

The knowledge that Brenton was a Ridgeway was just another piece to the puzzle, but I didn't think it was the big piece I'd originally thought it was. The important thing that Brenton's application hadn't been able to tell me was *why* exactly Brenton changed his name—from what Stephanie had said, it had been his choice and not something his family had pushed him to do. Something had happened that had been stressful enough to contribute to their father's death. What? Was it an affair, or something more?

I would be going to Ridgeway Farm, with Sam tomorrow, but I hoped for more answers today.

I'd never been to Brenton's house, but I knew where he lived. I thought it was time to visit him. I hoped I wouldn't run into Sam, and I really hoped that Brenton would be as pleased to see me as I was eager to talk to him.

Twenty

Monson's residential areas were separated into distinct though
small burgs. Ian and his landlord, George, had previously
lived in the Ivy League district, where the short streets were
all named after the educational elite: Harvard, Princeton,
Yale, etc.

Brenton lived in the alphabet neighborhood. When entering the neighborhood, the first street's name was Alpine, followed by Butler, Cascade, Devonshire, Estate, and so on.
Brenton resided on Fulmer, a street lined with trees similar to
those in the Ivy League neighborhood, but made up of houses
built closer to the 1950s than the Harvard-Yale early 1900s
houses. Each plot of land in the alphabet neighborhood was
extra-large, making each house seem oddly far away from its
neighbors, but comfortable, with plenty of elbow room.

Brenton's house was a wide, white, welcoming one-story
with a black front door and black shutters framing the one

large and two regular-sized front windows. The property would have been well suited to a white picket fence, but I knew Brenton would prefer the open space of his green front yard with no fence, even a picket one, closing him in.

I was surprised to find him outside in the front. He was on his hands and knees next to a big white bucket. It looked like he was patching a square of concrete on his front walkway. There was not a Christmas decoration in sight. He probably spotted my truck the moment I turned onto his street. He sat back on his heels and smiled hesitantly as I parked and waved.

I was probably making him uncomfortable, but I'd do what I could to make my visit easy and friendly.

I got out of the truck and walked toward him as he stood and wiped off his knees.

"Becca, everything okay?" he asked.

"Everything's fine. Sorry, go ahead and finish. I can wait."

Brenton looked around. I wasn't sure what he was looking for. He turned back to me and said, "No, it's okay. I got it smoothed out. It just needs to dry now. You want to come in?"

I inspected the concrete. It was definitely smooth. I didn't think I'd be interrupting a project that needed more immediate attention. "I'd love to," I said.

I hadn't expected an invitation inside. I thought that at best he'd talk to me at his front door.

After he covered the bucket with a snug lid, he led me into the house.

"You want something to drink? I'm warm from working, but it's a little cool out there. You want some coffee?" Brenton asked.

"Sure, thanks. Can I help?"

"No, have a seat. I'll be right back."

"Thanks."

Brenton's front room was appealing in an older, masculine way. His tan couch and brown recliner were both well used, and his coffee table was covered in newspapers and handyman magazines, the main theme being woodworking projects. I wondered if he enjoyed woodworking or if he just liked to read about it.

Brenton's dog biscuits were made from human food ingredients, which was one of the reasons so many people became loyal customers. Brenton took great care in using healthy "real" food, with no preservatives. His house smelled like a spicy bread bakery, and I sniffed with exuberance as I took a seat on the couch.

"Coffee will be ready in a second. Can I get you anything else? You hungry? I have some people food around here somewhere." He smiled.

"No, thanks," I said as I smiled, too. This was not the same moody Brenton I'd recently met; this was more like my friend Brenton, the one I'd known for a long time. I hoped he was back for good.

He sat in the chair and took off his Yankees cap.

I smiled again. "I hardly ever see you without that cap."

He looked at it before he dropped it on the coffee table. "Well, it's not just one cap, you know. I have a few and I do buy more. My customers have gotten to know me with it. It's become part of my business. I didn't plan it that way, but it's good to have a trademark of sorts."

"I didn't know it wasn't a plan," I said.

"Yeah, Linda has her old-fashioned clothes, you've got your overalls, and I've got the cap."

I laughed. "Believe it or not, these weren't a plan, either. They're comfortable and I'm not a very creative dresser. I still don't really think about them much, but I suppose my customers would be surprised to see me in anything else."

Brenton laughed, too. "Lucky accidents."

His short, brownish, curlyish hair that I hadn't seen all that much of was crushed a little, and I noticed that the cap also make him look a little younger than his fiftysomething years. I didn't voice that observation.

After a brief lull, Brenton said, "What can I do for you, Becca? Sam said you'd be stopping by."

"He did?"

"Yes, he was just here a little bit ago. He told me you probably wouldn't be far behind."

"Hmm," I said. No wonder Brenton was being friendly. He'd been warned.

"Yeah, I think he knows you pretty well. You two are good together."

I blushed. No matter that I was well over the age at which these sorts of comments should bother me—they still did. As usual, I chalked it up to the fact that I'd been through two divorces. I was still embarrassed by the failed marriages; I'd probably never feel deserving of someone thinking I'd made a positive contribution to a romantic relationship.

"So, you know then that I know you used to be Brenton Ridgeway?"

"Yeah, I know. But as I told Sam, I wasn't really ever trying to hide it. Honestly, I thought everyone knew. It's part of my reality. As I told him when he came by today, the day he took me down to the station I was angry enough not to want to discuss it with him or anyone, but . . . well, it's been a long time since I was *that* person. I even thought Allison understood why I was so upset. When she wanted me to explain it to her, I was surprised she didn't get it. I guess what I mean is that when I became aware that I was the one making my past a big deal because I'd done such a good job of keeping my secret, I was caught off guard and I behaved terribly. I'm taking some time off from the market. I'm going to have a good conversation with your sister after the New Year, after the Ridgeways are long gone, and after I've had time to get over my anger as well as my behavior. I was so angry—angrier than I'd ever been—when I saw my old family at Bailey's. I left that existence, Becca, and I saw them being at Bailey's as an invasion of my life. We've coexisted in the same area for a long time without needing to cross paths."

I nodded. "That makes sense. Allison will be fine, Brenton. You don't need to worry about any of that."

"I hope not."

"You haven't gotten along with the Ridgeways for a long time?"

Brenton shook his head and half smiled. "Yeah, and here's the crazy part—Billie and I had a chance to talk last night at the parade. We might have made up if I'd just stretched my comfort zone a little. I've never wanted to before, but when I saw her last night, I had a small urge to want to try to make things better. Isn't that strange and ironic? All that anger, and them being at Bailey's and me being forced to see them might mean I'll be able to . . . well, to at least be civil to my siblings again. I would never, ever have guessed that would happen. Never."

"That's great. Family's important."

He waved away the comment.

"What in the world happened to cause such a falling-out?" It was the bottom-line question, and the answer to which may lead to the other answers that we all needed. I had to ask.

"I can't tell you, Becca. It's none of your business. I didn't tell Sam, either. I'm not under arrest; he can't hold it against me that I won't tell him." Some of that angry, defensive Brenton was showing, but just a little.

"But what if the answer leads to a killer? Don't you think you should tell Sam, just in case?"

"I don't know who killed Reggie Stuckey, but I don't think my decision to part ways with my family, or the things that were behind that decision, had anything do with his murder. That was a long time ago, Becca."

"Do you have any idea who might have killed him?"

Brenton looked at me with true surprise. "I don't have even a small clue that could help. I haven't spent time around tree farmers, or Reggie Stuckey, for years."

"But the Ridgeways had, right?"

"They were all in the tree business. Maybe they had work, business things together. I just don't know what any of them have been doing."

I nodded slowly and hoped he'd add more. He didn't.

"Let me grab the coffee," he said as he stood and went back to the kitchen.

It seemed like knowing that Brenton's last name used to be Ridgeway *should* answer a multitude of questions, but now I wondered if that knowledge would only lead to more questions.

After he handed me the coffee and sat in the chair again, I decided to try something else.

"Brenton, have you been making and leaving me Christmas ornaments?"

"What? No."

"Shoot. I wish it were you."

"What's going on?"

I sighed. I counted on the fact that I wasn't wrong about my instincts regarding Brenton. I counted on the fact that for years I'd known Brenton, the homemade dog-biscuit guy, and we'd been friends enough that we could trust each other with at least some of our more minor secrets. I could tell him about the ornaments and my idea that they were clues, puzzle pieces that might lead to a killer. If I shared a little, maybe he'd share more about his breakup with his family.

When I was finished describing each and every ornament, he said something that turned out to be the biggest surprise of our whole conversation, something that unfortunately only led to even more questions.

He sat forward in the chair, his elbows on his knees and his eyes absently locked on the baseball cap. "Becca, I might know who is making them. I'll find out first and get back to you."

"Really? Why can't you just tell me now?" I said.

"Because I think you're 100 percent correct. I think the ornaments are clues, and I think they might lead to a killer, but I just want a little more information before I make such an accusation."

I gulped a mouthful of coffee. I'd hoped for more information, but this was even bigger than his family breakup. "Brenton, please tell me."

"I'm sorry, Becca. I can't. Not yet."

"Will you at least tell Sam?"

"When I know for sure, he will be the first I tell." Brenton smiled, but it was a gentle, somewhat sad smile. "But I'll be sure and tell you second."

"Thanks," I said. I couldn't help myself.

Twenty-one

Sam was expecting my phone call, but he wasn't expecting the news that Brenton told me that he may know who made the ornaments. I didn't see how I could have kept that from the police. Sam said he would go directly back out to Brenton's house to get the rest of the story.

I was a little thrilled that I'd been able to wrangle more out of Brenton than he had. Sam was just plain appreciative, and also worried.

He was also adamant that I was done investigating for the day. He didn't want me talking to anyone else until he understood what Brenton thought the ornaments meant. He told me to go to Bailey's or to help my parents get ready for the night's parade festivities, or to help Allison with something.

I thought he was cute when he was so adamant, but I didn't tell him that.

I was also out of questions. I'd asked everyone everything

I thought was pertinent. I'd wanted to ask Brenton how it had been to be married to Stephanie Frugit, but that was just plain curiosity. Maybe someday I'd find out more. But I'd learned lots about past personal lives of people I knew, people I'd just met, and people I'd only heard of. If nothing else, my perspective had changed. Reputations weren't always to be believed.

But sometimes they were—this thought, this simple idea, took root in the back of my mind and didn't want to let go. People sometimes did, in fact, live up to their reputations. But though the thought wouldn't leave me alone, I couldn't attach it to anything important regarding the murder.

I shook my head, mumbled something even I didn't understand, and then steered the truck downtown.

Both Allison and I had thought our parents would leave Monson shortly after the holidays. We thought they'd pack up the motor home and head out on another wide-open road adventure, but they hadn't said or done one thing to confirm those suspicions. They'd moved into a small house they owned but had previously rented out on the edge of downtown, and instead of it seeming like a temporary situation, they'd been doing upkeep on it that made it seem more permanent.

I even thought I'd seen a sketch of some spring garden ideas. When I told Allison about the sketch, we decided not to question or push them to tell us their plans. They still had just enough hippie left in them that they might rebel against our wishes that they stick around. Rebellion would always be a familiar behavior pattern.

Jason and Polly Robins had probably experienced more than their two daughters ever could imagine. As parents they didn't talk openly about all of those experiences, but frequently Allison and I would catch a look, a glance, a shared smile that tied them together, perhaps because the end result had been a short stint in jail, an adventure into something that was illegal, or at least skirted along the edge of legal.

Anyway, neither my sister nor I wanted the details. We were fine not knowing all of our parents' secrets or even most of them.

Jason and Polly had changed since they'd left for their previous road trip about two and a half years earlier, though. They'd become more conservative in their dress and less vocal when it came to discussing issues that were important to them. They'd never been particularly argumentative, just firm in their beliefs—and firm that everyone else had a right to believe whatever they believed; live and let live. Now my parents just didn't feel the need to talk about their causes as much.

Allison thought it had something to do with the fact that Mathis was, at the age of almost three, a sponge to the world and the people he loved and spent the most time with. He'd pick up a word or a mannerism so quickly that we all tried to be as well behaved as possible around him.

I disagreed with my sister on this point, though. I thought our parents were simply mellowing. They still cared fervently about their causes, but they preferred to spend their time baking bread, fixing the roof, or sketching plans for a spring garden rather than throwing themselves completely into causes.

And, despite the panicked nature that must have characterized Vivienne Norton's plea for decorating help, I imagined my parents were thrilled to take on the task, even if it had required that my mother take extra doses of allergy medication. One of their biggest causes, their biggest loves, was their hometown of Monson. Being able to help make the Christmas parade a more enjoyable and better event was right up their collective alley.

I found them both on Main Street and both on ladders this time, but neither of the ladders was high or wobbly. They were placing poles with wide weighted bottoms next to each of the fully decorated trees. Then, they'd step up onto a short step ladder and thread a pennant onto the top part of the pole. Each pennant had been painstakingly drawn with the tree winner's name.

"Did you paint all of these?" I asked Mom as I handed her the pennant she was reaching for.

"Your dad helped. It wasn't too difficult."

"Oh, Mom, I should be a better help to you."

"My dear, you have a million things going on, and you've had to bake all those cookies. They're delicious, by the way."

"Thank you."

"Polly!" Dad called from a few trees down. He was standing next to a tree that was all silver and gold—tinsel, ornaments, miniature wreaths. At the moment, the entire tree was sparkling from a thin ray of sun, which had peeked through a slit in the gathering and darkening clouds.

"Yes, dear?"

"I don't think I have the right winner. Who was highest bidder on this one?"

Mom reached into her back jeans pocket and pulled out a folded sheet of paper. "Dell, the pharmacist."

"Nope," Dad said as he looked at the pennant, "this doesn't say Dell."

"Check the stack on the library steps." Mom pointed behind him.

"Should I do it for him?" I asked.

"Don't be silly. He's right there, he'll figure it out."

"Is it really just the two of you doing this? There must be fifty trees this year."

"Fifty-three, and no, Vivienne and a couple of the other officers helped with the other side. They had to leave. Sam called them in for something. They'll be back if they have the time."

I glanced down the street, past Dad and past the line of trees, to the building that housed the small police department. I wanted to run down and see what was going on, if Sam had any more news from Brenton, but I couldn't have abandoned my mom even if she'd told me to.

I grabbed some poles and some pennants and followed along on her list as the three of us finished the task. Sam and I had bid on a few trees, but we hadn't won any of them. The train tree went to someone I didn't know from Smithfield.

After the pennants were set up, we brought out the tables and set them up in the middle of the street so that people could sit and visit or eat their treats, or just look at the trees. The tables had been stored inside the shoe store. Once we pulled them out, we taped holiday-decorated paper tablecloths onto them.

Neither rain nor snow was in the forecast, but the clouds made me wonder if we might end up with a little weather anyway. South Carolina didn't see much snow, but we sometimes got a little in Monson. And, sometimes the white stuff would actually accumulate in the higher elevations. I'd even heard of a few incidents of blinding snow up toward the Ridgeway Farm. A light dusting would be a welcome addition to the evening's event, but the paper tablecloths would quickly become soggy if there was too much moisture.

Mom, using her Mom superpower and her sometimes achy-with-a-storm-on-the-way knee, predicted that nothing would fall from the sky until at least the next day. I'd never known her to be wrong.

The setup duty from the day before had been the biggest chunk of work, so today's labors were somewhat lighter, but I was glad I'd come along to help at least a little.

Once Mom okayed that we were done until the festivities began, or until a strong wind caused a disaster that we'd have to clean up, I convinced them to walk around the corner for a break at the local Maytabee's Coffee Shop. My jams, preserves, and syrups had a good chunk of shelf space at the chain's five South Carolina shops. The Monson location had just acquired a new manager and she didn't know that I was one of their suppliers. I could shop them and my inventory anonymously. Today, I was startled to see that my product supply was low—I didn't know if I'd missed an e-mail requesting more or if the new manager hadn't figured out all the ins and outs of her job yet. I bought three coffees, and as I carried them to a table in the back I made a mental note to call or e-mail the owner for an update before Monday.

"We spoke with Allison briefly last night, but we haven't had much time. Is she okay—I mean, after the terrible murder at Bailey's?" Mom said after she took her first sip.

"I think she's okay. It was bad, though," I said.

"I can only imagine. Does Sam have any good leads?" Mom asked.

Both she and Dad had taken to Sam easily. They'd done the same with Ian and my two ex-husbands. Had they suspected I was facing something more challenging or dangerous than flakiness from my husbands, they would have jumped in and battled to defend me. And I was certain they felt a kindred connection to Ian, with his long hair and his seven tattoos, but they hadn't squawked when he and I had parted romantic ways. They seemed to be very fond of Sam.

"I think he has a bunch of weak answers. Hopefully, something will lead somewhere." I took a gulp of hot coffee. "You two have always been interested in the South Carolina political scene, right?"

"Sure," they both said.

"Do you remember a state senator from the late eighties named Evelyn Rasmussen Stuckey?"

Mom and Dad both laughed.

"Of course," Mom said. "We both worked on her campaign."

I should have known that Mom and Dad would either have worked for a politician or against them. It hadn't even occurred to me to ask them earlier. I needed to use my connections better.

"She was married to the guy who was killed, Reggie Stuckey."

"That's right! It's been so long that I forgot about all that," Mom said.

Dad said, "Evelyn's husband was so behind the scenes that he didn't have much to do with her work. I don't think

I ever even met him, but I knew he had a Christmas tree farm. I think he supported her career aspirations just fine, but then after his alleged affair—well, things were bound to go south from there."

I blinked. "So it was Reggie who had the . . . an affair?"

"Well, we think that's what happened. It was the best conclusion we could come up with at the time. Reggie had an affair. Evelyn was so embarrassed and horrified by the infidelity that she just quit. She didn't want her personal life to become public."

"The best conclusion?" I said. "You don't know for sure that that's what happened?"

"No," Dad said. "Times were different back then, Becca. Affairs and scandals are the common stuff of today's politics, and even though the same things went on back then, it was truly cause for a politician's ruin. Something happened that saddened Evelyn or humiliated her to the point that she gave up on her ambitions. We all suspected that there was an affair, and I think someone had some pictures or something. Do you remember, Polly?" Dad said.

"Kind of."

I took a sip of coffee and pondered the fact that in today's world, a politician or one of their family members could exhibit unacceptable behavior and still remain in politics. "Was she maybe being blackmailed with the pictures?"

"Uh, not sure I remember that," Dad said.

"It's terrible that her career was ruined because of her husband's indiscretion," I said.

"Yes. Now such circumstances would create a few news stories, some twittering, or whatever that's called, and it would most likely blow over. The politician could easily continue to serve. Different times back then. Evelyn just didn't want to deal with it, I guess," Dad said.

"Do you know who was the affair with?" I said. I'd literally crossed my fingers around my coffee cup with the hope their answer would give me a big, more important piece of the puzzle.

Mom shrugged. "That's probably the biggest reason Evelyn quit, so the press wouldn't take a deeper, closer look at the details. I never knew who the affair was with. As far as I know, she mostly kept it to herself."

"I would think the press would have looked more closely when she quit. They'd want to know why. They'd find out about the other person and report the details," I said.

"Well, maybe, but her quitting probably had a different effect then than it would nowadays. Yes, there was some investigation, but journalism was different and journalists liked Evelyn. Maybe they just respected her privacy," Mom said.

"And," Dad said thoughtfully, "I really do remember something about some pictures, but not much happened with them."

"I can't help but think blackmail was involved then," I said.

Mom tapped her finger on her lips. "No, I think she simply didn't let it get that far. Again, if I remember correctly, she just quit. She might have actually wanted the pictures to surface once she stepped down. She was very bitter toward her husband, who became her ex-husband very soon after she left the public eye."

"Excuse me a minute," I said. I pulled out my cell phone. Sam answered on the first ring, though I could tell he was in a hurry. "Sam, Reggie *was* the one to have the affair."

I explained to him my parents' memories and then asked him if he'd learned anything new.

"No, I haven't, but I'm having a hard time finding Brenton. I went to his house after you and I talked and he wasn't there."

"He must have left right after I did."

"I'd like to find him. I will. I'll let you know when I do."

"What's wrong?" Dad said after I ended the call.

"Sam appreciates the lead and he's going to talk to Evelyn," I said, not wanting to worry them with other details.

"Evelyn's still around?" Mom sat up straight.

"Yes, she goes by Evie and she has an egg stall at the Smithfield Market."

"We'll have to go see her," Dad said.

"She's odd, probably very different than when you knew her," I said.

"We're kind of different, too," Mom said. "I look forward to seeing her no matter what."

I tried to help jog their memories about who Reggie might have had the affair with, but it didn't help at all. I had my own suspicions, but I didn't want to plant false seeds so I kept those thoughts to myself.

Finally, I sent them home to take a nap before the evening's parade. I also went home to Hobbit. I still had cookies to bake, and even thought I doubted I'd be able to stop my mind from whirring enough to close my eyes, a nap might do us all some good.

Twenty-two

"That's it, I'm installing cameras and maybe a safe room for Hobbit," I muttered to myself as I pulled onto my driveway.

A car was parked at the bottom of the drive, close to the house. But Hobbit sauntered around the old, white sedan with her ears perked and her tail wagging; she wasn't distressed by whoever was visiting.

I parked the truck at an angle that would accommodate both me hoisting Hobbit into the passenger side and then us making a quick getaway, if need be.

My visitor appeared from around the house and waved happily.

"Mamma!" I said as I got out of the truck. "I didn't even know you had a car. I thought you just drove a truck."

Mamma laughed. "Well, gas being the price it is, I got this old thing to help with mileage. Traveling back and forth between Monson and Smithfield was getting expensive."

"Makes sense to me. Come on in. I'll get us something to drink."

"No, I can't stay." Mamma looked at her watch. "I've got to meet Carl. I thought I might see you tonight at the parade, but I wanted to talk to you as privately as possible. Sorry I didn't call first."

"No problem," I said. "What's up?"

"Well, I felt so awful about my thoughts about Evie that I tried to talk to her, be friendly, you know."

"How'd that go?"

"At first she was pretty snippy, but I hung in there and soon enough we started chatting in a more civilized tone." Mamma cringed but recovered quickly. "I kind of pride myself on being open-minded and friendly, Becca. It takes an open mind to look at me and not see a floozy, I know that. I look the way I want to look. I assume that other people do the same. But I think I forgot myself with Evie. She's cantankerous and grumpy, but once we sat together and really talked, I realized that she's probably just a lonely old woman who could use a friend or two. Well, anyway, enough of my shame." Mamma sighed. "She actually started opening up about her past. I had to push her. I had Addy fill me in on what he knew and I . . . well, I asked her some direct questions."

"I bet she either disliked or respected those direct questions."

Mamma smiled and nodded. "She respected them, just not immediately."

"Sounds about right."

"Anyway, she divorced Reggie because he had an affair."

I didn't want to ruin her excitement by telling her I already had the news she thought was new so I just said, "I wondered. Did she tell you a name, by chance?"

Mamma shook her head. "It's why she left politics, though. She was embarrassed and knew that Reggie's indiscretion would be used against her, or she thought it would."

"Back then it probably would have," I said.

"Maybe, but I think there's more. I think Evie, Evelyn, was proud of her position, proud of her marriage—maybe too proud. She couldn't handle being seen as imperfect. I really think that had more to do with it," Mamma said. "It was all about her ego."

I thought about it and then nodded. I wasn't much for psychology, but Mamma's words made sense. Lots of people in lots of different professions, politicians included, were frequently driven by ego.

"So," Mamma continued, "here's something else that surprised me. Evie said that before her ex-husband was killed, she and he had started talking again. He'd called her out of the blue and she'd wondered why. Well, he was friendly for a while, but then he told her that he'd recently started seeing the woman again, the woman he had the affair with all those years ago. Evie was under the impression that Reggie was seeking her approval."

"Let me guess, she didn't approve," I said.

"Not at all."

"I'm not surprised."

"She said it . . . what was the word she used? Riled? Yes, it riled her feathers—not ruffled—something fierce. Even after all these years, it upset her. She didn't like that it upset her."

That was a long time to hold a grudge, but infidelity wasn't ever easily forgiven.

"Did she get upset while she was talking to you?" I asked.

"Yes, and . . . well, this is rotten of me, but now I have to tell on her."

"Tell on her?"

"Yes, the day you all found Reggie? Well, Evie didn't come in to the market that entire day. She always comes in to the market. It's what she does, all she does as far as I can tell. Addy was worried about her, I remember."

"There could have been a good reason," I said as I tried to imagine Evie stabbing Reggie with a tree spike. It wasn't all that difficult to picture.

"Yes, there could have been, but she said one more thing that got my attention. She said that she's 'going *back* to Monson tonight, to visit the tree parade.' She said 'back,' so I asked her when she'd last been to Monson, and she quit talking."

"Interesting." It was, but I wasn't sure it meant much of anything.

"I thought so, too, particularly if her last visit was the day Reggie was killed. Anyway, I stopped by the police station but Sam wasn't there and I don't really know any of the other officers. Your house is on my way to Carl's, so I stopped. I hope it's okay that I was walking around."

"Of course," I said. Mamma didn't need to know she might have prompted me to finally improve my currently nonexistent security system.

"Good. I gotta go, but it's the last thing that Evie told me that probably kept me from telling the other officers. Sam . . . well, Sam's a friend, and I knew he wouldn't think it was weird, but even though Evie wouldn't tell me who the affair was with, she did tell me what the woman looked like."

"And?"

"Me. She looked like me—according to Evie, pretty, blonde, with a big bosom—and I'm quoting that last part. I'd just say 'boobs.'"

The world wasn't full of women who looked like Mamma Maria, at least not naturally. The doll ornament had made me hyperaware of pretty, blonde women. I knew Mamma hadn't had an affair with Reggie; she was far too young. Mamma's conversation with Evie made me realize I'd been on the right track, though—the doll had been meant to portray Reggie's illicit girlfriend. At that point, I thought that Patricia Archer or Stephanie Frugit must be the other woman. In my mind, I thought I could narrow it down further. Stephanie Frugit might live a lonely, isolated life, but I didn't think she'd sought out an old love. She didn't strike me as a person who ever went backward. If anyone, at the moment, Patricia was the most suspicious.

As for Evie not being at the Smithfield Market the day Reggie was killed, that might be important news. Sam needed to know about that, and he needed to know that she had plans to be at the parade that evening.

"I'll tell Sam," I said.

As Mamma walked to her car, she added, "Look for her tonight. Have Sam look for her. I can't imagine that she's attending the Christmas tree parade in Monson without a mission in mind. Maybe she's going to confront the other woman—or something worse."

Could she really be a threat? Anything was possible.

"I'll call Sam right away," I assured her.

Hobbit and I watched as Mamma steered the sedan up and out of the driveway.

"Did you hide inside first or did you just greet her without regard for your own safety?" I said to Hobbit.

The tail wag told me she'd done the second one. I sighed. "Come on. Let's call Sam."

Sam still hadn't tracked down Brenton. I told him the latest addition to the case and my thoughts about Stephanie and Patricia, but he was still hesitant to base suspicions on looks.

He was also interested in Evie's actions, both this evening and the day of Reggie's murder.

We made arrangements to meet at the parade. I was glad we'd spent yesterday evening enjoying our time together, because it sounded like Sam might be pulled a few different directions this evening. Duty called.

Hobbit would be a fine date anyway.

After some baking time and a short, restless nap, I loaded more cookies into the truck. I helped Hobbit into the passenger side and we headed for downtown. I'd switched into jeans and a thicker sweater because of the increasing chill in the air. The quickly darkening sky showed no sign of stars or moon. The chill was a good fit for the upcoming holiday and the air smelled perfectly clean and crisp.

Somehow the clouds formed a sort of pocket, and the lights from the decorations—those on the trees and those everywhere else—bounced off the bottom of the dark ceiling above and made it seem like downtown Monson and the parade were parts of our own little private, well-lit party. UFOs wouldn't spot us under the cloud cover this night. I liked the pocket, but I also suddenly hoped for a little snow.

No matter the paper tablecloths, a dust of white would be a perfect touch.

With no sign of Sam yet, Hobbit and I traveled slowly down one side of the parade and up the other. The crowd was huge, but only a little bigger than normal. The Saturday-night group was traditionally bigger than Friday's, and last night's had been healthily large. The thirty-minute trip from Smithfield was usually too far for a big influx, but I suspected the neighboring town's contingent was larger this year than in previous years. Finding a place to park had been unusually difficult and the number of unfamiliar faces meant the parade's reach was only growing.

I enjoyed looking at the trees again and consuming a multitude of treats, but I was anxious, too. I hoped I'd find or hear from Sam soon. I hoped he'd found Brenton and someone who looked like Mamma Maria who claimed to have had an affair with Reggie. I hoped Evie wasn't spiking someone to death.

"Miss Becca," a voice behind me said.

"Evie, hi! What a surprise," I said when I turned. Speak of the devil. And, there were no spikes in sight.

She was different. It was as though she'd cleaned up, brushed her hair. I wasn't much for frou-frou, but Evie carried herself a little differently, as though she'd been infused with a boost of confidence; or maybe it was self-respect.

"I haven't been to this neck of woods in a long time. It's good to get out a bit," she said.

If that was true, she hadn't come to Monson the day Reggie was killed like Mamma had perhaps thought. I hoped it was true.

I didn't truly understand why Evie had come to the parade, but I thought her appearance must have something to do with the fact that there was no chance she'd be running into her ex-husband. I hoped that wasn't because of something she'd done. For some reason, I'd taken a quick liking to her.

"It's good to see you. I'd love to grab you a hot chocolate or something." *And let Sam know you're here,* I thought.

"Oh, no, I'm fine. I don't want to hold you up, either. I'm here to look around, hopefully get into the holiday spirit some. Hello there," she said to Hobbit as she leaned over to scratch behind my dog's ears. Hobbit liked making new friends who knew how to scratch behind her ears.

"I wanted to talk to you again soon anyway. I was talking to my parents about our visit and they not only remember you, they worked on your campaign."

Evie straightened up and her eyebrows rose. "Really?"

"Yes, their names are Jason and Polly Robins."

Evie smiled. "This world just gets smaller all the time. I'll be; you're their daughter?"

"One of them. My sister, Allison, is the Bailey's manager."

Evie laughed. "I'll be," she repeated. "Any chance your parents are here?"

"I'd say there's a huge chance. We'll find them."

We walked together, very tall Evie and short me, with Hobbit in between us. I thought about asking her for details about the woman who looked like Mamma Maria, but I didn't want her to regret that she'd confided in Mamma, so I kept that to myself. For now.

It wasn't until I'd reunited Evie with my parents that something very obvious became a solid and probably important thought.

Evie—Evelyn to Polly and Jason—was hugging Mom and telling her that she actually looked better now than she did in the eighties, that she'd made a good hippie but the grown-up clothes and hair suited her much better. Sam had also probably contributed to the idea that pinged in my head when he was reticent to base suspicions on looks.

I agreed with Evie that Mom looked great, and so did Dad, but they also looked different. It would have been impossible not to look older, no matter how well you took care of yourself.

And Mamma Maria's twin from the 1980s just might not look like the Mamma of today.

I stepped away from Mom, Dad, and Evie and gathered my thoughts as I looked out to the crowd. Unless I had snapshots from the past, how would I know who might have looked like Mamma and the ornament?

Or perhaps the woman had aged extraordinarily well and had just changed her hair color. That took me back to Stephanie. Had she been blonde instead of strawberry-blonde back then? I didn't know.

Sometimes chance plays a big role in what feels like a futile search, but it is a rare gift and one that should never be ignored.

As I was drowning in my own disconnected ideas, I happened to glance across the street and see two people I'd recently met: Joel and Patricia Archer. They'd been cagey, uncomfortable, and distant. And what had Gellie said about them? That they used to work for Reggie and that they offered to help out again this year with the trees. They were currently inspecting a patriotic tree, all red, white, and blue. They were deep in conversation with each other. I looked at Evie and considered her quick transformation into someone who might want to step back into society. I hated to interrupt, but not enough.

"Excuse me, Evie," I said as I put one hand on her shoulder and pointed with the other one. "Do you know them?"

She squinted across the street, even lifted her glasses once, replaced them, and squinted some more. "I don't think so."

"They're Joel and Patricia Archer. They used to work for Reggie, but I'm not sure when."

She shook her head. "I don't remember them, Becca, but it has been a long time."

I looked at Evie, then at Mom and Dad, who had both raised their eyebrows slightly. They knew I was searching for something.

"Okay, good to know. Sorry to interrupt."

I left them to their conversation again, turning back to watch across the street. My thoughts were still jumbled, but they came to quick order a second later.

Patricia Archer peered furtively in every direction. The crowd was so busy enjoying the parade that she thought no one was paying any attention to her, but there we were, Hobbit and I, watching her every move.

Once convinced she could get away with it, she reached to the tree and plucked off a small three-by-five flag ornament. I didn't know for sure, but I thought it was painted wood. She dropped it into her bag and then turned to Joel, who'd been blocking her from one side as well as pretending not notice what his wife was doing.

My mouth fell open. I was torn between yelling and telling my mom on her. A part of me wanted to run across the street and confront her; another part just wished I hadn't seen the theft.

I didn't excuse my quick departure. I just stepped away from my parents and Evie and into the street. The large crowd and my short stature made it difficult to both see and move quickly.

A bunch of "excuse me's" later, Hobbit and I reached the other side of the street and the red, white, and blue tree. Joel and Patricia had moved on, but I didn't know in which direction.

I pulled out my phone and was relieved that Sam answered on the first ring.

"I just saw someone steal an ornament," I said.

"Who?"

I told him the details and he instructed me to meet him at the police station.

Hobbit and I hurried.

"There have been a lot of thefts," Sam said. "There always are, apparently. Considering the ornaments you've been given, we've been asking more questions of those who've decorated trees. A bunch of ornaments go missing every year. It's a hazard of having the parade out in the open and amid a crowd. Gus said there are so many fingerprints on the goldfish that we'd never be able to figure out who gave it to you."

"What about the cameras? Anything?"

"I'm afraid not. None of them were pointed toward the goldfish tree."

He handed me a cup of what I knew was the worst coffee ever brewed, and sat in the chair behind his desk. We were the only ones in the station.

"That's not very helpful in trying to find whoever's been leaving me the ornaments." I took a sip; I was right, it was terrible. I tried to control the reactive face contortion that always came with police station coffee, but I was sure I wasn't successful. Sam either didn't notice or had seen the reaction so often that he ignored it.

"Not at all." Sam sighed. "Vivienne's tracking down Joel and Patricia. She'll get the flag back and she'll scare them enough that they'll admit if they've been your Secret Santa. She's good at that."

"What do you suppose Patricia used to look like? I mean, she has the long, blonde hair, but when she was younger, maybe she looked like Mamma," I said.

"Maybe, but I think her act of theft makes her more suspicious than her hair."

"You think I'm being silly?"

"No, Becca, I don't think you're being anything but you. I may not understand the way everything in your mind works, and I assure you, sometimes you make me want to laugh like I've never laughed before, but only in good ways. And then sometimes you put it all together despite not one iota of proper police procedure. It's probably one of the things that made me . . ." He stopped.

I froze as I waited, but he took too long, and I've always had such a problem with patience.

"I'm crazy about you, Sam Brion," I said, bitter coffee aftertaste and all.

Sam smiled and the phone on his desk rang. He put his

hand on the handset but didn't lift it right away. "It's about time you realized that. And, just in case you haven't figured it out, I feel the same way about you. I'm head over heels for you, Becca Robins. I have been since the first moment I questioned you regarding the gruesome murder of Matt Simonsen. We'll graduate to the *L* word soon, I'm sure of it." He picked up the handset. "Sam Brion."

I was sure I'd care about who killed Reggie Stuckey again soon, just not for a few minutes.

Twenty-three

Such romantic moments would be typically followed up by more romantic moments, but it wasn't meant to be that night.

I lost count of the leads Sam mentioned that he had to chase down, and then I lost track of him. I wasn't able to find my parents again. I wasn't able to find anyone. Hobbit and I wandered a little, helped some of the highest bidders load their trees, and then we went home.

I woke early the next morning, excited about the idea of Sam and I cutting down our own tree but concerned he wouldn't be able to take the time away.

I got ready quickly and pulled out my phone just as I was hurrying to the kitchen to start the coffee and let Hobbit out.

"Hey, Becs," Sam said as he answered. "I wanted to call, but then it got late and I didn't want to wake you."

"Everything okay?"

"Oh, yeah, just police stuff. Don't know much more of

anything yet. Still looking for Joel and Patricia, and Brenton. It can take time."

"I know your work should come first, but do you think you'll able to go up to Ridgeway Farm?"

"Yes, but I'm in Smithfield now. Should we just meet there?"

"Sure," I said, more pleased that he'd be able to go than disappointed we wouldn't be going together. "What's in Smithfield?"

"Evelyn Rasmussen. I didn't get a chance to talk to her last night. I'm going to in about twenty minutes. I don't expect it to take long. If you leave there in about a half hour, we should both make it up to Ridgeway at about the same time."

"I can do that. Oh, Sam!" I'd made it to the kitchen and had finally taken the time to look out a window. "It's snowing."

Sam laughed. "A little."

"That's perfect; a perfect day for going to chop down our own tree."

"I agree. The roads aren't bad, but drive carefully and I'll see you in about an hour."

"Good luck with Evie."

"Thanks."

"It's snowing, girl!" I said to Hobbit.

I threw on a jacket and we ventured outside to the chilly air and the lightly falling snow. A dusting of white covered everything, but it wouldn't last long and it didn't seem like it would get heavy.

The morning was perfect; Hobbit agreed. Our morning run made both my lungs and toes cold, but the chill was welcome.

Ridgeway Farm was in a hilly pocket of South Carolina.

It would probably have been fine to take Hobbit along, but I'd forgotten to ask Denny, Billie, or Ned about their rules regarding pets, and I didn't want her to have to sit in the truck and look out longingly to trees she'd never be able to explore if they didn't welcome dogs on the property. Reluctantly, I left her home again, but since it was cooler she chose a spot by the couch inside. If and when it warmed up, she'd use the doggy door and go back outside.

I had another heart-to-heart with her regarding the importance of being aware and being careful. I thought she might be getting tired of the lecture.

She looked at me with one high eyebrow as if to tell me it was time for me to get over being concerned about leaving her alone. We'd had one scary incident but no others.

"Okay, girl, I'll work on it," I said before I left, making sure the door was securely locked behind me. I might stop lecturing, but I doubted I'd be able to stop double-checking the door.

As I drove, I sang Christmas carols aloud because I couldn't find any on my AM-only radio.

Though the concern about Reggie's killer had returned, it was close to impossible not to be content and downright happy about so many things. My life hadn't ever been tragic or sad, but I'd made my share of mistakes and had my share of lonely holidays. Both my divorces had become final during the month of November. I'd had two particularly strange Christmases where I didn't want to be around anyone but myself and, after the second split, Hobbit. And I'd been the one to prompt the separations. Divorce was usually awful, even if it was necessary.

But this year was different and wonderful.

"And, I'm not going to jinx it by dwelling on it. I'm just going to enjoy it as long as possible," I said in between "Jingle Bells" verses.

The turnoff to Ridgeway Farm from the main highway was marked by two large hand-carved signs. "This way to Ridgeway," they both read, each with large arrows pointing off into the hills. The borders of both signs were made up of wood-burned pine trees.

For the first time ever, I turned onto the road. I couldn't believe I'd never been there before. I hoped Denny would let me use the ax to cut down the tree. I hoped I could handle it.

The elevation increased as I drove on, which meant there was more snow, but still not too much, and not enough to be of concern.

The forest on each side of me was full of leafless oaks. I kept an eye out for when the oaks transformed into pines, but it looked like I'd have a number of hilly curves to maneuver before I made it to the farm.

The road was twisty enough that when my cell phone buzzed I pulled over before I answered it.

"Sam? You on your way?"

The only words I heard were, "Yes . . . there . . . careful . . . file . . . Evelyn."

"I'm almost there," I said with the hope that he'd understand more from me than I did from him. "The road isn't too snowy, just curvy."

"Wait . . ."

"Yeah, I won't start without you." I laughed.

The phone went dead, so I dropped it on the seat and put the truck back into drive.

I may have thought that Reggie Stuckey's farm was

spectacular and wonderful in a Christmas card kind of way, but Ridgeway Farm was a whole new level of stunning.

The curvy road suddenly ended and straightened out as though it were an arm gesturing forward. *Just take a look at this place.*

Ridgeway Farm was a little slice of heaven. The forest of oak trees was suddenly behind me, and after a short, fifty-yard drive, those tall trees weren't even in my peripheral vision. Somehow I had been deposited into a wonderful and scent-filled pocket of pine, and only pine, in never-ending, neat rows. Because of the slopes and hills I could see that the rows were made up of different-sized trees. I'd ask Denny about harvest time and how long a tree needed to grow before it could be harvested. I'd ask about what it took to take care of the trees. I suddenly wanted to know everything there was to know about growing Christmas trees.

Amid the trees, in a small but groomed clearing, were two giant barns flanking a house that was so idyllic it was probably made of gingerbread.

"Wow," I said as I stopped the car. The entire scene might have been as charming without the thin layer of fresh white snow, but I felt privileged that I'd chosen this day to come up and chop down my first Christmas tree.

Denny had mentioned that the farm would be busy, but currently there were only a few vehicles parked in a small area next to one of the barns. I followed the obvious ruts in the path and pulled my truck next to a newer-model red version and stepped out into the heady-clean, crisp, naturally scented air. I wondered if I could get drunk if I sniffed too deeply for too long.

"Hello!" Ned called from directly outside the closest barn.

He was dressed in a red-plaid flannel shirt and jeans and had a Santa hat on his head.

"Hi," I said as I walked forward to meet him. "This place is amazing!"

"Thank you. We don't ever get tired of it. Your boyfriend here, too?"

"He's on his way, should be here in a minute."

Ned looked behind me toward what must have been the doors of the magical wardrobe I'd driven though. Surely this was the edge of Narnia.

"Is there a reason to be concerned?" I said.

"No, not at all," Ned said. "It's the first real snow this year, but it's not bad. There are no road issues yet."

"Yet?"

"There won't be, I'm overreacting. I always do with the first snow." Ned laughed.

I turned to look toward the oak forest. No Sam yet, but he was close behind, I was sure. I looked up at the thick clouds above. A few small, light snowflakes landed coldly on my cheeks, but I didn't think we were about to face a big storm.

"It's fine. Really," Ned said. "Go on into the barn. We've got warm drinks and places to sit while you wait. I need to head out to make sure a couple customers are doing all right out there, but Denny and Billie are both around. Make yourself at home. When your friend gets here, one of us will show you the ropes." Ned smiled reassuringly before he turned and stepped around the barn.

The tall, wide doors to the barn were closed but I could probably get in with just a pull of one of the handles. If I hadn't caught sight of Denny going toward the other barn across the property, I would have pulled one of those handles and gone into the warm place with the hot drinks and lots of seats.

I hello'd and waved at Denny, but he was focused on whatever task he'd set out to do. He wasn't dressed as Santa, but he did wear red jeans, a white sweater, and a hat that matched Ned's. He walked with long strides, his attention on the ground in front of him, his face serious as he pulled open a door and went inside. He carried an ax with sure authority; I wanted to hold an ax that way.

I was curious enough to follow him over to the other barn, but I wasn't sure what the rules were. Were customers invited anywhere, or just the barn that Ned had directed me to go into?

I looked around, and not finding anyone to ask, shrugged, and hurried across to the other barn.

Someone would stop me if I was doing something they didn't want me to do.

One of the two doors on the second barn was slightly ajar, and a yellow band of light trailed out to the dark ground that was now flecked with bits of snow.

"Denny?" I said as I leaned into the opening. There was no answer, but I thought that this barn might have been off-limits to customers. This was a storage barn, full of equipment, tools, and the random parts of things that could be found on most farms. "Denny?" I said a little louder.

There was still no answer but something metallic crashed somewhere toward the back corner, a corner that was mostly blocked and hidden by an old tractor.

I threaded my way through the opening and stepped carefully over and around debris.

The light became brighter as I got closer to the corner and then the space became fully illuminated when I moved all the way around the tractor.

I should have said "hello," or repeated "Denny," but I was struck momentarily silent by what I saw.

Santa's workshop would have been the first way to describe the corner space. A long worktable served as the focal point, but it was surrounded on three sides by shelves of tools and . . . toys? No, not toys; ornaments. Christmas tree ornaments filled the shelves. The ornaments were made of all different materials. Many had been painted, but some were just plain wood or metal or other material.

Denny had set the ax on the table and picked up something else. I was sure it was another ornament. In fact, it was a big ornament, made of wood and painted to look like an elf; an adult female elf.

Nothing I saw was in itself scary, but I was scared nonetheless. I felt like I needed to leave that barn. Quick.

But Denny finally heard me when I took a step backward, my heel hitting something wheel-like and creaky.

Denny's head shot up. He saw me and his face fell at first, but he tried to cover his surprise, and maybe disappointment, with a quick smile. "Becca, hello," he said, but he didn't put down the ornament. "I didn't know you were here yet."

"I just got here. Sorry to interrupt. I saw Ned and he told me to wait in the other barn but I saw you come in here . . ." I was talking too much.

"Oh, well, it's okay."

But it wasn't—I could hear that much in his voice.

Denny finally put the ornament on the table. As he walked

around toward me, I took another step backward, but this time I fell. As I went down, I reflexively put my hand out and it hit something sharp.

"Ow!" I said, but I still tried to get up.

Denny was by my side, pulling me up by my arm an instant later.

"I'm okay, I'm okay," I protested.

"No, you're not. You're bleeding. Profusely."

I looked at my hand. He was right. I didn't look down to see what had cut my palm because I was so surprised by all the blood dripping down my fingers.

"Come here, there's a sink and some towels over here," Denny said as he pulled me toward the workshop and farther from the front doors.

"I'm okay," I said again, but we both knew I wasn't.

Denny had my hand under running water only a few moments later.

"I've got to clean it. It'll sting," he said, and he didn't hesitate to squeeze a pile of liquid soap onto it.

It stung meanly; the pain would have made my knees buckle if I weren't so hyped with adrenaline. I had the presence of mind to notice that the goose bite was on my other arm, so now I was injured on both sides. I needed to get out of that barn.

"Here, we need to keep pressure on the towel. You don't need stitches, but I'll put some bandages on it."

I held my good hand over the towel as Denny continued to direct me by holding on to my arm. He guided me to a stool next to the table and told me to sit. I did, but I was plotting how I was going to get around both him and the table when even the briefest opportunity presented itself.

He clasped my hand and the towel between both of his hands. He was putting pressure right over the cut, but I could tell the bleeding hadn't slowed much. I still needed to get out of there. I eyed the ornament on the table. I'd been correct; it was in the shape of an adult female elf. It was made of a piece of wood and cleverly carved to show the elf's curvy features and pretty face. It wasn't Mamma Maria's face, but it was still familiar.

"You're a wood carver?" I asked, my voice cracking.

Denny's hard, focused gaze moved from our hands to my eyes. "I guess."

"You make a lot of Christmas ornaments?"

He kept hold of my injured hand as he pulled another stool a little closer. He sat and looked at me again.

"About that . . ." he began.

I swallowed hard.

A *clunk* sounded from the direction of the old tractor. I hoped more than I'd ever hoped for anything that it was Sam.

But it wasn't.

"Denny!" Billie said as she came into view. "I've been calling . . . oh, hi, Becca. You okay?" She hurried toward the table.

It might not have been Sam, but I was still happy to see her. At least there'd be a witness when Denny bludgeoned me with the ax.

It didn't take but another second, though, to realize that the trap I'd unintentionally walked into was now more deadly because Billie had joined us.

Like her brothers, Billie was dressed for the occasion. As at the parade, she was again dressed as an elf, her short, green dress tight around her thin but curvy frame. No matter how old she was, she still looked great. I looked at her pretty face and her short, brown hair—and I realized that she looked almost exactly like the carved ornament on the table. I would have bet a thousand jars of jalapeño-mint jelly that she used to have long, blonde hair.

Even though I'd pondered the idea of the killer changing her looks or her hair, now wasn't the moment to be proud of my investigative or deductive skills. No matter what, I'd still walked into a trap. But there still might be a way out of it.

"I'm okay." I laughed. "Denny's taking good care of me. I should probably just get home and get cleaned up better. I'll replace the towel."

"Oh, don't be silly," Billie the elf said. "You can clean up here. I'll take you into the house."

"It's . . ." I began.

"Denny, what's this?" Billie said as she reached for the ornament on the table.

"It's just another ornament for someone's tree," Denny said, but when his eyes landed on mine this time, I was sure he was telling me not to tell Billie about the other ornaments he'd made for me. It was such a simple glance, but I suddenly knew so much more. I put the pieces together in my head, or at least what I thought were the pieces.

Denny had been making the ornaments to lead me to Reggie's killer. Billie and Reggie had had the affair. That act of infidelity led to their father's stress-induced death, and Brenton leaving his family, Reggie and Evelyn divorcing, and in some way to Brenton and Stephanie's divorce, too, but that must have been some sort of aftershock. And, finally, that affair had somehow, some way, led to Billie killing Reggie. I could have been completely wrong, but I suspected I was close to the facts, just not the exact reasons behind them. Now wasn't the time to ask clarifying questions.

"It looks like me," Billie said. "I don't understand."

"Aw, Old Girl, I thought it would be a nice surprise." Denny shrugged.

Old Girl. It was a horrible nickname, but one that didn't seem to bother Billie. Somehow it must have become a term of endearment. And, her e-mail address.

And, Old Girl, Billie, was upset. She looked at Denny and then at me. She knew the reasons behind everything, of course, but she didn't know what I suspected and she didn't have all the facts. She didn't know about the ornaments I'd secretly received. I smiled weakly. But, unfortunately, she wasn't stupid.

"That day we saw you with the metallic tree ornament— where'd that come from?" Billie said to me.

"A friend," I said. Okay, so maybe she knew a little about the ornaments.

Billie's eyebrows came together and she blinked. She knew something was up, but she still didn't have all the pieces. "Denny?"

"Let's get Becca into the house, sis. Let's get her cleaned up before she bleeds all over the place," Denny said as his grip tightened on my arm and he pulled me off the stool.

"No. Wait." Billie moved to the other side of the table as if to form a barricade. She wouldn't have been able to manage blocking both of us if Denny hadn't left the ax right where she could grab it.

"Stop," she said when she had the ax in hand.

"Billie, come on, you're overacting to something," Denny said. "What's the problem, Old Girl?"

But she didn't buy into his act.

"No, something's going on and I want to know what it is," she said.

Denny sighed. He knew his sister, and I could tell he knew that stalling wasn't going to work much longer. He pulled me around the table, but Billie and the ax stopped us.

In the next instant, Denny threw me around his sister and toward the old tractor. "Run, Becca!" he said.

I stumbled but regained my footing and managed a quick glance back at the brother and sister before I hurried through the rest of the barn. Billie had the ax raised, but it looked like Denny might be able to fend her off. No matter what happened, I knew I needed to get out of there and get some help.

It seemed to take forever to step over and around all the junk but I finally made it outside—and right into a rare South Carolina blinding snowstorm.

I was so surprised that I froze in place for a second. I knew in which direction the house and other barn were located, but I could only see the outline of the house. The barn was hidden by a whiteout.

"Help!" I yelled.

I needed to keep moving, but the new layer of snow not only made everything blindingly white, it made for slick footing.

If I could just get to my truck, I could at least lock myself inside it. But I realized that wasn't the best plan when it came to getting away from an angry woman with an ax. And, I was leaving a bright-red trail of blood.

"Help!" I said again, but it felt like I'd been put into a vacuum. It seemed like my voice didn't travel much farther than my own nose.

I wrapped my hand more tightly with the bottom of my jacket and hoped the bloody trail wouldn't continue to form as I made a quick decision and ran into the space between the barn and the house and toward the trees.

I slipped and slid, but somehow I moved forward. When I came upon a tree, I hurried around it, hopefully hiding myself from the ax-wielding elf. If I kept going deeper into the copse, I'd hopefully find someone who was cutting down their tree and would have an ax I could borrow.

There'd been other vehicles out front. There were people here somewhere.

But I didn't even make it to the next tree before I heard Billie.

"Becca!"

How did I hear her when I could barely hear myself?

I froze in place again as huge snowflakes stung my warm face and got trapped by my eyelashes. I couldn't run. I wouldn't win.

But I could hide.

The pine tree next to me was huge, too huge, I thought, for any normal home. It belonged in a place like Rockefeller Center or perhaps the White House. Its lowest branches were close to the ground. I dove under and hoped for the best.

And I came upon the most wonderful surprise. It wasn't an ax, but it was something that might help. I'd seen something similar in Reggie Stuckey's garage and I thought I might have found a useful weapon.

I wasn't far from the barn, so I wasn't far from whatever outlet was needed to power the mechanism. It had a cord extending out from under the branches that was covered with snow once it was in the open, and I hoped it was plugged in. I couldn't sit up because of the branches, so I lay on my back with my head up against the trunk. And waited, though not for long.

"Becca, I know you're in there. The snow isn't falling fast enough to hide your footprints. And you're still bleeding. Come out," Billie said.

I remained silent.

"Fine. I'll come in then."

Billie started chopping at the low branches with the ax, causing my headroom to shrink and bits and pieces of tree to fall down on me. I tried to remain steady and keep my eyes clear, but it was difficult not to panic.

It took her only a few more seconds to create an opening where I could see her legs, but I didn't think she'd spotted me quite yet. I pulled my knees up and got ready.

Another three chops later, most of her was exposed.

Right before I thought she'd lean over and finally know without question that I was there, I aimed with my bloody hand, and fired.

And much to my relief and satisfaction, it worked.

Billie might have seen my footprints and blood, but the snow had completely covered the cord attached to the flocking gun that had been left under the huge tree. She had no idea I'd found a weapon. I hadn't been sure myself, but I'd been hopeful.

As I pulled the trigger, Billie's face quickly became covered in white. I didn't know if the substance stuck, stung,

Twenty-four

I found Denny still in the barn. As I hurried around the tractor, he was coming to. He said Billie had hit him, but fortunately had only used the side of the ax blade to knock him out. I helped him up and then we made sure Billie couldn't do any more damage to anyone.

The snow subsided about three minutes after we tied the elf's hands behind her back, and suddenly there were people everywhere. Ned and the other customers had been in the other barn, waiting out the quickly passing storm with hot cider and an assortment of candies and cookies. They had no idea what had gone on in and behind the other barn.

Sam's cruiser appeared from the oak forest and sped toward me when he noticed I might be injured.

Sam handcuffed Billie and put her in the backseat of his cruiser. He deposited me in the front seat, insisting that he take me to someplace where someone could look at my hand.

We'd retrieve my truck later. He might have someone make sure Billie's eyes were okay, but he made no promises.

He called in and requested that other officers get to the Ridgeway Farm quickly because he had an injured party he was going to take care of. I insisted on getting the whole story from Denny before we left.

It was what I'd finally concluded, but bigger. Yes, Billie and Reggie had had an affair and that was the reason Evelyn quit politics and she and Reggie divorced. Brenton, the youngest Ridgeway sibling, was devastated when the stress of learning of the affair killed their father, or so he concluded. Brenton's father's love of his home state of South Carolina ran deep, so deep that his respect for its political leaders couldn't be rattled. He wanted the parties involved in the affair to come forward, tell the world what they'd done, and confess, come clean like any honest citizen would do. Instead, everyone—except the youngest sibling, Brenton—insisted on keeping the truth hidden and secret. Mr. Ridgeway was devastated by what his daughter had done to another family and to a rising political career. When his father died, Brenton thought that it was the stress that killed him, but no one could ever be sure. Brenton became so angry at his siblings that he left them and hoped to never have close contact with them again.

Of course, Brenton was a great guy, but his loner ways were the result of choices he'd made, choices that were all about being alone and not being a part of the family that he was born into, a family that had disappointed him deeply. He wasn't just a private person; it turned out that he was a lonely, somewhat tortured private person. It wasn't discussed, but I suspected that those personal choices had played a big role in the failure of his marriage to Stephanie Frugit; the tragedy of this broke my heart.

After he and I had spoken and when Sam had gone in search of him again, Brenton hadn't left town, hadn't disappeared; he'd only gone to talk to Stephanie. Though he couldn't sustain a marriage, and though they hadn't remained close at all, she knew about his past. He could talk to her if he really needed to, and he suddenly felt like he needed to. He needed to talk through his suspicions regarding who he thought had murdered Reggie Stuckey. Even though he'd felt betrayed by and had left his family, it hadn't been easy for him to accept that one or all of them might have been involved in murder. He felt like Stephanie was really the only one who would understand. It didn't even occur to him that Sam might look for him again.

No one brought up the fact that it seemed Brenton was gone from his home overnight. I didn't know if he'd spent the night at Stephanie's house. If the police knew, I didn't push them, or Sam specifically, for the answer. It was none of my business, and I felt no need to overstep that boundary. I hoped a little, though, that a spark might have somehow been reignited between Brenton and Stephanie. I blamed it on the spirit of the season. Happy endings make good Christmas stories.

Billie and Reggie had been seeing each other again, but Reggie had tried to stop the re-acquaintance; this upset Billie. She told the police that originally she was only going to mess with him by calling him, disguising her voice, and pretending to be a representative from Bailey's inviting him to sell trees at the market. She thought she would make her ruse even bigger if she called the Bailey's owners telling them she represented Reggie. She would tell them that he wanted to sell his trees at the market. She expected to be told that the Ridgeways had the exclusive contract and that no one else was welcome, making Reggie look even worse when he showed up at the market with his truck full of trees. She was surprised when Mel told her he'd send her a contract just in case it worked out. She was so caught off guard that she gave him a made-up fax number. Then she doctored the Ridgeway contract and faxed it to Reggie. She hoped to put him in an inconvenient and uncomfortable situation; this was easily accomplished by his mere appearance at Bailey's. Billie claimed that she hadn't intended to kill Reggie. She claimed to become so angry with him, and that the stake was "right there. It just happened."

When he was greeted by Allison in the Bailey's lot, it didn't take long for Reggie to suspect that the mixup had somehow been caused by Billie. After the initial conversation, and without anyone noticing apparently, he called her to his truck and confronted her. She claimed that his accusations and continued insistence that they weren't going to ever be together again angered her enough to "just react" with the spike. She said it wasn't premeditated, and it might not have been, but we all hoped she'd never leave jail.

Billie had never gotten over the affair that had ruined so many lives. Over the years, Denny had watched her closely with the hope that she'd move on. Billie wouldn't tell anyone how she and Reggie had recently reconnected, but Denny blamed himself. He'd finally let down his guard, finally quit checking her whereabouts all the time, quit looking at her computer.

I shared with him the old adage—where there's a will, there's a way. If Billie wanted to get in touch with Reggie, she was going to find a way, even if it took her almost thirty years to do it.

Denny had known who'd killed Reggie, or he had suspected it. But his family was already broken, and he didn't want to be the one to turn in his sister. He'd lost a brother. If he was going to lose his sister, he didn't want it to be because of him. His loyalty was strange and misguided, but the idea of leaving ornament clues for me, for the person he knew was dating a police officer, was at least creative. The police didn't like his reasoning, but I hoped he wouldn't end up in too much trouble.

Later, all the ornaments and their messages made sense, sort of. The messages would have been difficult to interpret no matter what, but the last elf, if it had been delivered, might have brought everything together. Denny had stolen the eggs from Jeannine and the corn husks from Barry. He said he hadn't been sneaky about his crimes, but it seemed that most everyone trusts the guy who looks a little like Santa, particularly during the month of December. He did purchase the onion from Bo, though. As they were completing the transaction, the small copy of the state seal fell from his pocket to the ground. He counted on Bo not noticing or caring. In fact, Bo had noticed, but he just hadn't remembered the specifics of the moment until later when he heard the whole story. Denny had also stolen the fish ornament off Wanda's tree. He'd seen Billie and me beside the tree, and he hoped that our shared few moments of conversation would make me think of Billie when I saw a fish ornament again. His plan hadn't worked. He admitted it had been a desperate and poorly thought out attempt.

Billie had had long, blonde hair when she was younger, when the affair started. Actually, we did have proof of how she'd looked back then, but we hadn't noticed it. In the file full of Ridgeway articles we found in Reggie's desk were pictures from as far back as the late eighties. There was one small article, with one small picture of Reggie and Billie together at a tree farmers' event. They were young, happy, and in love; there wasn't any other way to describe the two people in the picture. I was still baffled that the affair hadn't been bigger news, or at least big enough for a reporter or two to dig up the dirty details. I'd never understand how covering those sorts of stories had changed so much over the years.

Since Sam and I still hadn't figured out what Denny was trying to tell us with the ornaments, he'd made one final gift, a well-crafted one this time. One that he hoped would clearly tell us that we needed to suspect Billie. He'd planned on leaving a note with it in my truck on the day we came to cut down our tree, though he still hadn't figured out what to say in the note. We didn't get that ornament.

And, we never did get a tree.

But, we had a pretty poinsettia plant.

"They were just thieves?" I said as I took the cup of hot chocolate from Sam.

He sat next to me on the couch. "Yep. Joel and Patricia Archer had worked for Reggie years earlier, but just by helping with the trees. This year, they also decided to steal some ornaments. They've stolen a lot of things. I think we're going to find lots of criminal behavior as we take a closer look. They're scam artists, but they aren't big-time as far as we can tell. They took advantage of Reggie's death to jump in and earn his money. I think they were trying to figure out how to steal the truck."

"They wouldn't have gotten far," I said.

"Probably not. Oh, Patricia's the one who faxed the contract back to Allison."

"Why didn't she tell you that when we talked to her?"

"After she faxed it, she put it in her jacket pocket, just in case there might be something written into it that she could somehow use against Reggie. And, she never told her husband what Reggie had asked her to do. It seems that Reggie was perfectly aware that Joel and Patricia weren't completely above board, so he had told them to stay out of the garage, and away from his papers, messy though they were. She wanted to keep the contract to herself, just in case. Apparently, even Joel and Patricia didn't trust Joel and Patricia."

"Why did Reggie hire them again?"

Sam shrugged. "Hard to know, but I think he must have been an okay guy. Maybe he wanted to give them a second chance."

It was Christmas morning, and Hobbit and I were both at Sam's; we'd been under his watchful eye since my hand had, in fact, needed to be stitched. He still needed to be available for work and his house was closer to the police station, so he'd insisted we stay there. Hobbit and I were both fine with it. We'd spend the afternoon with my family, but the morning was just for us.

"Oh, and you'll be happy to know that Batman will be

well taken care of. Evelyn—Evie—gave Reggie's house and the farm to Gellie."

"Wow! That's quite a gift."

"Evelyn didn't want it. Gellie will leave it for her daughters and their families. A good idea, don't you think?"

"I do. Sam, how'd you get Evelyn to finally tell you everything?" I asked.

Sam had told me that his last visit with Evelyn had been productive almost to the point of too much information, but he hadn't shared his pressure techniques with me. She told him everything that had happened all those years ago and all the players involved. She shared details of how she found out about the affair, and she told him that she'd suspected Billie had killed Reggie all along, but she, of course, didn't have any evidence.

Sam took a sip of his coffee and glanced at me over the brim with his amazing eyes. They were particularly stunning this morning and I found it difficult not to just stare into them. He finally said, "I suspected the Ridgeways were somehow involved, though I wasn't sure how. I knew Evie had taken a liking to you. I told her you were on your way to confront them and she spilled everything."

"Oh, that was such a good idea," I said appreciatively.

"It would have been better if Evelyn had come forward with the information sooner, but even after all these years, I think she was ashamed about her husband having an affair. I think your parents were correct; I think the marriage breaking up was more about Evelyn's ego being bruised than about Reggie's infidelity."

"Ouch."

"I also wish I'd reached to you tell you to stay away from

them until I got there. I didn't plan on your phone not working in those trees. I'm sorry about that."

"No problem. I'm fine." I didn't want him to feel bad about what happened, but I knew he would for a while. "Hey, look, it's snowing again."

It was snowing lightly. With Hobbit at our feet, we sat comfortably on Sam's couch. He'd lit a fire in the fireplace, covered my legs with a quilt, and served me all the bacon, eggs, and hot chocolate I could consume. And the poinsettia was beautiful. We looked out the large picture window next to the plant and watched the snow fall on the neighborhood and the orange truck parked out front.

"I've got something for you," he said as he reached to a drawer in the coffee table.

"I thought we weren't going to exchange gifts until we went to my parents' house."

"This is just a little something."

He pulled a small box out of the drawer. It was wrapped with a simple bow, and it scared me speechless.

Sam laughed. "Becca, what's in here will hopefully show you how much I care about you, but I'm not buying you a ring until you're good and ready. Just open it."

I tried not to show my relief. I wasn't quite good and ready. Yet. Soon maybe, but not quite yet.

I untied the bow and pulled off the lid.

"It's a key," I said.

"It is. Not long ago, you claimed I'd only let you drive my cruiser when I cared enough about you. I'm pretty serious about the department's cruisers. . . ."

But he couldn't talk anymore. It's difficult to talk and kiss at the same time.

Recipes

Best Basic Holiday Cut-Out Cookies

¾ cup butter or margarine, softened
¾ cup superfine sugar
1 teaspoon baking powder
¼ teaspoon salt
1 egg
1 tablespoon milk
1 teaspoon vanilla extract
2 cups all-purpose flour

ICING:

1 cup sifted confectioners' sugar
¼ teaspoon vanilla extract

1 tablespoon milk
A few drops of food coloring, in various colors
   (optional)
Sprinkles and edible glitter (optional)

Using an electric mixer, beat the butter or margarine in a large bowl on medium to high speed for 30 seconds. Add the sugar, baking powder, and salt; beat until combined. Beat in the egg, milk, and vanilla. Beat in the flour. Divide the dough in half. Cover with plastic wrap and chill for 3 hours or until the dough is easy to handle.

Preheat oven to 375 degrees.

On a lightly floured surface, roll out half of the dough to a ⅛-inch thickness. Using 2- or 2½ inch cutters, cut the dough into desired holiday shapes. Place cookies 1 inch apart on ungreased baking sheets.

Bake for 7 to 8 minutes, or until edges are firm and bottoms are light brown. Remove cookies from baking sheets and transfer to wire rack to cool.

In a small bowl stir together the confectioners' sugar, vanilla, and enough of the milk to make an icing of piping consistency. Divide into batches, one for each color that you are using, and place each batch into a separate small bowl. Add drops of color and stir icing until color is mixed in. Use a piping bag or a plastic bag with a small corner cut off to decorate the cookies.

Makes about 3 dozen

Becca's Strawberry Jam-Filled Cookies

¾ cup butter, softened
½ cup sugar
1 egg
2 teaspoons vanilla
¼ teaspoon salt
1¾ cups all-purpose flour
¼–½ cup fruit preserves, any flavor (of course,
   Becca uses strawberry, her specialty)

Preheat oven to 350 degrees.

In a medium bowl, cream together the butter, sugar, egg, vanilla, and salt. Using a spoon or a plastic spatula, mix in flour a little at a time until a soft dough forms. Roll dough into 1-inch balls. Place balls 2 inches apart on ungreased cookie sheets. Use your finger or a similar-sized implement to make a well in the center of each cookie.

Place preserves into a small plastic bag and cut off a small corner piece. Divide preserves evenly among each cookie well.

Bake for 8 to 10 minutes, or until golden brown on the bottom. Remove the cookies and cool on wire racks.

Note: Keep dough in refrigerator when not baking. Dough should not be stored for more than a couple days.

Makes about 2½ dozen

Orange Meltaways

1 cup butter, softened
½ cup confectioners' sugar
½ teaspoon orange extract
1¼ cups all-purpose flour
½ cup cornstarch

FROSTING:

2 tablespoons butter, softened
1½ cups confectioners' sugar
2 tablespoons 2 percent milk
¼ teaspoon orange extract

Preheat oven to 350 degrees.

In a small bowl, cream butter and confectioners' sugar together until light and fluffy. Beat in extract. Combine flour and cornstarch. Gradually add the dry mixture to the creamed mixture, and mix well.

Shape into 1-inch balls and place 2 inches apart on an ungreased baking sheet. Bake for 10 to 12 minutes, or until bottoms and edges are light brown. Remove to wire racks to cool.

FROSTING:

In a small bowl, beat butter until fluffy. Add the confectioners' sugar, milk, and orange extract, and beat until smooth.

Spread, or use a plastic bag with a corner cut off to put a small design on each cookie.

Note: Keep dough in refrigerator when not baking. Dough should not be stored for more than a couple days.

Makes about 2½ dozen

Gingerbread Biscuits

½ cup light molasses or honey
½ cup firmly packed light brown sugar
2 tablespoons unsalted butter
2½ cups all-purpose flour, divided
2 teaspoons ground ginger
Pinch ground cinnamon
Pinch ground cloves
Pinch cardamom
1 egg yolk, room temperature
½ cup milk
1 teaspoon baking soda
1 tablespoon tepid water

Preheat oven to 350 degrees. Line baking sheets with parchment, and set aside.

In a saucepan over low heat, combine the molasses, sugar, and butter, and stir gently until the butter is melted and the sugar dissolved. Remove from heat and allow to cool.

Sift together 2 cups of the flour, ginger, cinnamon, cloves, and cardamom into a mixing bowl. Add the egg yolk, milk, and molasses mixture and stir to combine.

Dissolve the baking soda in the water and add to the flour mixture. On a lightly floured work surface, gradually knead in as much of the remaining flour as needed to obtain a firm dough. Roll dough to ½-inch thickness, and cut out desired shapes. Place on prepared baking sheets and bake for 10 to 12 minutes. Cool on baking sheet for 5 minutes, then transfer to a wire rack to cool completely.

Makes about 2 dozen

Brandy Snaps with Pastry Cream

2 tablespoons corn syrup or light molasses
¼ cup unsalted butter
⅓ cup packed brown sugar
¼ cup all-purpose flour, sifted
1½ teaspoons ground ginger

PASTRY CREAM:

3 egg yolks
¼ cup sugar
2½ tablespoons all-purpose flour
1 cup milk
1 teaspoon vanilla extract

Preheat oven to 350 degrees. Line two baking sheets with parchment paper, and set aside.

Combine syrup, butter, and brown sugar in a saucepan set over low heat and stir until butter is melted. Remove from the heat and stir in the flour and ginger. Drop mixture by 2 teaspoonfuls, 3 to 4 inches apart, onto a prepared baking sheet. Make only 3 to 4 snaps at a time. Bake for 5 minutes—they'll be thin and bubbly. Remove the parchment with the brandy snaps from the sheet and allow to cool on rack for 1 minute or until the snaps are warm and moldable. Gently roll each snap around the handle of a wooden spoon to make a tube. Allow to cool on the handle for 2 to 3 minutes, then transfer to wire racks to cool completely. Repeat with remaining dough.

To make the pastry cream, whisk the egg yolks and sugar in a bowl until pale—about 3 minutes. Sift in the flour and mix well. Heat the milk to boiling and gradually whisk it into the yolk mixture. Pour this mixture back into the saucepan and stir, constantly, over low heat until the mixture is thick, about 7 to 10 minutes. Stir in vanilla. Cool mixture, then pipe into the brandy-snap tubes.

Makes a dozen

Super-Easy Pumpkin Cream Pie

1½ cups milk
2 (3.5-oz.) packages instant vanilla pudding mix
1 cup canned pumpkin puree
1 teaspoon pumpkin pie spice
1 cup frozen whipped topping, thawed
1 9-inch pie crust, baked

Combine milk, pudding mix, pumpkin, spice, and whipped topping in a bowl. Beat with an electric mixer on lowest speed for about 1 minute. Pour into cooled pie crust.

Chill until set, about 3 hours. Serve.

Cranberry Cream Pie

1 cup fresh orange juice
1 cup sugar
5 ounces shortbread cookies
½ cup roasted almonds
4 tablespoons unsalted butter, melted
1 (8-oz.) package frozen cranberries, thawed and
    patted dry with paper towels
1 (¼-oz.) packet unflavored gelatin
2 cups heavy cream

Warm the orange juice and sugar in a small pan over low heat until the sugar dissolves. Transfer to a large bowl and refrigerate until just cool, about 30 minutes.

Meanwhile, pulse the cookies and almonds in a food processor until finely ground. Add the butter and pulse to combine. Press the cookie mixture evenly into the bottom of a 9-inch springform pan and set aside.

Clean the food processor, then puree the cranberries with ¼ cup of the cooled juice.

Sprinkle the gelatin over the remaining juice and let stand for 1 minute. Stir until the gelatin dissolves. Add pureed cranberries and stir to combine.

Beat the cream in a medium bowl using a whisk or electric mixer until soft peaks form. Fold the whipped cream into the cranberry mixture until well combined. Pour the cranberry cream into prepared crust. Place on a rimmed baking sheet and refrigerate until set, at least 4 hours.

Whipped Shortbread Christmas Cookies

1 cup butter, softened
1½ cups all-purpose flour
½ cup confectioners' sugar
1 teaspoon pure vanilla extract
¼ cup red maraschino cherries
¼ cup green maraschino cherries

Preheat oven to 350 degrees. Line cookie sheets with parchment paper and set aside.

In a mixing bowl, combine butter, flour, confectioners' sugar, and vanilla extract using an electric mixer until mixture is a smooth consistency. Be patient.

Spoon dough by teaspoonfuls, or by tablespoons for larger cookies, onto prepared cookie sheets, about 2 inches apart.

Cut maraschino cherries into quarters and place one piece in the middle of each cookie, alternating red and green cherries.

Bake for 13 to 15 minutes or until bottoms of cookies are light brown—do not overbake. Remove from oven and cool on cookie sheets for about 5 minutes. Transfer to wire racks to finish cooling.

Makes about 2 dozen

Cranberry–White Chocolate Muffins

¼ cup chopped walnuts
⅓ plus ¼ cup brown sugar, divided
2¼ cups flour, divided
3 tablespoons butter, melted
¾ cup sugar
1 teaspoon baking powder
½ teaspoon baking soda
2 eggs
½ cup vegetable oil

1 cup sour cream
1 cup chopped fresh or frozen cranberries
½ cup white chocolate chips

Preheat oven to 375 degrees. Spray 16 muffin cups with baking spray containing flour; set aside.

No mixer needed. Using a spoon, in small bowl, combine walnuts, ⅓ cup brown sugar, ¼ cup flour, and butter, and mix until crumbly. Set aside.

In large bowl, combine remaining 2 cups flour, sugar, remaining ¼ cup brown sugar, baking powder, and baking soda, and mix with wire whisk. In medium bowl, combine eggs, oil, and sour cream, and beat with whisk until smooth and blended. Add egg mixture to flour mixture and stir just until combined. Add cranberries and white chocolate chips. Stir until blended.

Spoon batter into prepared muffin cups; divide brown sugar mixture evenly over tops. Bake 20 to 25 minutes or until muffins are brown and firm to the touch. Let cool in muffin tins for 3 to 4 minutes, then carefully remove to wire racks to cool. Serve warm.

Makes 16

Becca Robbins is happy to help research a farmers'
market and tourist trading post—until she has to
switch her focus to finding a killer...

AN ALL-NEW SPECIAL
FROM NATIONAL BESTSELLING AUTHOR

PAIGE SHELTON

Red Hot Deadly Peppers

A Farmers' Market Mini Mystery

Becca is in Arizona, spending some time at Chief Buffalo's trading post and its neighboring farmers' market to check out how the two operate together. She's paired with Nera, a Native American woman who sells the most delicious pecans—right next to a booth with the hottest peppers money can buy.

When Nera asks her to deliver some beads to Graham, a talented jewelry maker inside Chief Buffalo's, Becca is grateful to get a break from the heat. Little does she realize that the heat's about to get cranked up even more—because Graham has been murdered, and she's the one who finds his body. She soon discovers that Graham was Nera's cousin, and that her uncle was recently killed, too, after receiving a threatening note. Becca begins to think the murders may have something to do with the family's hot pepper business. Now she must find the killer, before she's the one in the hot seat...

Includes a bonus recipe!

paigeshelton.com
facebook.com/TheCrimeSceneBooks
penguin.com

M1144T0813